FOLLOW MY VOICE

Content warning:
Discussions of suicide, eating disorders,
mental illness, bullying, and the use of a slur.

FOLLOW MY VOICE

a novel

ARIANA GODOY

translated by Frances Riddle

PRIMERO SUEÑO PRESS

ATRIA

New York Amsterdam/Antwerp London
Toronto Sydney/Melbourne New Delhi

PRIMERO SUEÑO PRESS

ATRIA

An Imprint of Simon & Schuster, LLC
1230 Avenue of the Americas
New York, NY 10020

For more than 100 years, Simon & Schuster has championed authors and the stories they create. By respecting the copyright of an author's intellectual property, you enable Simon & Schuster and the author to continue publishing exceptional books for years to come. We thank you for supporting the author's copyright by purchasing an authorized edition of this book.

No amount of this book may be reproduced or stored in any format, nor may it be uploaded to any website, database, language-learning model, or other repository, retrieval, or artificial intelligence system without express permission. All rights reserved. Inquiries may be directed to Simon & Schuster, 1230 Avenue of the Americas, New York, NY 10020 or permissions@simonandschuster.com.

This book is a work of fiction. Any references to historical events, real people, or real places are used fictitiously. Other names, characters, places, and events are products of the author's imagination, and any resemblance to actual events or places or persons, living or dead, is entirely coincidental.

Copyright © 2022 by Ariana Godoy
English language translation copyright © 2025 by Frances Riddle
Originally published in Spain in 2022 by Penguin Random House Grupo Editorial, S.A.U. as *Sigue mi voz*
English language edition copyright © 2025 by Ariana Godoy
Published in agreement with Writers House

All rights reserved, including the right to reproduce this book or portions thereof in any form whatsoever. For information, address Atria Books Subsidiary Rights Department, 1230 Avenue of the Americas, New York, NY 10020.

This Primero Sueño Press/Atria Paperback edition September 2025

PRIMERO SUEÑO PRESS / ATRIA PAPERBACK and colophon are trademarks of Simon & Schuster, LLC

Simon & Schuster strongly believes in freedom of expression and stands against censorship in all its forms. For more information, visit BooksBelong.com.

For information about special discounts for bulk purchases, please contact Simon & Schuster Special Sales at 1-866-506-1949 or business@simonandschuster.com.

The Simon & Schuster Speakers Bureau can bring authors to your live event. For more information or to book an event, contact the Simon & Schuster Speakers Bureau at 1-866-248-3049 or visit our website at www.simonspeakers.com.

Interior design by Kyoko Watanabe
Manufactured in the United States of America

1 3 5 7 9 10 8 6 4 2

Library of Congress Control Number has been applied for.

ISBN 978-1-6680-9897-4 (pbk)
ISBN 978-1-6680-9898-1 (ebook)

This book is for you.
It's for me.
These words are an escape valve and proof of life.
I hope they may provide a refuge from the storm.

Prologue

HIS VOICE.

It wasn't his eyes or his looks that got me; it was his voice: delicate, soft, but at the same time confident and masculine. I never imagined I could be so fascinated by someone based solely on the sound of their voice, without an idea as to what they look like. But he was the only person I've allowed inside the four walls of my room, which I guess created the perfect storm.

My name is Klara. I'm a nineteen-year-old girl who, for the past eight months, has been unable to leave the house for more than fifteen minutes. Faithful listener of the radio show *Follow My Voice*.

1

Listen to Me

I'M MESMERIZED BY the sound of the popcorn popping in the microwave and the smell that floods the kitchen. *Mmm, delicious*, I think, smiling as I pour Coke into a glass. This is the event I wait for all day, the one thing I look forward to in all the hours I spend inside this house. I take the popcorn out of the microwave, pick up the glass with my other hand, and move down the hall to my bedroom, walking on air. It's silly how much I cherish this moment; we often learn to appreciate the little things in life after being on the verge of losing it all.

I sit on the bed, place the popcorn on the nightstand, and put on my headphones. They're purple—my favorite color—and big, covering my ears entirely, and they tend to pinch my head. Even so, I don't want to get new ones; they were a gift from my mother and hold sentimental value for me. I open the radio app on my phone and find the usual station. I shove a handful of popcorn in my mouth, checking the time: My favorite show is about to start. The host of the six o'clock hour signs off energetically, and they go to commercials before the seven o'clock show begins.

Then the moment arrives. I hear his voice, and my heart races.

"Good evening, folks," says that voice I love so much, the voice that has been with me through so many hard times. "Thank you for tuning in tonight. Without further ado, I welcome you to tonight's evening show: *Follow My Voice*. I'm Kang, your friend and companion for this hour."

Kang.

The first time I heard him, it was by chance: I was in the living room, bored, playing *Candy Crush* on my phone, and my sister, being old-school, had left the radio on some random college station. Kang's show began and, when I heard his voice—so smooth and comforting—the way he spoke, his comments on the different topics, and the songs he'd chosen, I was instantly captivated. As I listened to him, I got to know him, and I learned that we share the same passion for pastries, poetry, and music. He's even mentioned my favorite bakery in the city several times. He's very smart; I can tell by the way he talks, with the confidence of someone completely secure in their knowledge.

I have no idea what he looks like, and I have no intention of finding out. I like the platonic feelings I have for him, far removed from any romantic sentiment. I don't want anything more than that—it would only complicate things and that's not a luxury I can afford at the moment.

"Tonight we have a beautiful full moon, have you seen it? If you're at home, I want you to look out your window right now; if you're driving, please keep your eyes on the road, you can see it later."

I get up and walk to my window; he's right, as always. The moon hangs clear and luminous in the night sky.

"Nights like this make me think about the infinite perfection of the universe."

I can't take my eyes off the moon.

"We're merely tiny specks in this gigantic galaxy of ours, yet, even so, there are days when we feel like everything revolves around us. We humans can be very self-centered. But we are also capable of amazing things. I suppose, like with everything, we have our good and our bad."

I place my hand on the window and outline the shape of the full moon with my index finger, a perfect circle. I wish I was the moon, not a person living in this defective shell of a body that struggles to survive every day.

"I'm going to start with a song I like a lot, by a local band. I hope you like it." A slow, melancholic tune begins to play:

I just need a minute to process all these
feelings.
You are silence,
my calm in this storm,
the cure to this pain that I feel.
Please, don't go;
please, don't go.
I'm all out of words, the silence hurts,
your glances burn
and I blaze with feelings.
Feelings . . .
Feelings for . . . you . . .

There's a silence when the song ends and Kang sighs before speaking. "A pretty sentimental song, huh? You've just heard 'What I Feel,' from the band P4. Don't forget to support our local talent by following them on social media and listening to their songs."

I walk back over to the bed and take a sip of Coke.

"I chose that song to kick off tonight's topic. We get messages every day from people asking for heartbreak songs. I think love is an incredible feeling, but it can bring with it other emotions that aren't so incredible if that love isn't reciprocated. Have you ever had your heart broken?"

Love is not something I've given much thought to this past year; love isn't for people like me, infected and defective. It's for people like Kang: successful, with a bright future ahead of them. The curiosity is killing me; I hope he says something about this aspect of his life. That's what I like most about his show: He first talks in general about a topic and then gives us his opinion and shares his personal experiences.

"I have to admit that I've never been in love, so my thoughts on the matter might not be very insightful. But I've seen a lot of people in love, and I've witnessed the effects it can have. In some cases, it changes people for the better, in others, for the worse. But don't worry if you've had your heart broken; time heals all wounds, and you'll find someone new to make you twice as happy. Like I always say . . ."

"We have to learn from the bad and turn the page to move forward," we recite in unison.

"We'll go now to another song, and when we come back, I'll read some of your messages about tonight's topic. Don't forget, that number is . . ."

The next song starts after he finishes giving out the number, which I know by heart despite the fact that I've never sent a message to the show. Why would I? Like I said, it's enough for me to just listen. I don't want or need anything else. I couldn't deal with any more complications right now.

Kang, it's enough for me to enjoy your show and hear you say, "Follow my voice."

2

Follow Me

I PASS THE days one after another, mainly stuck in the four walls of my room. There's my bed, in the middle, white Christmas lights wrapped around my bedframe from a few Christmases ago that I never bothered taking off. To the right is my nightstand with a lamp, a book, and my favorite pictures of my mother and me. To the left is my desk, with rolled-up canvases on top that haven't been touched in years. It used to be a place where I liked to sit down and paint, but now I just use it to read or watch TV dramas when I get tired of being on my bed.

I wish I could say I'd made it more appealing with posters on my walls, pictures of and with friends, but that would be a lie. The most I have are some white hanging shelves reserved for my favorite novels—the rest of my books are scattered throughout my room—and some random knickknacks that my sister added so it wouldn't look so empty. While this is my safe space, sometimes I grow tired of it. But, with the exception of days I practice exposure therapy, the farthest I go is to a different room inside the house, to be stuck in a different set of four walls. Regardless of how my day is spent, for the most part, it's always the same: The sun filters in through my window until it finally disappears, only to be replaced by the moon, and then everything starts all over again. Every day is exactly the same, monotonous, except for that one hour every other day, when I get to hear *his* voice.

I go through my evening routine. It's almost time for Kang's show, so, popcorn and Coke in hand, I head to my bedroom. But my little bubble of bliss is burst when I run into my sister in the hallway.

"Ah! You scared me!"

Kamila crosses her arms. Yes, Kamila with a K; my mother loved the letter *K*.

"You know you shouldn't be eating that junk, it's not healthy," she scolds me. I see she has her white doctor's coat folded over one arm.

I give her a huge smile to soften her up. "It's just this once."

She narrows her eyes and furrows her brow. "That's what you said yesterday."

"Are you on call?" I ask, changing the subject—usually the best course of action.

"Yes, one of my patients"—she stops for a moment, always so careful with her words when she talks to me about her work—"had a setback."

Setback. That's her favorite euphemism to avoid naming the mental health situations she encounters in her job day-to-day. Kamila started working as a psychiatrist four years ago, and I'd like to say it's been easy for her, but no, it's been exhausting and heartbreaking. She's the strongest person I know, which is why she's been able to handle it so well.

I believe that everyone has a calling in life. Some find theirs and live happily with their decision; others don't and simply let themselves be pulled along by the flow of life, withering and dying without ever having found a dream, goal, or objective for their existence. Before everything changed, I had so many dreams and

I was so full of energy, I wanted to eat the world, achieve the unachievable. Then my mother got sick. And one blow after another gradually destroyed that young dreamer, eating away at me until I became what I am today. Now, I'm an empty shell, barely surviving.

"How are you?" Kamila asks, looking at me cautiously, always analyzing me. I can't blame her; it's her job.

"I'm good."

"Dizzy spells? Vivid dreams?"

I shake my head. "No side effects this time."

Kamila sighs with relief. "If you have any symptoms, you need to let me know, Klara; antidepressants are not something to be taken lightly. Trust—"

"Is the most important thing," I finish her sentence for her. "I've never lied to you." And it's true; I've always been honest with her when it comes to anything that has to do with my mental health, it's just that I don't like it when she goes into doctor mode on me. But I have to put up with it since, apart from being my sister, she monitors every step of the treatment laid out by my psychiatrist, who, along with my therapist, sees me once a month. My sister makes sure that I stick to my medication; she takes care of me.

"Have you had any unpleasant thoughts?"

That makes me smile. I don't understand why she thinks she has to be so cautious with her words. "I haven't had any suicidal thoughts, Kamila, if that's what you're asking."

We had this same conversation when I started my previous antidepressants. The first few weeks, as my body got used to the medication, I felt even lower and more depressed—something that can happen before you begin to notice any improvement. I call it a roller coaster: sudden lows followed by new highs. Kamila was by my side then, too.

"Andy will be home from work soon, so you won't be alone for long. You can call me if you need anything."

Andy is Kamila's husband, and I live with them. He's a nice man.

I swallow, because being alone scares me more than I want to admit. "I'm fine, go."

Kamila pulls me into a hug. "I love you, K."

I respond with a couple pats on her back. "I love you too, K2."

We've used these nicknames for each other since we were little. Even though she was a teenager when I was born, our age difference never kept us from being close.

I watch her walk away, and then I go into my bedroom. When I hear Kang's voice opening the show, I relax and begin to eat my popcorn. The topic tonight is family.

"I think that who we are, our personality, has a lot to do with how we're raised and the things we see on a daily basis growing up."

His voice sounds a little sad. Does this topic upset him? If so, that makes two of us.

"What do you guys think? Let me know in a text message as we listen to the next song."

As I begin to get lost in the lyrics, I feel a tap on the shoulder and open my eyes. Andy is standing in front of me, wearing an impeccable gray suit, a light-blue button-down shirt, and a striped tie to match. His dark hair is combed back perfectly, not a strand out of place.

I put my headphones around my neck. "Hey," I say, greeting him with a smile.

"Just wanted to let you know I was home. Keep listening to your show," he says, as he checks his watch. "It's your favorite one, right?" I nod and he points to my hair. "Pink looks good on you."

I roll my eyes. "According to you and Kamila, everything looks good on me."

"It's because we love you."

Andy is a very sweet man, and, despite the fact that he's only a few years older than my sister, he's become like a father to me.

"Sorry, but your opinion doesn't count for much."

"That hurts," he says, grabbing his chest.

"You'll survive."

He turns around and walks to the door. "Enjoy your show."

I put my headphones back on just in time to listen to Kang reading one of the many messages he's received. "This next one is from a very dedicated listener. Thank you for always tuning in, Liliana. Today she says: 'I love the way you express yourself so well and how you help others understand complicated topics. I find it very... sexy.' Umm... Thanks so much for this message of support. I do it for our listeners—I couldn't do it without you guys."

Liliana sends messages all the time, and it irks me, though I don't know why. Maybe it's the fact that Kang thinks of her as a dedicated listener when there are so many other people like me who've been listening to the show for ages. But it doesn't matter.

Kang says good night as the show comes to an end. "Don't forget to follow us on social media. You can find *Follow My Voice* on YouTube, Instagram, and X. Good night from your humble host, Kang. Have a great evening. I'll leave you with this song titled 'More of You,' from the band Broken Dreams."

More...
It's not enough.
What if it's not enough?
If everything changes,
no matter how much I pay attention...
to you...
For you...
these sweet words for no reason,
life doesn't matter at all
or how high you might fall
No...
It's not enough, not today, not tomorrow,
having you only in my mind.
I want more, much more of you.

As I listen to the chorus, my finger hovers over the Instagram app, trembling. I have an old account that I haven't checked in over a year. I don't know if it's because of what Kang said about Liliana or because of the song that's playing, but I feel suddenly curious. The second part of the song hits me even harder.

What if my emotions explode?
If my feelings take over,
and I can't hold back anymore.
What if I lose control?
Because of you . . .
For you . . .
these sweet words for no reason,
life doesn't matter at all
or how high you might fall. No . . .
It's not enough, not today, not tomorrow,
having you only in my mind.
I want more, so much more of you.

My mind made up, I open Instagram and search for *Follow My Voice* before I have time to regret it.

3

Look at Me

I SPENT MOST of Friday reading *Pride and Prejudice*. It's my third time reading it—what can I say, I'm a cliché when it comes to Jane Austen. The pages are tearing at some corners because it's an old book—it was a library book before it was donated to a big book warehouse sale. Mom used to hunt those down to take me; we could get so many books for just a few bucks. It was one of our things. I loved those days; even in the heat of summer when those warehouses were too hot, I was happy. In a way, all the old books around my room carry a story, a memory of a happy day with my mother in a random warehouse. She's here with me, in these books, in these walls. I'm safe here, and only here.

"Time to eat!" Kamila yells from the hallway, and I sigh before heading out of my room.

The clinking of silverware echoes through the dining room as I sit at the table with Kamila and Andy. I force myself to eat. I'm not hungry, but I know I still need to put on weight and, based on the way my sister is looking at me, she's not going to let me skip a meal. I glance at the clock and I start eating faster; it's almost time for my show.

Andy notices my anxiety. "You still have twenty minutes before it starts, don't worry."

My sister takes a sip of juice. "I'm glad you found that show you like so much, but have you thought about looking for other things you might like to do as well?"

Andy shoots her a disapproving look, and she lobs one right back at him. "What? I don't want her focusing on just one thing when there are so many other activities out there that I know she'd enjoy. Have you thought at all about getting back into painting again?"

I grip the spoon. I've completely lost my appetite. "No."

Kamila gives me a sad look. "I'm not trying to make you uncomfortable, K, I just want the best for you. Painting could aid your progress; it could be a very positive thing for you."

Painting used to be my passion, way before literature and TV dramas. My biggest dream was to open my own gallery and exhibit my art, the product of everything I imagined when I was alone with my brushes. The smell of paint was the smell of home to me, my safe place. But, after everything that happened, it's now just a reminder of everything I will never be.

"I'm never going to paint again. I've already told you that." I stand up and fake a smile. "It's time for my show. I'll be in my room."

Outside in the hallway, where I'm sure they can't see me, I stand with my back against the wall. I can hear them talking about what just happened.

Andy starts out: "Very subtle, Kamila. You know you can't talk to her like that during dinner; it ruins her appetite."

"It's for her own good, babe, and you know it. She needs to branch out and find other interests. If she focuses all her energy on a single thing, and for some reason it falls through, where will she be then? She could experience a major setback."

"And how is a radio show going to fall through?"

"My God, Andy, so many things could happen to that show... The host is just a college kid. What's gonna happen when he graduates? How do you think K is going to take that?"

I feel a tightness in my chest. She's right. Why haven't I thought of that?

"You seem to have given it a lot of thought."

"My little sister, who's going through a really rough time, has only one thing she likes. But there's so much more to life than a radio show."

"You're incredible."

"Thank you."

"It wasn't a compliment," Andy says. "Just let her enjoy her show. If it ends, we'll deal with it."

I go into my room with my sister's words still echoing in my head: *What's gonna happen when he graduates?* Slouching, I pick up my phone. Last night I followed the show on Instagram, but I didn't have the nerve to look at any of the posts. Now, after hearing my sister, I'm feeling bolder. My heart beats desperately in my chest as I scroll through a bunch of photos of the radio station: the microphone, the red "On Air" light, a set of headphones. There are pictures of gifts from the show's listeners, including drawings and knickknacks, even food sent for the entire staff. But there are no pictures of Kang.

I'm about to give up when I come to a group shot of the entire team dressed up for Halloween. No one is tagged, but the bottom of the picture lists everyone's names from left to right. I scan them until I find Kang. He's a little taller than everyone else, and he's wearing a creepy clown mask that covers his entire face.

My heart continues to beat faster than normal, and it scares me a little bit. I'm surprised at the relief I feel over not being able to put a face to the voice I listen to every day. I know that, once I see him, I'm going to want to talk to him, but I know I won't be able to do it.

I put my headphones on and sit down beside the bed as I

look at one of the pictures on my nightstand: my mom and me, both wearing huge smiles, at a carnival a few years ago, the lit-up Ferris wheel behind us. Neither one of us was perfect, but that moment was.

I remember how hard it was to convince her to purchase the picture once the photographer told us the price. She'd never been a big spender, always scrimping and saving, so cautious and careful. Her efforts paid off when it came time to send Kamila to college; Mom had more than enough, and was even able to start her own bakery business. She made the best cakes in the world.

As if Kang can read my mind, the topic tonight is the loss of a loved one.

"It's very hard to deal with the loss of someone we love. Each person experiences it differently. It's harder for some of us than for others. Unfortunately, that's the way life goes. Sooner or later, we will all face a loss of this kind, and all we can do is take a deep breath and keep moving forward in a way we think honors that person."

It's been a while since I've cried, but I now feel the tears building up behind my eyes. I take the picture of my mother in my hands and run my thumb over her bright smile.

"I don't want to minimize what you feel when I say you have to move on. We are human beings, it's normal to feel pain, sadness... It's normal to cry. Let yourselves feel all of your emotions but keep moving forward, always at your own pace; there's no correct or incorrect amount of time when we're talking about grieving the death of someone we love. And know that you can always carry that person in your heart the rest of your lives."

Kang seems to understand everything so perfectly; has he been through something like this? Tears stream freely down my face as he continues speaking. "The next song is very special to me, so please listen with me as we honor those who are no longer with us."

Why?
I'd like to ask, to bring you back,
look into your eyes and ask: Why?
I don't understand, maybe that's why I can't let you go.
Tell me, answer me, why? Why did it have to be this way?
At the top of my lungs, I shout over and over. Over and over.
Why? Why, if I love you so?
Why, if I gave you my all?
My love can't be the air you breathe.
I'll breathe for you, if need be.
I'll dream for you on sleepless nights,
I'll go up against any enemy.

I rip off my headphones. I can't listen anymore; it hurts too much. I throw myself onto the bed, burrow under the covers, and cry inconsolably into my pillow. It's the first time I haven't listened to Kang's show all the way to the end. The first time that I don't want to hear him.

4

Write to Me

"IT'S ALL RIGHT, we'll be with you the whole time," Kamila says, patting me on the back. "We're going to try to make it to the park this time. Mondays are not crowded at this hour."

I want to try leaving the house, I really do. This is one of the exercises that my therapist recommended, a kind of exposure therapy for my agoraphobia. *"One step and one breath at a time, Klara!"* I remember his words and try to control my breathing, which is coming fast.

"What if I have a panic attack? I'm scared." I'm terrified of causing disappointment just as much as I am of unfamiliar settings. Today will be the day we make it all the way to the park—the farthest I've ever gone—but instead of coming right back, we'll be staying for as long as I can manage.

Kamila gives me a comforting look. "I'm a doctor, remember? No one is more qualified than me—I won't let anything happen to you."

"But I could get run over or someone could try to hurt me. I could stop breathing and you won't be able to do anything. What if my heart stops while I'm crossing the street? How many minutes is it to the nearest hospital?" My mind races with catastrophic thoughts. Fear takes over, and I feel my agoraphobia intensifying, urging me to return home, where it's safe and secure.

My sister takes my hand.

"You're a young, healthy woman; your heart and lungs are fine. You're not going to die. Don't listen to your thoughts, just walk, right here, with me."

I swallow and feel my heart hammering against my ribs. I can do this, I really can.

Andy smiles warmly and stands on the other side of me. "We'll be with you every step of the way."

We leave the house and begin to move down the sidewalk. The sun blinds me for a moment, which happens every time we do this task—too many hours without exposure to natural light.

Kamila talks to distract me: "Remember Drew, Paula's dog, from next door? She just had a litter of adorable little puppies."

I try my best to smile, picturing them. I saw them through the backyard fence the other day; they are precious and so playful. "Yeah, they're cute," I answer.

She nods as we walk. I can see the park in the distance. "Well, Paula told me that you can go see them whenever you want."

I swallow and feel a tightness in my chest. "Yeah, I'll stop by." As if it were that easy.

I think about all the people who never understood what was happening to me, who said that I was exaggerating or trying to get attention. I've heard it all:

"Oh, yeah, like leaving the house is so hard!"

"You're crazy."

"We all have it tough, don't be so dramatic."

"Just come out! Just walk through the door! It's not that big a deal!"

"There's nothing wrong with you, you're just trying to get attention."

"Depression is an excuse."

"Anxiety disorder? God, what will she come up with next?"

"What's wrong with you now?"

"Just get over it and move on."

Some people don't understand that our minds can get sick just like our bodies. When someone has the flu, no one says, "Just think about something else and it'll go away." If someone cuts themselves badly, others immediately say, "You should go to the hospital to get stitches!" But when you're depressed, which can be a much deeper and more complex wound than any physical injury, no one believes there's really anything wrong with you. And then these same people are so shocked when someone dies by suicide, claiming they never saw it coming, that they don't understand how something like that could've happened, that they would've helped if they'd only known. So hypocritical. They could start by listening when someone needs to be heard, by not ignoring their pain as if that will make it magically disappear. I know some who are struggling might not want to be helped; some don't give any signs that anything's wrong. But there are individuals who do ask for help and are ignored or told that there's nothing wrong with them.

"There are plenty of people who have it way worse in the world and you don't see them complaining all the time."

Is that supposed to make me feel better? Is the fact that there are others in worse situations supposed to make my feelings just go away? Does it somehow magically erase who I am, what I've been through?

"You're such a crybaby."

"You're so needy."

"You hurt yourself, that's insane."

Depression is not a decision; no one decides to move through life feeling hopeless, with the weight of surviving making every step taken feel heavier than the last. Who in their right mind would want to live every day with a pain so strong it's practically suffocating?

I wish I could correct people who are dismissive of mental illness. Crying is simply expressing your feelings. No one complains when someone smiles, no one asks them to explain it. Happiness is not the only emotion in the world, so why does sadness have to be justified?

Expressing your needs is brave. It takes courage to set your fears aside and ask for the help you so urgently need.

Hurting yourself means you're desperate. If someone has gotten to that point, I hope they find the help they need. I'm lucky that my sister is a psychiatrist and she understands what I'm going through; I can't even imagine what other people are up against without someone close who will listen to them, who believes them.

In the park, Andy spreads a picnic blanket on the grass and we sit. "I'm so proud of you."

I uncross my arms and reach down to touch the grass, so cool and soft.

Kamila rubs my back. "You did so well today."

We've been going out little by little for a few months now. We started once a month, then once a week, and now we are doing it every other day, adding more distance each time but never more than fifteen minutes. In the beginning, I could barely get out the door; now I've made it all the way to the park. My progress is mostly thanks to my sister's hard work and Andy's support. They've both been so patient. They never push me to attempt other outings; they know this is what I'm comfortable with for the moment, a somewhat familiar routine.

After a few breathing exercises, it begins to feel good to be here, sitting on the grass, feeling the sun on my skin, even though I know I'm only able to do this because I have Kamila and Andy with me. I hope to one day be able to do it on my own, but I should still count this as progress.

I can see the lake in the distance surrounded by tall trees that still hold on to their lush green: my mother's favorite place. We used to come here a lot, in the end; even after she could no longer walk, we would bring her in her wheelchair to watch the sunset. I remember her sad smile as she said to me, *"The view is so beautiful here. It's interesting how we learn to value the little things when our time is limited."* I smiled back and she patted my face. *"We should all live as if we were going to die tomorrow; we would have much fuller lives if we didn't assume we had all the time in the world."*

I feel like I'm failing my mother every day that I spend locked away inside the house. The memory of her frail figure and pained expression interrupts the peaceful moment. My chest tightens. Death seems to be staring me in the face as I become acutely aware that I am outside, exposed to the world. A cruel and dangerous world, a place that is not safe; it was not safe for my mother, and it isn't safe for me, either. The heaviness in my chest grows and I know it's time to go home: my safe place. Where nothing and no one can hurt me. I take one last look at the hills in the distance, apologizing to my mother.

I'm sorry, Mom, I'm not strong enough to smile through it all. I'm not as strong as you.

◆ ◆ ◆

When we get home, I take off my shoes and rush to my room. Kang's show must be about to start, so I throw on my headphones as fast as I can.

Halfway through the show, he begins reading messages from listeners. Liliana again.

Maybe it's because I accomplished staying outside for a few minutes, and I'm feeling good about myself despite my last-minute setback, but I don't think twice as I take out my phone and type a message to the station. My heart jumps into my throat as I hit *Send*. He probably won't even read it; he must get so many texts.

But, as if life suddenly decided to throw me a bone today, Kang picks my message. "Okay, I'm going to read the last message of the day. It says, 'Dear Kang, your voice is a comfort for people who are having a hard time like me; you brighten my day and calm my nights. I will always follow your voice. With gratitude, K.'"

Silence. Kang says nothing for a few seconds, and I swallow. *Did I scare him? Did I sound too obsessive? Is this not something a nineteen-year-old girl would say?* I can't help but think this is yet another thing taken from me, the ability to be and act my age.

He clears his throat and finally speaks. "That's very kind of you to say, K. Thank you for your message. I will always try to be here for you."

It's the first time I've communicated with him and, although it's not the same as a face-to-face interaction, it's a big step for me and it makes me feel good. *Really good.*

5

Respond to Me

"I'M LOSING YOU. I'm losing you," I sing loudly as I make myself a ham and cheese sandwich.

I've been in a really good mood lately. Maybe the new medication is finally starting to kick in—after trial and error with a few others, I think we've finally found one without serious side effects—or maybe it's because I've been able to go to the park with my sister these past few weeks without having any panic attacks. Perhaps it's a combination of everything. I set the sandwich on the table and, noticing that the trash can is full, I grab the bag to take it out. I get to the door, open it, and stop dead in my tracks.

What am I doing?

I grip the garbage bag tightly and peer into the danger of the outside world. I'm safe here, I can't go out. Kamila and Andy aren't home—if I have a panic attack out there no one will help me.

I close the door and put the garbage bag back in the trash can. My good mood vanishes into thin air; I guess there's a lot more progress I still need to make.

◆ ◆ ◆

"Today I'm going to try to get caught up with some of the messages we've received. We've had a lot of activity lately," Kang says later that night.

I'm one of the listeners who's been sending messages to the program regularly, ever since that first day. Sometimes he reads mine on the air, sometimes they seem to go unnoticed; regardless, I've already gained a reputation for being a loyal listener, like Liliana. Of course, Kang doesn't know who I am; I simply sign my messages as *K*.

"Liliana says she's sending us lots of love today. Thank you for the donuts you sent to me and the entire crew. I want to reiterate that no one should feel obligated to send us anything—just being a faithful listener is the greatest gift—but we appreciate your thoughtfulness." Kang pauses. "Today, we also have a message from K that I want to share." I sit up straight in bed. "It's another quote, this time from Benjamin Disraeli, and it reads: 'There is no index of character so sure as the voice.' Is that true? If it is, you guys must know my character better than anyone. I think that was what K, whoever he or she is, meant to imply. And, K, feel free share your pronouns with us; we don't know how to refer to you, and all of us on the team are curious. I can tell from the quotes you send in that you must be a big reader; something we have in common."

I have the urge to write into the show and tell Kang that my name is Klara and my pronouns are she/her, but I hold back. I like being somewhat anonymous; he might as well keep thinking of K as an abstract person he'll never meet, because he never will.

"Well, before we get to the last song of the hour, I want to let you all know that I'll be gone next week, taking care of a few personal matters."

"What?!" I say out loud.

"But I'll be leaving *Follow My Voice* in the very capable hands of my fellow radio host Erick, who you may know from the six o'clock program, *Riffing with Erick*. I'll be back soon. Try not to miss me too much."

"No. No." I shake my head at the phone.

"I'll miss you guys, but I hope you have a great week. We'll go now to our last song. This is Kang, your friend and companion, bidding you farewell."

"No..."

Before I realize what I'm doing, I type a quote from a favorite novel of mine, *Gone with the Wind*: *"Oh, my darling, if you go, what shall I do?"* —K.

I send it and then realize what I've just done. I cover my mouth with my hand. What was I thinking? The guy has a life and things to take care of. But what am I going to do for a week without him? Kamila was right, I shouldn't place so much importance on one thing; with Kang gone, I'll feel lost.

I let out a long sigh. What's wrong with me? I'm such a mess. I need to wake up to my reality. I should've never tried to interact with Kang—what was I hoping to accomplish? I'll never meet him, so why am I getting all carried away? It's dangerous; in the long run, I'll only be let down.

I walk from the bedroom to the kitchen with my shoulders slumped. I open the fridge to grab a bottle of water and I'm about to return to my cave when I hear a tiny barking sound, or is it a whimper? I head over to the front door and press my ear against it. The mini barks continue. I crack the door open, nervous, and the cool night air flows into the house. My neighbor's golden retriever puppies are playing on the front yard. They're so cute. But what are they doing out so late?

My stomach drops when one of them rolls off the curb into the street and a car passes, almost running it over.

Oh, no! I instinctively rush through the door, but, as soon as I'm outside, I realize that I'm alone. I look around, searching for some kind of assistance, but there's no one. I think back to how soft their fur was and the way they licked my hand through the backyard fence when I played with them on one of our walks to the park. My heart twists in my chest. I clench my fists at my sides, frustrated with myself for not being able to help them.

The other puppy slips off the curb into the street, trying to follow his brother. I'm hyperventilating now, and I have to look away when another car passes.

You can do it, Klara. Even if you're having a panic attack, those little dogs need your help, I tell myself. And then I take off running. Desperately.

The puppies are now in the middle of the road, and a car is approaching. Overcoming my fear, I step in front of the puppies and hold up my hands. "Stop! Wait!"

The vehicle screeches to a halt just inches away from me. "Out of the way! Are you crazy?!"

I scoop up the two golden retrievers and jump back up onto the sidewalk, my heart in my throat. I feel eyes on me and, when I look up, I see Kamila and Andy with bags from the corner store in their hands, watching me in shock.

What just happened?

Miss Me

ERICK IS AN idiot.

It has nothing to do with the fact that I miss Kang; Erick is just obnoxious. He's the type of guy who constantly makes sexist jokes and thinks he's hilarious. I listened to him the first night after Kang left, willing to give him a chance; but no, Erick can't hold a candle to Kang. I don't even know how they let him stay on the air with such inappropriate comments.

So I haven't been able to listen to my show for an entire week, and, while I'm bummed about it, I'm not doing as badly as I feared I might. I think the puppies licking my hands right now are a big part of that. Paula, our next-door neighbor, has asked me to look after them while she's at work since she still needs to fix the fence around her house and she doesn't want them to escape again and get hurt. So I'm a puppy sitter, which I never imagined would be so therapeutic. I sit on the couch, and they immediately jump up and climb onto my lap or nestle in next to me. I love to pet their soft ears and heads.

"You're adorable, do you know that? Of course you do, everyone tells you all the time," I say, smiling. "And you love me no matter how awful I look or what a mess I am. If that's not true love, I don't know what is."

I'm in a good mood. I keep taking steps in the right direction, and it brings me a sense of hope. There's a refreshing normalcy in the air and it feels great. There's just one thing missing: Kang, although I know it's strange to miss someone I've never met. I don't know him, but I feel like I do, because I listen to him speak for an hour every other day and his voice has become so familiar to me.

◆ ◆ ◆

"Have you given any more thought to starting college next semester?" We're at the table and Kamila just can't keep herself from bringing up my biggest fear.

I continue chewing. I saw it coming. My sister, seeing my slight improvement, is ready to launch me into the outside world. I can't blame her; she just wants me to get my life back on track, but she hasn't been subtle about it, "accidentally" leaving college pamphlets all over the house.

"I don't think I'm ready."

Andy puts his hand on my shoulder. "That's fine."

But Kamila won't let it go so easily. She wipes her mouth and goes on: "You've improved a lot, K. I think it would do you good to go to campus. Who knows, you might even make some friends."

Friends . . . The word brings a bitter taste to my mouth. Because the people I considered my friends in high school vanished as soon as my mom got sick.

I huff. "Make some friends?" I say sarcastically, pointing to myself. "With the mess that I am?"

"Klara . . ."

I stand up. "Let's be honest, who would want to be friends with someone like me?"

Andy reaches for my hand, but I pull away. "Klara, don't . . ."

I go to my room, close the door behind me, and lean my back

against it, pressing my lips shut tight to keep from crying. It hurts. Because I do want to make friends. I want to be normal. To do all the things people my age do—socialize, date, go to parties, and yes, attend college. I want that more than anything in the world. But I can't, and every time someone reminds me of it, it hurts.

I look to the picture of my mother with that dazzling smile. I remember like it was yesterday the rainy evening she came home and asked my sister and I to have a seat on the sofa, because she had something to tell us. A thousand things flashed through my mind, but I could've never imagined what she was about to say: *"I just came from the doctor's office. A few weeks ago, I noticed a lump in my left breast . . . I've had several tests done, including a biopsy."*

At this word, my entire body went cold.

"It's cancer."

And with *that* word, I was frozen solid.

You hear people talk about the disease, but you never think it will affect you or someone you love; like some abstract, distant danger. My grandmother died of cancer, but it was so long ago that I never thought it could happen to my mother.

Tears, explanations, doctor's appointments, like an avalanche, and, as it was happening, it seemed unreal. It was as if I was watching it all from a distance, like a scene I wasn't even a part of. Every morning I woke up wishing it had all been a bad dream.

Then came the discussions about treatments, chemotherapy, mastectomy. I watched the life leave my mother's body in a slow and painful process; I saw her lose her beautiful black hair, become so thin I was afraid to hug her too tightly. I sat with her for hours on the bathroom floor while she threw up after her chemotherapy sessions. She suffered so much. Why her? It's a selfish question, but seeing my mother go through all that, watching her crawl slowly to her death, was the most painful thing I've ever witnessed—something that marked my life forever.

My mother always tried to stay strong, to fight, but I will never forget the night we came home after the doctor told her that the cancer had spread to her lungs and there was nothing to be done. That she didn't have much time left.

I help her to the bed and she pats the spot beside her. She hugs me close. "Everything will be fine, Klara."

Tears flood my eyes, but I try to be strong for her. "I'm so sorry, Mom."

She kisses my head. "You're sorry? It's not your fault, baby."

"I wish . . ." *My voice breaks.* "I wish I could take all this pain away from you, I . . ." *More tears stream down my face.* "I would do anything for you, but I don't know what to do."

"I know." *Her voice sounds so sad.* "I'm in so much pain, baby," *she says, crying.*

My heart aches for her. I press my lips together, letting the tears come. "I know."

"I'm ready to leave this world. I don't want to suffer anymore; I want all this pain to end. I just can't take it . . ." *She takes my face in her hands.* "I want you to know that I'm going willingly, peacefully, and I want you to listen to your sister, okay?"

I nod, unable to respond.

"I love you, Klara, I love you so much. You and your sister are the best gifts life has given me."

"I love you so much, Mami."

It was just a few weeks later that my mother died. I went into her room with breakfast to find a scene that will remain etched in my brain forever. She was lying in bed, clutching her chest, not breathing. I dropped her breakfast on the floor, shouting for my sister to come, and rushed over to help her. But there was nothing more to be done. My mother was dead. Her body, thin and weak, grew cold in my arms as I held her and sobbed.

"Mom, please, I love you so much. Please don't go."

Kamila tried to pull me away, crying. *"Klara..."*

"No!" I shouted, hugging my mother tighter, kissing her head. *"I won't leave her alone! I can't, she needs me."*

When I looked down and saw how pale her face was, I realized that I would never see her smile again, I would never hear her voice. An overwhelming pain blazed up inside me. She was gone.

Kamila and Andy pulled me away. I cried and wailed until I ran out of breath, until I couldn't take it anymore and I fainted.

7

Message Me

KANG IS BACK and once again I have something to look forward to every other day. I decide to do things differently: Instead of staying cooped up in my room, I go out into the backyard and watch the puppies play as I get ready to listen to tonight's program.

"Good evening, folks. This is Kang, your friend and companion for this evening's radio program, *Follow My Voice*. I missed you all this past week."

I missed you more, I think.

"But I'm back now, ready to play you some songs and discuss some important topics with you, as usual. Today I want to piggyback off a previous topic and talk about the people we miss when they're not around, whether it be a partner, a friend, or someone who is no longer with us. But, before we get into it, I want to welcome a special guest who's stopped by to visit us tonight. You already know him, none other than Erick Lamb, who was gracious enough to sub for me on the show while I was away."

I frown.

"Hey, guys, it's me, Erick, hangin' out with my man Kang tonight."

Kang laughs. "So, in case you're wondering what's going on, I've decided to have special guests on the show every now and then, so we can get different perspectives on our daily topics."

Why? You're perfect all by yourself, I think.

Erick clears his throat. "Don't worry, I won't steal all your time with Kang. I'll just chime in every once in a while."

Kang starts talking about what it feels like to miss someone, but just as I'm beginning to relax and enjoy his voice, Erick interrupts, spoiling everything.

I send a message to the show, praying that Kang will read it. *You don't need Erick. The show is perfect with just you.* —K.

Kang reads out some messages without mentioning mine. But then, unfortunately, Erick speaks up. "Wow, okay, we have a message here from K and, apparently, she is not too happy to have me here."

"She?" Kang asks. "What makes you think K is female?"

"It's crystal clear. I've seen all the messages she sends you and this last one talks about how perfect you are . . . I mean, the *show* is. It's obvious that she's a chick. And I think the audience would agree with me."

I'm mortified. I wrote that message for Kang. Even though I wanted *him* to see it, I knew he wouldn't read it out on the air, because that's just not the way he is. Erick is another story; he likes drama and is constantly creating awkward situations.

Kang is silent for a few seconds. "Well, K, is Erick's sixth sense correct?" he finally says.

Erick laughs and the sound is grating to my ears. "Yeah, babe, just confirm for everyone that I'm right and I promise not to interfere with your darling Kang's show ever again."

I bite my lower lip. I really don't want Kang to have Erick back on the show, and confirming that I'm female doesn't seem like a big deal.

"We have a message from K," Erick says. "But, since I like to keep you on the edge of your seats, we'll play the next song and when we come back, we'll read it to you."

Fear...
In your world of love, and sadness,
let me fear you.
Let me heal you.

The song continues and I like it; Kang always chooses great songs. But I'm finding it hard to listen, kicking myself for having sent that message to the show.

The song ends and Erick begins speaking: "Well, we're back, and I know you can't take the suspense any longer. The message from our darling K says, 'Yes, I'm female. Now, Erick, will you keep your promise?'" Erick lets out a chuckle. "Apparently K is not a big fan of mine... Too bad, babe, your loss! But, all right, let's get back to our topic for today."

Kang talks more about the feeling of missing someone. "People sometimes struggle to admit how much they miss someone, thinking it's a sign of weakness. But as Fyodor Dostoevsky writes in *The Brothers Karamazov*: 'What is hell? I maintain that it is the suffering of being unable to love.'"

"Well, I'll just come out and ask the question on everyone's minds right now," says Erick. "Kang, have you ever missed anyone?"

"Of course."

"A friend? A family member? Or a girl you like?"

My heart stops. I don't want to hear about a girl Kang misses, but I'm unable to take off my headphones.

Silence.

Erick laughs and continues, "I wish you could see the expression on Kang's face right now; I really think it's a girl."

Ouch.

Kang finally speaks. "I don't think people are interested in that, Erick. It's time to say goodbye for tonight. But before we go out with a song, I'd like to read a quote from one of my favorite poems, 'Annabel Lee' by Edgar Allan Poe. 'We loved with a love that was more than love.' Now, to our song. It's about missing someone, to go with our topic of the day. I hope it makes you feel something, anything, even if it's pain, for it's better to feel any emotion than to keep it locked inside. Enjoy, and have a good night."

The song begins and I listen to it as I go back to my room. I lie down on the bed, close my eyes, and start to doze off before I'm woken up by the feeling of my phone vibrating on my chest. I'm a very light sleeper, something left over from the nights when I had to stay alert to care for my mother when she was sick.

Soothing music is playing in my ears; I take off my headphones and sit up to check the message, the light from the screen so bright it blinds me for a second. Kamila and Andy are the only people who text me. Pathetic, I know. But, to my surprise, it's a message from an unknown number.

Unknown: Hello.
Me: Who is this?
Unknown: Kang.

And right there, lying in the darkness of my room, I forget how to breathe.

8

Convince Me

I STARE AT the screen, unable to move, unable to react. Did I read that right? I must be dreaming. I rub my eyes, but the message is still there.

Kang? Kang sent me a message? How? Why? The questions crash into each other inside my head. The border between fantasy and reality has been breached and it terrifies me. Should I answer him?

> **Me:** Kang? From Follow My Voice?
> **Unknown:** The one and only. Sorry to text out of nowhere, don't want to scare you.
> **Me:** How did you get my number?
> **Unknown:** I got it from the radio station message board.
> **Me:** Why?
> **Unknown:** I don't know, K.

What kind of answer is that? My heart feels like it's on the verge of collapse. I'm talking to Kang, whose voice has gotten me through so much for so long.

Me: You're going to have to come up with a better answer than that.
Unknown: I know, I guess I'm just curious about you.
Me: You're curious about one of your listeners?
Unknown: Yes . . .
Me: Is this something you do with all the fans of your show?
Unknown: No, only with you.

I feel a strange tingling in my stomach. *Is this really happening?*

Me: Why?
Unknown: I already told you, curiosity.
Me: How do I know you're really Kang?
Unknown: Ask me anything you want.

I chew on a fingernail as I think about what to ask, and when I glance at the book on my nightstand I get an idea.

Me: Tomorrow during the show, say a quote from Jane Austen at some point; then I'll believe you.
Unknown: Okay. But can I talk to you today?
Me: We can talk tomorrow, person claiming to be Kang.
Unknown: Talk tomorrow, K :)

I put the phone on the bed and hug the pillow tightly, burying my face to stifle a squeal. Did that really just happen? This feeling is new to me. Before my mom got sick, I never thought much about boys. Is this what being interested in someone feels like? If so, Kang is the first guy I've ever really been interested in and I don't even know what he looks like.

I walk out of my room with a smile on my face and run straight into Kamila.

"Oh, I forgot how pretty you look when you smile."

"What? I smile at you often."

"Not like this. This one seems genuine."

I avoid eye contact, still smiling. "It's . . . a beautiful night."

Kamila raises an eyebrow. "I'm guessing your good mood is thanks to that guy's radio show, am I right?"

I nod. "Yeah, you could say that."

Kamila hesitates for a second, and I imagine I'm not going to like what she's about to say. "Have you looked at the university website like we talked about?"

My good mood goes right down the drain.

"Do you think you're ready to visit campus yet?"

"No."

Kamila lets out a long sigh. "Klara, you have to try. Taking even just a class or two this semester would give you a lot to think about, something to do besides sitting home alone filling your head with negative thoughts. The distraction might do wonders for you."

"Kamila, I know I've made some progress, but going to college is completely different. Not only would I have to adjust to an entirely new environment, navigate academic expectations—something I'm so out of touch with, might I remind you—among other things, but what if I have a panic attack in front of everyone? There will be tons of people there. I'd die of embarrassment. I can't. I don't want to."

"I'm not going to force you into anything you don't want to do, you know that. Just think about it, Klara. You're a very smart young lady with a lot of talent and a whole life, experiences, and yes, even challenges ahead of you."

Just as I'm about to snap at Kamila, Andy walks in.

"There they are, my favorite girls."

I give him a tight-lipped smile.

Kamila plants a quick kiss on his lips. "I thought you weren't going to be home until later."

Andy rubs his neck. "I left early—it was a rough day." His eyes move from my sister to me. "Why is everyone so serious?"

"Kamila, once again, was trying to convince me to start college," I answer.

Andy turns to my sister. "I thought you said you weren't going to pressure her."

Kamila crosses her arms over her chest. "When did you two team up against me?"

I shrug. "When Andy stopped making such a fuss about my eating habits, like the Coke and popcorn that you claim are 'unhealthy.'"

Kamila sends her husband a murderous look. "Andy!"

He throws up his hands. "You know I can't say no to her."

Kamila laughs. "All right, just think about it, okay, K?" She takes Andy by the hand. "Come on, I'll give you a massage."

Andy throws me a military salute. "Good night, K1."

I salute back then head to my room, my mind still stuck on the conversation with Kamila. I grab my laptop and look up our city's community college out of curiosity. I scroll through the slideshow that appears on the home page, and I begin to wonder if that could be me one day. I decide to venture further and click on the *Programs and Pathways* tab. I scroll to the bottom and see a photo of a classroom full of students. Frustrated at myself for missing out on so much, I shut my laptop and grab my phone instead, choosing to do something that will distract me: reading my exchange with "Kang."

That night I dream of a radio station, a university campus, and the outline of a guy whose face I can't see.

◆ ◆ ◆

I wake up feeling a little uneasy the next two days, thinking about the conversation with Kamila. She has no idea how much I wish I could be a part of the world, be a normal teenager, experience life.

I think about all the things a nineteen-year-old should be

doing—decorating a cramped dorm room with a roommate, pulling all-nighters, cramming for an exam I forgot to study for, going to football games, joining clubs just to socialize.

I spend the entire day ruminating over the possibilities and my limitations, weighing the pros and cons of going to college, until I finally give up and decide to curl up in bed with a book to pass the time until Kang's show comes on.

But as luck would have it, even my favorite pastime decides to mock me today.

"Welcome back to our show, folks. This is Kang, your faithful friend and companion for this hour of *Follow My Voice*. You might need to break out your sweaters tonight. We're going to see lower temperatures as the summer heat eases and we get ready to welcome a cool, autumnal breeze." He sounds almost excited about it. "Most people prefer summer, but I love the cold; watching snow fall outside my window is one of my favorite things. I wonder if you listeners out there agree with me. Are you winter or summer people?"

I like the cold, too.

"Anyway, with the new semester having started this week, today's topic is how education has changed in the past few years. These days we can't help but mention the impact of the internet and technology..."

I tune out Kang as I begin to think about the topic, back to the pandemic days, when we were forced to take school online. I could do that now, but I know Kamila won't like that; she wants me to leave my bubble, enjoy society. Am I able to? Thinking of the progress I've made so far makes me believe I could...

Sitting by the window, looking at the dark sky, I leave my thoughts behind and realize the show is about to end and Kang hasn't read a quote to his listeners. Was the person messaging me someone else pretending to be him? The thought makes me feel both hurt and relieved at the same time. It's better this way because if I started texting Kang, I'd probably start wanting to meet him, and that's a risk I can't take.

"Well, that's all for now, I hope you enjoyed the songs and theme of tonight's show. Thank you for your messages; even though we don't have time to share them all on the air, I assure you that I always read each and every one as soon as *Follow My Voice* ends. This is your friend and companion, Kang, bidding you farewell. Have a wonderful evening."

I'm so disappointed . . . I'm about to rip my headphones off when I hear Kang's voice again. "Oh, and our quote for today is from *Northanger Abbey* by Jane Austen: 'The person, be it gentleman or lady, who has not pleasure in a good novel, must be intolerably stupid.' Good night, folks."

For the second time in less than three days, Kang leaves me breathless.

9
Surprise Me

"KLARA."

The sound of the water running as I wash the dishes almost drowns out the insistent voice calling my name. My body is present, but my mind is elsewhere. Even though it's been two hours since Kang's show ended, I can't stop replaying his last words over and over, confirming that he in fact sent me those messages the other night.

A hand waves in front of my face. "Klara." Someone shakes my shoulder, bringing me back to reality.

"What is it?"

Kamila appears at my side, studying me like always. "What are you thinking about? You're on the moon."

"Oh..." I soap a cup with the sponge. "Nothing."

She raises an eyebrow. "Are you sure? That's the fourth time you've washed that same cup; I'm sure it's more than clean by now."

I rinse the cup, turn off the tap, and dry my hands with a dish towel. "You wanted to talk to me?"

She nods and gestures for me to follow her to the living room sofa. I can already guess what she wants to talk about, so I'm not surprised when she begins. "We didn't finish our conversation the other day. Now, before you get worked up, I just need you to hear me out. The fall semester just started, and I want you to sign up for classes before the window for registration closes." She tries to sound firm, but her eyes are wary, attentive to my every reaction. "I know it seems fast, but I've checked with your therapist and he agrees that you're ready to take this next step. He wants to see you before you start your first day."

"What, like he's going to be able to prep me for it?"

"He wants to give you some advice in case you have any difficulties at first."

"Difficulties? Do you mean like a nervous breakdown or a panic attack?"

Kamila purses her lips; the possibility obviously concerns her. "I can go with you on the first day, if that would make you feel better."

"Of course, what better way to keep from attracting attention than to have my sister there as a bodyguard!"

To my surprise, Kamila smiles. "Your sarcasm is back, that's good."

I look out the window behind the couch. My chest constricts with fear as I imagine myself surrounded by dozens of college students, all examining me, expressions of disgust on their faces; the girls who used to say they were my friends, whispering about me.

That was high school, Klara, my subconscious reminds me. *Maybe college is different.*

Can I really give it a shot just because I hope the mean teenagers from high school have matured, though? It seems like wishful thinking. Dr. B. would probably say something like "*How bad can it be? If it doesn't work out, then we'll try something else.*" I bite my lip, considering my options. What if it's too soon? We can wait another month, right? That's probably a safer approach, and that's what I need: to be safe.

I'm about to say no when I look away from the window and my eyes land on my sister. I face her hopeful expression, the glint in her eyes and those small wrinkles between and above her eyebrows that have gotten worse since Mom died, and I can't say anything for a minute. She's been with me through everything and she lost her mother, too. And she almost lost me. In this instant, as I stare at her, I can't take that hope away from her.

Maybe *Follow My Voice*'s topic was meant to land on my ears. Thinking of remote classes makes me believe there's a way I can appease my sister while still protecting myself as much as possible.

I take a deep breath because I need to believe that I can make an effort for myself and for her, too.

"I'll give college a try, on two conditions," I say.

Kamila's eyes widen in surprise; she obviously didn't expect a positive response so readily. "Sure, whatever you want."

"I want to start with just one in-person class, and if it's too much, I'll drop it. The rest of the classes will be online, and I'll choose them."

"Okay, what's the second condition?"

"I want to start out at community college."

Kamila frowns. I have a feeling it's because she was hoping I'd want to attend Duke University, the school she graduated from with honors. But my ex-best friend now attends Duke and I have no desire to run into her. Besides, the acceptance process takes months, and even though Kamila still knows people there and could probably pull some strings, that feels wrong, unjust to others.

Kamila thinks about it for a second. "All right, I'll see about getting you enrolled in community college. You'll probably start a few weeks late, since classes have already begun, but I'll try to make it happen as soon as possible."

I give my sister a tight-lipped smile and take her hand. "Thank you. I really appreciate everything you do for me."

Kamila squeezes my hand gently. "It's my pleasure, K."

We hear the sound of the front door opening and shortly after, Andy appears, loosening his tie. "What do we have here? Girls' meeting?"

Kamila lets go of my hand. "Klara has just agreed to start college this semester."

"I agreed to give it a try," I correct her.

Andy can't hide his surprise. "Really? That's great." He sits down with us and we chat for a while about a case he's working on that has been keeping him in the office longer hours than usual.

Andy is a lawyer and has just started his own law firm with a couple friends from law school. He's been a little stressed, but he assures us it's nothing he can't handle. But when the conversation switches to community college, it's me who begins to wonder if it's something *I* can handle. My mind starts spinning with every possible thing that could go wrong, and I feel my heart starting to accelerate. I can't help but excuse myself, pretending I'd like to get a head start and look at possible college courses. I don't want to burst Kamila's bubble, even though by the way she's looking at me, I can tell she's already worried. She's about to say something, no doubt ask me if I'm okay, but I stand and wish them a good night.

When I get back to my room, I nervously check my phone in hopes of finding a text from Kang: zero messages. I toss it onto the bed; what did I expect? I demanded that Kang confirm his identity and now that he has, am I supposed to text him? I'm not going to.

I sit on the bed, stretch out my legs, and pick up my laptop. I navigate to the webpage I use to watch my favorite K-dramas and click on an episode, but I can't concentrate, constantly glancing at my phone. It would be better for everyone if Kang just never messaged me again, a sign for me to come to my senses and stop feeding these impossible delusions. He wrote to me because he doesn't know how messed up I am. It was simple curiosity, as he himself said.

It's late now, almost eleven o'clock, and I know he's not going to text me tonight. Why does it make me so sad?

You're an idiot, Klara. Don't get your hopes up, don't expect anything from him. That's the only way to keep yourself safe.

That's what I'll do. Everything will be fine.

My phone buzzes, announcing a new message, and all my previous thoughts go out the window, because I know it can only be him. No one ever texts me, with the exception of Kamila and Andy, and they're home, so they would come to my room if they had something to tell me. I pause the Korean drama and open the message.

> **Kang:** Are you there?
> **Me:** Yes.
> **Kang:** Forgive me for writing so late.
> **Me:** No big deal.
> **Kang:** I got tired of waiting for you to text me.
> **Me:** Was I supposed to?
> **Kang:** I thought you would after I confirmed my identity.
> **Me:** Oh, sorry . . .
> **Kang:** Am I bothering you, K? If so, just tell me. I'll understand.

I hesitate for a moment. If I say yes, he'll stop texting me and my heart will be safe; if I say no, we'll keep talking and I know my interest in him will only grow.

What should I do?

My finger scrolls up and down the screen, scanning through the conversation with Kang as I try to make a decision. I have to stay inside my safe zone. I'm not sure it's a good idea to keep talking to him since I'll never be able to get to know him in person.

Gritting my teeth, I prepare to lie and tell him that he is indeed bothering me.

"We should all live as if we were going to die tomorrow; we would have much fuller lives if we didn't assume we had all the time in the world." My mother's sweet voice echoes in my mind. No one knows better than I do that we don't have all the time in the world. Before I have a chance to regret it, I respond.

Me: No, you're not bothering me.
Kang: Sweet :) What's your name?
Me: Just call me K.
Kang: You're shy, aren't you?
Me: I guess so.
Kang: Well, what are you doing up so late, K?
Me: I was watching a Korean drama.
Kang: Why does that not surprise me?
Me: What do you mean?
Kang: They've become very popular.
Me: Have you watched any?
Kang: Yes.
Me: Really? I didn't expect that.
Kang: My sister forces me to watch them with her.
Me: I like your sister.
Kang: What about me? From your messages to the show, I could've sworn you liked me.

I remember all the messages I sent professing my admiration for Kang and the show . . . but I did so thinking I would never talk to him.

Me: I really like your show.
Kang: My show, or me?

I didn't expect him to be so direct. I bite my lower lip, unsure of what to say. Kang seems to sense my discomfort.

Kang: Just joking, K.

I need to change the subject. I'm so careful with all of my responses; editing them over and over before I send them. I don't want to write something dumb or make any spelling mistakes.

Maybe I'm overthinking it, but I'm talking to the guy I've been listening to on the radio for the past year, so I think it's understandable that I want to be meticulous.

> **Me:** And what are you doing awake?
> **Kang:** Just thinking. I'm not sleepy.
> **Me:** I've been there. Thinking too much keeps me awake.
> **Kang:** And what do you do to get to sleep?
> **Me:** Chamomile tea helps.
> **Kang:** I have some, I'll give it try. Talk to me while I make it. What K-drama are you watching?
> **Me:** A romantic one.
> **Kang:** How specific!
> **Me:** Was that sarcasm?
> **Kang:** Yes.
> **Me:** Wow, I didn't know you could be sarcastic.
> **Kang:** There are a lot of things you don't know about me.
> **Me:** Like what?
> **Kang:** Like how curious I am about you.

My heart beats faster. Why did he have to say that?

> **Me:** Don't waste your time. I'm nothing special.
> **Kang:** That's hard to believe considering that you've quoted Edgar Allan Poe six times on my show.

Has he counted? I don't remember how many times I sent him lines from different poems, stories, and books I like.

> **Me:** So you're curious as to why I quoted a famous poet?
> **Kang:** No, because you've sent quotes from a lot of my favorite books.
> **Me:** So I've piqued your curiosity through literature?

Kang: You could say that.
Me: Seems a bit cliché.
Kang: Why can't I be cliché?
Me: You can be anything you want to be.

That's the big difference between him and me: He has a bright future ahead of him. I, on the other hand, have limited horizons.

Kang: I owe you one, K.
Me: Why?
Kang: The chamomile worked.
Me: Oh, I'm glad.
Kang: Think I'll be able to sleep now :) Talk tomorrow?
Me: Okay, good night, Kang.

I feel a strange sensation in my stomach as I type his name.

Kang: Good night.

I put my phone down, but another message comes in.

Kang: And you can be anything you want to be, too, K.
Talk tomorrow.

I lay in bed, a big grin on my face. I spend the next few minutes going through our conversation, wishing it could've gone on a while longer. As I read through our texts, I try not to think about one of the main things causing me to stress about community college—something I haven't allowed myself to voice inwardly or outwardly: I'll be attending Durham Community College—the same college Kang goes to.

10

Heal Me

MY THERAPIST'S OFFICE is the most colorful room I have ever been in. There are pictures of rainbows and multicolored landscapes, and the walls are painted in two different shades of blue. I don't know if it's supposed to be therapeutic, but it works for me. I also really like the paintings he has displayed, which were done using a unique layering process. This office is familiar to me and has become another safe space.

Dr. Brant, or Dr. B., as he likes to be called, is a tall, white-haired, balding man with round glasses and an almost permanent reassuring smile. "Klara," he says, bowing jokingly to greet me.

I have paraded through a lot of therapists' offices for close to two years, ever since my mother died, but Dr. B. is my favorite by far and has been my therapist for the past eight months. He makes me feel like I'm not a patient, just someone talking to a friend. He's helped me out so much, and has managed to take my agoraphobia from severe to almost moderate.

"Dr. B.," I say, returning the bow. We sit with his desk between us, facing each other.

"You're looking well, Klara. I'm glad."

"Yes, and I came here alone today."

Agoraphobia has robbed me of so many things, mainly my independence. The constant fear of what might happen to me if I go out alone has limited me greatly. Getting to this point has been a gradual process, another part of my exposure therapy. And since I'll be attending an in-person class in two weeks, I decided to come here by myself, push myself further. Even if this office is a safe space for me, getting in an Uber and sitting inside a car with an unfamiliar driver is not, and that part was terrifying. Coming to my appointment on my own feels like a huge victory.

"That's incredible." He gives me a thumbs-up. "And you're eating better, too, I can tell; that's important when you're on medication."

I nod. "I know."

"Have you been doing your breathing exercises?"

"Yes. I practiced them today on my way here."

"Good. Have you been keeping busy with activities?"

I nod again. "Yes, and I haven't had any panic attacks, even when I've done things outside my comfort zone. I've been staying outside at the park a little more, joining Kamila on small errands every now and then."

"That's excellent news, Klara. But you should still keep doing your breathing exercises in case you do experience a panic attack. Even if it happens, it does not cancel out all your progress up to now. You may experience a few more panic attacks before you say goodbye to them forever, or you may never have one again; only time will tell."

"I know."

"You also know why you're here. You're starting a new chapter of your life—going to college. How do you feel?"

"Very scared."

"And what are you scared of?"

"Everything: being around so many people, having a panic attack in front of everyone, being stared at, being criticized, being made fun of..."

He places both elbows on the desk and leans forward. "What will happen if people stare at you? Will you die?"

I shake my head as I voice my response. "No."

"What if they criticize you or make fun of you?"

I sigh. "Nothing."

"Exactly. Yes, you are going to feel uncomfortable, you might even feel bad, but the reality is that looks and words can't hurt you physically, Klara. And that's your biggest fear, physical harm, dying. Does this concern with people teasing you come from a fear that, for example, you might stop breathing and no one will help you?"

"Yes."

"Why would you stop breathing, Klara? Do you have a lung disease?"

"No."

"Pneumonia? A bad flu, by chance?"

I shake my head.

"So why would a young woman with a healthy pair of lungs suddenly stop breathing?"

Another sigh. "I don't know, they're just thoughts that come to me."

"And what have we said about those kinds of thoughts?"

"They are not facts, they are beliefs rooted in fear," I say, taking a deep breath.

"Where is the evidence to back up this belief that you will suddenly stop breathing?" he points out.

"There's none."

"Exactly. You want to know some facts? You're a young and healthy lady who doesn't even have a cold. You will not spontaneously stop breathing; that's not how our amazing human bodies work. They don't shut down out of nowhere."

"Do you really believe that?" My voice is filled with hope.

"Oh, I do, and my belief is not based on fear, it's based on evidence. Now, where does this belief that you will stop breathing come from? Any ideas? Have you ever experienced any kind of shortness of breath? Or seen something like that?"

I take a moment to process and think about what he's saying, and I bite my nails for a second.

"I . . ." A pause. "It's just . . ." Another pause. He doesn't say anything, nor does he pressure me to continue. He just waits for me, and then it dawns on me. "My mother," is all I say.

He nods. "Your mother?"

The sight of her holding her chest, not being able to breathe before she died comes back to haunt me. "She couldn't breathe—she clutched her chest, and then she died." My voice breaks a little.

His gaze softens. "I'm so sorry you had to witness that, Klara." He hands me a tissue as silent tears roll down my cheeks. "What's the emotion overwhelming you right now?"

"Sadness and despair," I admit, sobbing now.

"Because you couldn't do anything for her at that moment?"

"Yes, I just watched and screamed for my sister." The shame that statement ignites in me brings out more tears.

"It was out of your control." His voice is softer, compassionate.

"I should have done something, been faster, I don't know." I wipe my tears with the tissue.

"And you think that would have changed anything?" His question stings a little.

"Maybe."

"Do you really believe that?" he asks, and I don't answer. "Klara, your mother was very sick. She was at the end of her life, and from what you have said before, she was ready to rest. She had a beautiful conversation with you to make sure this wouldn't happen: the blaming, the guilt, the should haves. No matter what you did or think you should have done, she was still going to die. You couldn't control that."

"I know," I say, sniffling.

"This breakthrough is really important because now we know where this belief is coming from, and I want you to hear these following words and internalize them as much as possible: You are not your mother."

I stop breathing. Words have power, I learned that through therapy, and certain statements hit harder than others, like this one.

"I am not my mother," I voice softly.

"You went through some of the same pains, but you are not her. You're here with no medical reason to stop breathing."

Finding out the root of some of my fears is painful, but a relief comes after it, because the chaos and fear-based scenarios in my head lose strength. Knowing the root of them makes them less scary and more reasonable. Dr. B. and I discuss that belief before coming to the end of the session.

"Do you really think I'm ready to go to college, Dr. B.?"

"What do you think?"

"I don't know. Maybe . . . ?"

"Klara, the first day will be hard. I'm not going to lie to you. But it will get easier as time goes by, and eventually you won't even remember the fear."

"Do you really think so? Do you think I can have a normal life?"

"Of course. Did you think this would last forever? You went through something very scary and stressful that most women your age never have to face, but you're working through it and you're starting to heal. Nothing lasts forever."

My heart fills with hope, but I'm still a little worried. "What if I have a panic attack in the middle of class?"

"If it's something that can't be avoided, you just have to wait for it to pass. You know it will pass."

"I don't want to make a scene," I say.

"Well, if you feel a panic attack coming, go to a private place where you can do your breathing exercises to ride it out. I know it feels scary to be alone during one, but you know what it is, and you know that it will pass. I want you to focus on that part, and I want you to focus on your statements."

"I am calm. I am safe. I am protected."

"Yes, you are, Klara." He smiles at me, and I return it.

Mr. B. gives me more tips for my first day, and then my session is over and I bid him farewell. I feel more relaxed about how to handle starting community college and more hopeful that everything will go well. I *need* everything to go well. Starting college is the first step to regaining control of my life and getting back on the road to normalcy.

11

Think of Me

"GOOD EVENING AND welcome to your favorite program, *Follow My Voice*. This is your friend and companion Kang speaking."

I'm feeding my neighbor's puppies, so my phone is in my pocket and I have my headphones on.

"It's a nice, cool Monday night. You might need to bundle up a bit with a light jacket. I'm loving this drop in temperature so much that I've got a hot chocolate right here next to me, and it's really hitting the spot."

I smile; I love hot chocolate.

"Tonight's theme was chosen by you, our dear listeners, throughout the day today by voting on our X feed."

Donky, one of the puppies, licks my hand and it tickles.

"Out of several options, the winning topic is unrequited love. I was surprised that option won out, but I find it very interesting."

"Unrequited love, huh?" I rub Donky's neck. "Our love is not unrequited, Donky." The puppy sticks out his tongue and licks me. "Our love is pure and true. You and Sappy"—I pet the other puppy—"are my Prince Charmings." Sappy lets out a little bark, and they both melt my heart.

"Apparently, some of our listeners know what it's like to experience unrequited love, maybe because they fell in love with someone who's famous, out of reach, already taken, or unavailable due to other circumstances that made it impossible to be with them. Like Shakespeare's Romeo and Rosaline in *Romeo and Juliet* or Heathcliff and Cathy in Brontë's *Wuthering Heights*, two of the most impossible loves in literature."

Romeo and Rosaline.

Heathcliff and Cathy.

Kang and Klara.

What am I thinking? I shake my head to banish these crazy thoughts.

"I think the only advice I can give is, if circumstances won't allow you to be with a certain person, you need to let them go. I think by holding on to the impossible, you're wasting time and you may miss the opportunity to find someone you can truly be happy with. You may be letting a greater, more possible love slip away before your very eyes. As Benvolio tells Romeo, 'Forget to think of her . . . Examine other beauties.'"

This is the first time I've heard Kang sound a bit negative, although it's practical advice. *Have you ever had an impossible love, Kang?* But he said the other day on the show that he has never been in love.

"I have to admit that I haven't been entirely honest with you, folks."

That gets my attention. I sit down.

"The other day I told you that I'd never been in love, but that's not true. My first love was an unrequited love."

I don't know why it makes me uncomfortable to hear that.

"She was in love with someone else, so yes, I know how it feels, and I can tell you from firsthand experience that it's better to let that person go and move on."

It sounds to me as if he hasn't fully gotten over her. And it hurts.

It shouldn't—Kang is just a radio host whom I like to listen to and whom I've exchanged a few text messages with. It shouldn't bother me that he has feelings for someone else. But it does.

Kang introduces the next song, while I keep turning his words over in my mind. I need to forget about it; it's none of my business, I shouldn't care. Part of me is a little sad that he hasn't texted today, but he's under no obligation to do so. Besides, if I want to talk to him, I could write to him myself. But I won't; I'm not brave enough.

I'm putting water out for the puppies when the song ends and Kang speaks again: "Let's continue with our theme for today. I'd like to share a quote that reads, 'The worst way to miss someone is to have them sitting right next to you and know that you can never have them.' This line is by the incredible Gabriel García Márquez. What do you think? I agree that the most painful of all unrequited loves are the ones in which a person has to share their daily life with someone they long to be with but can't. Have you experienced anything like that? Share your thoughts with us."

Kang says he's going to read messages from listeners and first up is Liliana. "Liliana left us a message today. She says, 'Dear Kang, you are my unrequited love.'"

My jaw almost drops to the floor. *Really?!*

Kang laughs. "I don't think I'm anyone's unrequited love, Liliana, but I'm flattered."

What if Liliana piques Kang's curiosity and he decides to text her? I'm sure that, unlike me, she wouldn't hesitate for a second to initiate a conversation with him. *I don't care*, I tell myself.

When the show ends, I reluctantly take off my headphones. If it weren't for Donky and Sappy, I'd be in a bad mood. But these adorable puppies are a source of calm.

A few minutes later, Paula comes to get them and I cuddle them each one last time before she takes the pups home. As I say goodbye and close the door, my phone vibrates. Excited, I quickly open the message.

Kamila: Andy and I are getting dinner out, we'll be back in a few hours.

I'm disappointed. Kang is not going to message me.

I take a shower to pass the time, enjoying the hot water washing over me as I think about my first day of college and what classes I will take. But, as I'm rinsing my hair, my chest constricts. I try to take a deep breath, but I can't. It feels like I have something lodged in my throat, preventing me from breathing. Fear courses through my veins, my heart races, my arms and legs begin to go numb.

I can't breathe. I'm alone. There's no one here to help me.

Heat spreads to my face and now I'm suffocating. I turn off the water, wrap a towel around my body, and step out of the shower.

I'm going to die. No. No.

I pick up my phone, but my hands are shaking so badly that I can barely see the screen as I struggle to call Kamila. Before my sister has a chance to say anything, I pant desperately into the phone: "I . . . can't . . . breathe."

"K?"

Kang's voice on the other end of the line takes me by complete surprise. "I . . ."

"K? Are you all right?"

"No . . . I . . ." Tears flood my eyes. "I'm scared . . . I can't breathe."

"Why? Are you sick? What's the matter?"

"I . . ." I'm short of breath. "I . . . panic attack." My speech is incoherent. "Do you know what that is . . . ? I . . . My chest hurts."

"I do know what a panic attack is." Kang's voice becomes softer. "It's going to pass, K. I'll stay with you until it does."

"I'm so scared . . ." My voice breaks. I don't know why I'm telling Kang this, but he's the only person I have and his voice in my ear is soothing.

"I'm here with you, K. You'll feel better soon, you'll see."

Thick tears roll down my cheeks. "I can't breathe."

"Yes, you can, K. What you're feeling right now is going to pass and you're going to feel good again."

"No! That's not true. I think I'm having a heart attack."

"That's not going to happen, I promise. I'm right here, K. I'll help you through this. Try to breathe with me, think of something else while this panic attack passes . . . Do you realize the leaves will start changing colors soon? Don't you love the way the wind blows them gently from the branches, how they dance in the air until they reach the ground?" There's something about how he says his words that I find calming. My chest rises and falls rapidly as I listen to him. He keeps speaking. "I want you to think about the fall, K. Close your eyes. I want you to remember how the colorful autumn leaves float softly to the ground . . . Are you visualizing it?"

I close my eyes. "Yes."

"Now, every time you see a leaf fall, take a deep breath . . . Remember that you're the one imagining it and the leaves can fall at whatever pace you need them to."

I listen to him and follow his advice. After a while, I don't know how long, the panic attack, little by little, begins to dissipate and my breathing returns to normal.

"Kang."

"That's the first time you've said my name—I like the way it sounds when you say it. You have a very nice voice, K."

My heart is still beating quickly, but at least I can breathe now. "I . . . I don't know what to say . . ."

"You don't have to say anything. Are you feeling better?"

"Yes, thank you . . . for . . . You must think I'm . . ."

"Stop. I'm glad I could help."

"Really, thank you. I must have dialed your number by mistake, but you helped me so much. Thank you."

Kang sighs. "I'm glad you made that mistake, then."

"Why?"

"Because I got to hear your voice. I think it's only fair since you've heard mine so many times."

"My voice is nothing special."

"I disagree. It's nice and kind of growing on me, K."

Now that the fog of the panic attack has lifted, it hits me that I'm talking to Kang on the phone and I begin to feel nervous. "I should go."

"Okay, get some rest. If you feel bad again, you can call me by mistake anytime."

I feel a familiar tingling in my stomach. "Okay. Good night, Kang."

"Good night, K," he whispers, and I feel the tingling intensify. "Oh, and K?"

"Yes?"

"Thanks for letting me follow your voice," he says, before hanging up.

12

Remember Me

DEFEAT.

What I feel is utter defeat, infecting every particle of my being. I thought I was getting better; I thought I could lead a normal life. I've been so deluded, such an idiot. Everything I've achieved over so many months of effort all destroyed in matter of minutes. I sit on my bed, my back against the wall, hugging my knees to my chest as if I might somehow be able to hold my broken pieces together.

After Kang hung up, I sat without moving until Kamila and Andy got home. I was afraid that if I did anything else I might have another panic attack. Talking to Kang calmed me down, but it didn't cure me. My fears are still there, bubbling under the surface like lava waiting to erupt.

The voice inside my head has become mean and cruel. *You called him in the middle of a panic attack? Do you have any idea how crazy he must think you are?* Or, even worse: *Now he feels sorry for you. Couldn't you hear the pity in his voice as he was trying to calm you down? You're pathetic, Klara.*

Kamila gave me a long talk about how this was not a setback, and that my progress has not been in any way affected by this one incident. So why do I feel so bad about it? I rub my face, lie down, and burrow under the covers to try to sleep.

◆ ◆ ◆

What I hate and fear most about depression is the state of "deactivation," as I like to call it, where you just feel numb. Things happen around you but you can't participate, existing without any reason or motivation. It's as if life leaves your body and you're left an empty shell. You don't live, you don't think, you don't speak, you just exist.

"Good morning!" Andy comes into my room. "I brought you breakfast."

This is a surprise since Kamila is the one who usually takes care of me. I guess she can't miss any more shifts at the hospital. My phone is on my nightstand, but I haven't looked at it or listened to Kang's show in a week. I'm sitting in what has become my favorite position: back against the wall, arms around my knees with my chin resting on them.

"Paula asked about you. She wants to know when the puppies can visit again."

I don't respond.

"Klara, look at me."

I turn my head slightly toward him. The fine lines on his face become more pronounced, even through his facial hair, as he smiles kindly, his deep brown eyes staring at me intently. "You know we're not going away, Klara." He places a hand on my shoulder. "I'm not an expert like your sister, but I'll speak from the heart. You didn't take a step back. You had a panic attack, but those few minutes don't cancel out all the hours I know you were feeling good. Think about all the fun you had with the puppies. Or when you practice your exposure therapy. Or how much you enjoy that boy's radio show." He squeezes my shoulder. "Don't let a few minutes define things, okay? Just let me know what you need and I'll get it for you."

I think of how my mother used to take care of me when I was

sick as a little girl. She would make me vegetable soup and feed me, even after I was too big for it.

"Open up big for Mama." Her smile is contagious. "Come on."

"Mom, I'm not a baby anymore. I'm eleven years old," I say, rolling my eyes.

She pats my cheek. "You will always be my baby, now open up."

I reluctantly oblige and she feeds me a spoonful of soup. It's delicious. She looks at me with so much love in her eyes.

At the time I didn't appreciate the peace and security she was able to transmit with a simple glance.

Thick tears run down my face. "Soup."

Andy is surprised to hear my voice. It's the first time I've spoken in days. "You want soup?"

I nod, my voice hoarse from tears, as I respond, "Vegetable soup."

Andy pats my back. "Vegetable soup it is." He leans over and gives me a kiss on the head.

When Andy comes back a little while later, I don't move, but he seems to read my mind and picks up the spoon. "Okay, come on, open wide," he says, playing along as he feeds me a spoonful of soup. It might be the most childish thing in the world, but it's what I need right now. I don't know why, but this sense of being taken care of makes me feel safe enough to reenter the world, to reactivate. Andy pats my cheek just like my mother used to. "You're going to be fine, Klara, I promise."

His total assuredness makes me feel better. I am so grateful to have Andy in my life. Not just anyone would be willing to put up with what he's been through with my mom, my sister, and me. He has a wonderful, kind heart. Maybe life, when it rips people away from us, tries to make up for it by putting other people in their place.

"So, I've been listening to your radio show with that guy, Kang, right?" he says casually as he feeds me another spoonful. "He's very good at what he does—he seems quite mature for such a young man."

I can't believe Andy has been listening to the show. Yet another thing he does for me.

"He's mentioned you several times on the air."

I almost choke on the soup. "He mentioned me?"

"Yes. On more than one occasion. He said he wondered where K could be, asked if you were listening, and said he was surprised that you hadn't sent any messages. I assumed you were K, it's too much of a coincidence."

I continue eating in silence.

Kang mentioned me on *Follow My Voice*? I find that hard to believe. A tentative feeling of joy buoys to the surface, but the weight of my depression pushes it back down. When Andy finishes feeding me, I stand up and reach for a towel.

"I'm going to take a bath," I say, but I immediately freeze as I remember the panic attack I had in the shower.

Kamila has stayed with me while I showered the past few times. Andy seems to understand my fear. "I'll wait by the bathroom door. You won't be alone. I'll be right outside in the hall, okay?"

My lips are trembling. "Thank . . ." My voice breaks, so I try again. "Thank you, Andy."

He smiles. "You're welcome, K1, always."

◆ ◆ ◆

I feel a little better after showering, but I go back to bed and lay under the covers until I hear the front door open. Kamila must be home from her shift. I get up and start walking to the living room. When I reach the hallway, I come to a halt and watch as she stops in front of Andy, who's waiting for her in the kitchen. They say nothing, just look at each other for a few long seconds. Kamila starts to cry, and it breaks my heart. Andy hugs her, stroking the back of her head and whispering words of encouragement.

This is the side of Kamila that she never shows me. I know she hasn't had it easy, either. Just because she's a psychiatrist doesn't mean she's made of stone. She was deeply affected by our mother's death and her work is emotionally draining. A few months ago, a patient she'd been treating for years died by suicide, and that broke a part of her that I'm not sure can ever be put back together; she feels like she failed him.

I don't want to be a burden to her, to make things harder. Heartbroken for Kamila, I return to my room, determined to stay afloat and overcome my deactivated state. I think back to Kang's soothing words as he helped me through my panic attack. Kang...

"It's going to pass, K. I'll stay with you until it does."

"I'm here with you, K. You'll feel better soon, you'll see."

Hearing his voice on the phone was a thousand times better than listening to him on the radio. I'll never forget that feeling of having him so close.

Well, that was the last time, unless you're planning to make him talk to you again out of pity.

I run my hand along the window and feel the cold glass on my fingers. I try to tell myself that Kang doesn't pity me, that he understands what it's like to suffer a panic attack. He stayed with me until it was over.

I plug my phone in and leave it charging while I open the curtains so I can watch the leaves dance in the breeze. It looks so pretty and relaxing. Mom was the biggest fan of the fast-approaching season, and her enthusiasm made it grow on me. She used to say fall leaves were nature's confetti, that it was Earth's way to cheer us up. I guess that's why one of my favorite paintings is of an autumn forest with a little cabin in the distance. Cliché, I know, and some would consider it basic. In my defense, I could picture myself in that cabin, smelling nature and watching the leaves fall during a crisp morning. I'd wear a sweater while holding a cup of hot cocoa. I wonder if I will ever be able to do that: travel and stay in a remote place like that. It seems impossible now. What other things and experiences am I missing while staying here?

More sadness flows through me at all the possibilities of things I could be doing out there.

I settle back into bed and pick up my phone, now charged enough to power on, and I feel it vibrate in my hand. There are tons of notifications about new episodes of Korean dramas, voicemails from Kamila on the day of the panic attack, and . . . eleven messages from Kang!

My heart leaps as I open the chat thread to read from the first message to the most recent.

Friday

9:04 A.M. Good morning, K. Hope you're doing all right today. I was waiting for you to text me when you felt ready, but I grew impatient. I hope that's okay.

5:57 P.M. Ready for today's show?

8:16 P.M. No messages sent today either, huh? It's okay. Hope you're feeling better.

Saturday

10:35 A.M. I know answering messages should not be your priority right now. I just hope you're doing okay.

1:57 P.M. Now I get how listeners must feel when they send messages to Follow My Voice with no response.

7:03 P.M. I've decided to send you quotes, like you used to send to the show and brighten up my afternoon. Maybe they'll have a similar effect on you.

8:46 P.M. "Come what come may, time and the hour runs through the roughest day," from Shakespeare. Good night, K.

Sunday

7:56 A.M.   "No matter how long the storm, the sun always shines behind the clouds," by Kahlil Gibran.

2:47 P.M.   "The thing in the world I am most afraid of is fear," by Michel de Montaigne.

9:39 P.M.   "How sweetly sounds the voice of a good woman! It is so seldom heard, that, when it speaks, it ravishes all senses," by Philip Massinger.

Today

11:24 A.M.   "Like a dream the echo of her voice rings forever in my ears," by Ramón de Campoamor. I hope Google translated it correctly.

What are you doing, Kang? What are you hoping to find in someone like me? And why does your insistence buoy me up and make me want to feel again?

13

Lift Me Up

KANG DOES NOT give up.

I thought he would get tired of waiting for me to reply and stop sending messages, but two days have gone by and his texts are still coming steadily.

Kang: Good morning, K.

I stare at the chat thread, scrolling up and down with my thumb on the screen. I'm sitting on the bed with a pillow on my lap. Yesterday, as much as I loved reading Kang's messages, I couldn't bring myself to respond. The cruel voice inside my head began taunting me every time I even considered it: *You're going to write back? Really? You think a guy like him wants to get mixed up with someone who has as many problems as you?*

I recall my last conversation with Dr. B.

"And what have we said about those kinds of thoughts?"

"*They are not facts, they are beliefs rooted in fear.*"

I take a deep breath and process those thoughts. *There is no evidence he is sending those messages out of pity. Kang may just be curious about me.*

I have to make more of an effort. I can do it. I've been eating better, trying to find my way back to the path I'd charted with my life before everything that happened.

The doorbell rings and I know who it is. I stand up, feeling *almost* cheerful.

You can do this, Klara, I say to myself.

I open the door for our next-door neighbor Paula, carrying a puppy in each hand.

"Good morning, Klarita." Paula is a woman in her forties exuding elegance and style. Her makeup is always flawless and her hair is high in a perfect ponytail. She has never married; her dog, Drew, and now these puppies are her family. "Donky and Sappy have really missed you."

I smile. "I missed them, too."

"Great choice today. I love the purple; it's your color."

"Andy likes the pink."

"Andy doesn't know the first thing about style." Paula hands me the puppies and, after saying goodbye, I close the door and put them down.

Sappy and Donky hop around happily, wagging their tails so fast I can barely see them. I kneel down to meet them at semi–eye level. "I guess it's true. You really did miss me, huh, you silly doggies!" Sappy barks and licks my hand while Donky climbs into my lap and starts licking my chin. Immediately, I feel better; these puppies are like magic. Their love is unconditional, no matter my faults, no matter my weaknesses. I feel a knot forming in my throat. "I missed you little guys, too. I . . ." I swallow. "I had a little setback, but I'm getting better now."

Donky tilts his head to one side and stares at me. "You guys are going to help me, aren't you?" I wipe away a tear. "Of course you're going to help me."

Donky barks and pushes his little head against my chest, making me smile.

"I wish everyone was like you. So loving, never judging."

◆ ◆ ◆

I spend all day playing with Donky and Sappy. I feed them, take them out into the yard for a while to relieve themselves, and then sit on the couch with them. Through the double windows in the living room, I watch as it begins to rain.

The rain falls harder and it feels like a cruel joke, because it was raining just like this the day my mother told us she had cancer. And it was raining just like this the day of my mother's funeral.

My clothes are soaked, and my wet hair sticks to the sides of my face. My lips tremble from the cold and tears mingle with the rain pouring down on me.

"I'm so sorry, Klara."

"Sorry for your loss."

"Your mother was a great woman."

"She made the most delicious cakes."

"You'll get through this."

Everyone is talking all around me, but I can't hear anyone. A pair of arms guides me and hands squeeze my shoulder comfortingly, but I can't feel them. Why? Have I died along with you, Mom? Or is it that you're the only one capable of comforting me now?

The people dressed in black are beginning to disperse, time goes by, but still, I can't feel anything. An umbrella appears above my head. I don't know who's holding it until I hear Kamila's voice. "Klara, it's time to go."

My eyes are still fixed on the dirt that covers my mother's grave.

Kamila squeezes my shoulder. "Klara, are you listening to me? You're going to catch a cold. Let's go home."

Home . . .

How can we still call it home when Mom will no longer be there, when I will no longer be able to smell the cakes she bakes or hear her laughter, so loud it could be heard from several houses away?

Kamila tugs at my arm, but I refuse to budge.

"No," I whisper through my wet, shivering lips. "We can't leave her alone, Kamila, it's too cold."

"Klara . . ." My sister's voice is broken.

"My jacket . . ." I start to take off my coat. "She needs it, she must be so cold."

Kamila tries to stop me. "Klara, no, don't."

I push her away and kneel down to place my jacket over the fresh earth that has swallowed my mother. "That's better, Mom. Now you won't be so cold. I'm not going to leave you alone, don't worry." I press the jacket into the dirt. "I won't leave you alone, Mom. You always told me that you hated being alone and that's why you had two daughters. You told me that, because you were an only child, you never had anyone to play with. And I know how you always hated the rain. I'm here, I won't leave you alone with this rain and this cold."

I hear Kamila sobbing behind me.

"I love you so much, Mom." My eyes are blurred with tears. "How could I leave you here all alone? How could I?" I say hoarsely, still crying and pressing my jacket to the ground.

"How can I go on without you?"

Strong arms pull me up, forcing me to stand.

"No." I try to break free. "No . . ."

Andy does not loosen his grip, now pulling me away.

"No, Andy, no. We can't leave her alone in the rain."

Kamila turns my head so that I'm looking at her. Her face is red and her eyes are swollen from crying. "Klara"—she holds my face between her hands—"we have to go. Remember what Mom said, that she'll always be with us as long as we keep her here." She places a hand over my heart. "She'll never be alone; she'll always be with us."

My lips tremble, and I keep trying to free myself. "I don't want to leave her. It's raining so hard. I'm not going to leave her like this."

"Mom will not be alone."

"I'll stay with her until it stops raining," *Andy says, and his voice suddenly reminds me that he's still there.* "Go home and get some rest. I'll keep your mother company, okay?"

"You promise?" *I ask.* "Promise you won't leave her alone as long as it keeps raining? She doesn't like the rain."

Andy nods.

"I promise you, honey. Now go home."

Two tears slide down my cheeks as I remember that moment. The rain is still pounding against the window.

I miss you so much, Mom. I'm sorry I haven't been able to visit your grave. I wish I could go out whenever I want to . . . But I'm trying, Mom. For you, for Kamila, for Andy, for me. I'm trying my best to be able to visit you whenever I want, to keep you company on rainy days like this.

I wipe my tears, careful not to move too much since Sappy and Donky are asleep on top of me.

And then the phone vibrates in my pocket and I carefully pull it out to check the message:

Kang: Nice weather we're having today. It's strange how I love the snow, but hate the rain.

No, it is not strange, I want to say; I feel the same way. Another message comes in.

Kang: I miss your voice, K.
Kang: The show's about to start. Will you be listening tonight?

My heart skips a beat. I hesitate for a few seconds and stand up slowly so as not to wake the puppies. I find my headphones and put them on. Back on the couch, I anxiously tune into the program, because I've also missed the sound of his voice, so much.

"Good evening, folks. Welcome to tonight's evening program, *Follow My Voice*. This is Kang, your host and faithful companion during this hour."

And there, for the first time in days, with the puppies beside me, listening to the show, I feel truly motivated to get back on my road to healing, picking up right where I was before the last anxiety attack.

I smile, happiness warming my heart, reactivated, ready to feel again.

Call Me

Me: Great show last night, Kang.

I send the message without thinking twice. But it's okay—Kang deserves some sign of life from me after he sent so many messages without giving up. The fact that he cares so much about a stranger whose name he doesn't even know says a lot about him.

I'm vacuuming the living room carpet. After spending so many days in a state of deactivation, I feel the need to be productive and help out around the house. It's the least I can do for Kamila and Andy. I'm not yet ready to go back out, but if I'm going to stay inside all day, I can at least clean. I find it surprisingly enjoyable, in fact, because it's a great distraction.

My phone vibrates in my pocket, and I try to act natural but fail as I instantly turn off the vacuum and pull out my cell as fast as I can to read Kang's text.

Kang: I'm glad you liked it, K.

His message puts a smile on my face. I like that he doesn't mention what happened and refrains from pointing out that this is the first time I've texted back in days, after so many messages from him. It's as if none of that ever happened. I close my eyes as I think about what to say next to keep the conversation going. His reply was not a question, so I don't know if he even expects me to respond. My phone vibrates again as another text comes in.

> **Kang:** And what is the mysterious K up to today?
> **Me:** I'm cleaning. How about you?
> **Kang:** A little bit of homework. Now I'm composing :)

I furrow my brow. Composing? That word can only mean one thing.

> **Me:** You compose . . . songs?
> **Kang:** Yes, I like music. I think I'm kinda good at it, although I might be kidding myself.

I imagine him singing with that amazing voice of his and my heart races. I guess having a good radio voice doesn't necessarily mean he's a good singer, but something tells me he is. I can't imagine this guy being bad at anything.

> **Me:** Really? I would've never guessed.
> **Kang:** I don't tell a lot of people. Consider yourself lucky, you know my dark secret.
> **Me:** That's not a dark secret.
> **Kang:** Hahahahaha, you say that because you don't know the whole story.
> **Me:** And are you going to tell me? :O
> **Kang:** Depends.

Me: Depends on what?
Kang: I'll tell you about my singing if you tell me your name. ;)

I bite my lower lip, hesitating.

Me: Why do you want to know?
Kang: Isn't it obvious? So I can look you up on social media and stalk you.

I laugh out loud at his honesty, but I'm not worried, because I'm not on any social media; I deleted most of my accounts. All I have left is the old Instagram profile I use to check the radio station's account, but I don't even have any photos on it.

Me: Well, that doesn't really make me want to tell you.
Kang: Just kidding . . . Or maybe not ;)

I scratch my head, imagining the consequences of telling Kang my name. We live in a small city, as my mother called it: too many people for it to be considered a town but too few to be a major city. There are probably several Claras, but there is probably only one Klara with *K*. That unique spelling, causing problems.

Me: I'll tell you, someday.
Kang: It's okay, I understand.
Me: But I still want to know the super-secret story behind your music.
Kang: If you call me, I'll tell you.

I hold my breath. He keeps trying to move things along, always wanting to know more about me. *What is it you're looking for, Kang?* I feel nervous just thinking about talking to him on the phone; it's hard enough to send him messages, taking my time with every single response, but hearing him live, right in my ear, his beautiful voice would destroy me. The day I called him by mistake I was overwhelmed with panic, so I didn't feel nervous about talking to him then, but calling him now, when I'm calm, is another thing entirely. I can't do it.

> **Me:** You love to negotiate, don't you?
> **Kang:** Yes, you leave me no choice.
> **Me:** What do you mean?
> **Kang:** You won't tell me anything about yourself, not even your name. So I have to employ my best tactics, K.
> **Me:** Tactics for what?
> **Kang:** For getting closer to you.

Kang is an expert at leaving me speechless. I'm about to respond when I receive an incoming call from Kang. I stare at the phone, moving it from one hand to the other. Should I answer? Can I handle this? What if I stutter? What if he notices that I'm left breathless by certain things he says? I don't want to make a fool of myself.

"Forget the what-ifs, they won't get you anywhere, Klara," my mother told me on one of our many afternoons at the lake. *"Life is too short to worry about the multiple possibilities or outcomes that might result from every decision we make in the situations we face."*

I accept the call, squeeze my eyes shut, and lift the phone to my ear. "Hello?"

A second of silence, and then I hear that voice that I've heard so often, that voice that has helped me through so many dark moments alone, that voice that I have always followed tirelessly.

"Hello, K."

I swallow, trying to remain calm, but I feel my heart in my throat. "Hello, Kang."

He chuckles and my legs go weak. "Have I told you before how much I like the way my name sounds when you say it?"

This comment turns my legs to jelly. I can't say anything for a few seconds, so Kang speaks again.

"Thank you for answering, I thought it might scare you. Now I feel less guilty."

"Don't worry . . ." I need to get the conversation back around to him so that he can do more of the talking. "So, are you going to tell me the dark story of your music?" I ask.

There's that quiet laughter again. This guy is going to give me a heart attack.

"Yes, we made a deal, and I intend to keep my end of it, at least."

I frown. "I didn't say I accepted the deal."

"You were never going to accept it, K."

How does he know?

"You weren't going to call me. I knew you wouldn't."

"So you called me."

Sigh. "Yes, I think I'm getting to know you a little bit."

"Well, I still want to hear that story."

"Okay, so by day I'm Kang, diligent student; some evenings, Kang, host of the most popular college radio program in town. And, on some nights, I play my songs at a bar on Fourteenth Street."

That's not what I expected. How does Kang have time to do all those things? "I don't understand, what part of that secret is dark?"

"No one knows it's me."

"No one knows you play music at a bar?"

"No one who knows me knows anything about it. Well, except Erick."

"How mysterious. Why are you hiding it?"

"Well . . . it's a part of me that I don't want to show everyone. That's why I wear a mask."

The story just keeps getting better and better. This guy leads a double life. I feel like I'm talking to Superman. By day, he's a regular guy; by night, he's a mysterious, masked singer. I can't stop myself from giggling. I cover my mouth, but I realize he's heard me. "I'm sorry."

"It's funny, I know. You can laugh, K."

I press my lips together, holding in my laughter. "And what mask is it? Like the Flash?"

"Not far off. It's actually . . ." He clears his throat. "Batman."

I can't help but crack up as I picture him singing in a crowded bar wearing a Batman mask.

Kang feels the need to defend himself. "It was the best option I could find. I needed a mask that would cover my face but still leave my mouth free so I could sing."

I'm now laughing uncontrollably.

Kang groans. "Fine, fine, laugh all you want!"

I finally get ahold of myself, out of breath; a few tears have even escaped my eyes. I haven't laughed like this in so long. I'd forgotten how therapeutic it can be.

"K?"

"Sorry, sorry. I'm here. Thank you! I needed that. I'm still curious as to why you need a mask at all though?"

"If making you laugh comes at my expense, then I'm okay with it. I'm glad I was able to do that for you. Though it was as much for my benefit as it was yours . . ."

Silence.

Kang coughs, then proceeds. "Anyway, I'll save the story of the reason for my mask for another day. Now I know you'll have a reason to continue to talk to me."

Why are you saying these things to me, Kang?

I take a second to respond, willing my rapidly beating heart to slow down. "Well, then I guess this won't be the last time you hear from me. Either way, I really enjoyed learning your dark secret."

"I'd love for you to come see me play one of these nights. Are you twenty-one yet? I don't even know your age." Kang suddenly lets out an exaggerated gasp. "You're not secretly an old woman trying to seduce a young college guy like me, are you?"

"That's exactly it," I joke. "That's why I won't tell you my name. So you can't find me in the town's nursing home records."

"I knew it."

I grin like an idiot. "What kind of music do you play?"

"That's another part of the story you haven't yet unlocked."

"What?"

"My information for your information. Shall we resume negotiations?"

"Seriously?"

"Yeah. I mean, I don't mind telling you about myself, but I know that if I don't ask you for information in return, you'll never reveal anything about yourself."

I huff. "You talk as if you already know me."

"Am I wrong?"

I hold in a chuckle. "Well . . . Since I already have to wait to hear more about your mask—what do you want in exchange for telling me more about your music right now?"

"Your name."

"Fine, my name is . . . Claire." It's similar enough to my name, so I'm not technically lying.

Kang sighs. "Why are you lying to me, K?"

This guy is a mind reader. "How do you know I'm lying?"

"After all your reluctance, for you to just say your name so quickly seems suspicious."

"You seem to be able to read people pretty well without having met them."

"Actually, I'm very bad at it, but with you . . ."

My heart is racing again. "With me what?"

"I don't know, K, things feel so . . . easy."

I want to ask what he means, but I don't think I can handle his answer.

"Klara."

"What?"

"My name is Klara with a K. Nice to meet you, Kang."

15

Astonish Me

THIS IS A *bad idea*, I think, but I don't say it. I don't want to kill the excitement I see in Kamila's eyes as she walks beside me to the car. Andy is waiting for us with his hands on the steering wheel, smiling. I take a deep breath, clenching my fists at my sides.

It's going to be okay, Klara, I say to myself over and over again. I need to do this, I need to face life again, for Mom, for Kamila, for Andy, for myself. The sun feels nice on my face, like it's awakening my senses and charging me with energy. I've spent so much time indoors recently that even just exposing my skin to sunlight feels like an accomplishment.

I get in the back seat and Kamila sits up front.

Andy glances at me in the rearview mirror. "Black, huh? I liked the pink," he jokes.

I give him a nervous smile. "I like black, it's the color of my soul."

Kamila shakes her head and smiles. "Her dark sense of humor is back, Andy."

Andy starts the car and I swallow, tightening my grip on the seatbelt that runs across my chest. I take a deep breath and look out the window as we pass trees, houses, stores, people. I focus on the view in an attempt to stop myself from thinking obsessively about my breathing and the fear that I won't be able to stop thinking about it. After explaining my unique situation, Kamila managed to get us a private guided tour of the community college campus today, Saturday, when there will be few students around.

Familiarizing myself with the campus at a time when it's not crowded will help me feel more comfortable when I start classes. This was a recommendation from Dr. B., who said that a gradual, thoughtful adaptation process would be best. This campus visit is the first step and then I'll begin attending one in-person class three days a week this semester.

I have to admit that I'm terrified. My palms are sweating and strings of negative thoughts parade through my mind, but just when I'm ready to give up and go back to my room, those four walls that have become my safe haven, I think of Kamila's tears and I remember my mother's words. I remind myself that it will be hard, but, if I want to recover, I have to do my part. I wish there was some sort of magic cure for anxiety and depression. But the cold, cruel reality is that, no matter how much help I have, I will never overcome my depression and anxiety if I don't actively do something about it. It's going to take a lot, because mine was not a mild case by any means, but I've made some progress, and that makes me feel like I can do it.

"*You know what's good about hitting rock bottom? You can only go up from there,*" my mother once said. Those words have always stayed with me. She was such a wise, bold woman, an entrepreneur, so sweet and full of love to give. I put my hand on the window and feel the warmth of the sun through the glass. I miss her so much.

Andy parks in front of a large sign that reads DURHAM COMMUNITY COLLEGE in black and blue lettering. The main building looks much bigger and more modern than I expected; the pictures online don't do it justice.

"Ready?" Andy asks, opening the door for me.

I clutch the seatbelt, close my eyes, fill my lungs with air, and let it out slowly to relax the tension in my muscles. I open my eyes, unclick my seatbelt, give Andy a thumbs-up, and step out of the car.

The entrance to the main building is wide with metal and glass doors. We walk along as Kamila reads the names on several offices until she finds the one she's looking for. We knock and are greeted by a woman with short white hair and wrinkles decorating her face. Next to her is a younger woman with long black hair and a big smile.

"Welcome, Klara." The younger woman holds out a hand. "I'm Caitlin Romes, one of the counselors here at the college, and this is Mrs. Leach, head of Counseling Services."

I shake Ms. Romes's hand and then Mrs. Leach's.

"We're delighted to have you here. We'll do our best to make this process as smooth as possible."

They both seem nice—not like the kind of people who are just pretending to be nice out of pity.

"Well, let's get down to it, I'll show you around campus."

Ms. Romes guides us from place to place, each building rising between winding walkways and carefully kept green spaces. There's a cafeteria, a small fitness center, a library, a bookstore, a field used for various outdoor sports, an indoor court, and my favorite, a student courtyard. It's a vibrant open space with a blend of a neatly trimmed lawn, trees that provide plenty of shade, and paved walkways. Benches and metal tables are dispersed across the courtyard, offering various spaces to sit and relax. Walking through it, I can't help but hope one day I'll get to enjoy its calmness. As for the buildings, the different wings are modern and spacious: long corridors lined with classrooms, stairways that lead to different levels . . . just like any other campus, I assume.

Eventually, we arrive at the art exhibition rooms and painting studios, and I get the sense my sister requested that this be one of our stops.

I pause in a doorway, staring at all the tools—brushes, canvases, paints—and students' work displayed on the walls. And, for the first time in a long time, seeing the process of art being created doesn't hurt.

"Your sister mentioned that you're an artist," says Ms. Romes. "Have you heard of the artist known as Mann, the prominent painter? She's one of our art instructors here; you'd love her."

I nod, smiling, and walk away from the door. Getting back into painting is an idea I've rejected up until now. It may not hurt so badly to look at art anymore, but from there to painting again is a long way.

Let's take it one step at a time, Klara.

The campus seems so peaceful without any students around and I don't think I'd have any difficulty attending classes if it were always like this, but imagining the halls filled with college kids, all staring at me, gives me anxiety.

After the art studio, we head back to the counseling offices, where Ms. Romes shows me a list of college courses and different degree options. I'm not really sure what career I'd like to pursue, so I opt to enroll as Undecided. Kamila and I agreed I don't want to feel overstimulated and overwhelmed for my first semester, so I decide to only take two courses—one online class (ENG-231 American Literature I) and one in-person class (HEA-110 Personal Health/Wellness).

Once my classes are chosen and locked into my schedule, Ms. Romes hands me the campus map and a couple pamphlets, including the one that consists of emergency services and contacts. I see her name and number on the list, and it somehow brings me a sense of relief. She's promised to keep an eye on me and be available for whatever I need, and I'm grateful. Before we leave, she offers to accompany us to the bookstore to pick up my textbooks, and once everything is settled, we say our goodbyes, and she walks us out the door.

The drive home is quiet. Kamila and Andy ask about what I thought, how I liked the place, etc. I'm surprised at how positive I feel after visiting campus today, calm even. I walked by the room where my in-person class will be held and I know where everything is, so I won't be the typical new girl who has to ask for directions. I'll be able to get around on my own, without anyone's help, and hopefully go unnoticed.

◆ ◆ ◆

Kang called me after dinner and we've been on the phone for a while. I feel more comfortable chatting with him; I still get a little nervous, but since we've started talking almost every day, I've gotten used to his voice.

"I don't understand what it is you like about the secondary characters," he says.

I'm sitting down at my usual spot by the window, the one that holds many memories of past conversations between my mom and me. I just told him that when I watch Korean dramas, I often dislike the main love interest and I fall instead for the guy whose heart is broken by the main character who is hopelessly in love with the leading man. "The secondary love interest is always a sweet, tender guy who treats the protagonist well from the beginning. Why should we all fall for the bad guy who makes the girl suffer?"

"Well, when you put it that way, it makes sense. But in real life, the nice guy never gets the girl."

"That's not true. I, for one, am not into bad guys."

"So, you like nice guys, you say?"

I bite my lips—a habit I've picked up since I started talking to Kang—feeling nervous. "Who doesn't?"

"Girls always go for the 'bad boy' type, like Erick." Kang told me that he and Erick have been friends for a long time and that Erick is quite the ladies' man.

"Not all girls."

He laughs quietly. "And am I a good guy or a bad guy, Klara?"

As always, hearing him say my name melts me completely, immobilizes me in a good way, a completely different way from when I have a panic attack; I'll never get used to it. "I'm still trying to work that one out."

He laughs again. I'd like to make him laugh like that all the time. "How can I help make up your mind, then?"

"That's for you to come up with on your own. If I told you, that would be cheating."

"Fair enough. Though it would be a lot easier if you let me prove it to you in person. I'm a lot more charming that way."

I wish I could, Kang, more than anything.

"I'll think about it," I lie.

"Well, this guy, who could either be good or bad, is going to sleep now."

"Good night, Kang."

"Good night, Klara."

I hang up, cover my face with my hands, and squeal like a little girl. I love talking to Kang, and I worry it could be dangerous for me. The attraction I felt toward him at first was completely platonic. I only knew things about him that everyone else who listened to his show was privy to; but now I'm learning things that I'm pretty sure none of his other listeners know, and as I get to know him more, I like Kang, for real. That puts me in a very vulnerable place, and I fear I could end up getting hurt. I know I will never be able to date him, and he will eventually get tired of just talking on the phone. Anyway, he probably sees this as a friendship, nothing more, so I shouldn't get my hopes up.

Putting my fears aside, I fall asleep with a smile on my lips.

♦ ♦ ♦

The day has arrived. I watch from the car window as students stream onto campus. They greet each other, laugh, check their cell phones. My heart is pounding, and it feels like every part of my body is sweating profusely, so much so that I have to wipe my clammy hands on my jeans.

"Are you sure you don't want me to come in with you?" Kamila asks, examining my every gesture from the driver's seat. "You know I already feel awful for not being able to pick you up today after class."

"Don't worry—it's only a quick ten-minute Uber ride home. I'll be fine." I try to sound convincing as I take off my seatbelt and give her a hug. "I'm going to give it my best, Kami."

She hugs me tightly. "Okay, remember you can call me if anything happens. It's your first day. Just the fact that you're here is major, that's enough."

"My goal is to attend my scheduled class, no more, no less," I say. "I'll do my best to achieve it."

"I love you so much, K." She puts a hand on my cheek, eyes red. "Now, go out there and show them what you're made of."

"Yes ma'am, K2."

I get out of the car and wave goodbye as I watch Kamila drive away. I grip the straps of my backpack and spin around to take in the scene in front of me before flipping the hood of my sweatshirt over my head, covering my hair and part of my face. It's cooler than I expected, so I hurry inside.

Everything is different from how I'd pictured it. As I walk down the main hallway, no one so much as glances at me. Some students seem too engrossed in their phones to notice anyone else; others are talking to their friends. I'm relieved to see that I'm not drawing attention to myself. However, as I enter my classroom, that relief vanishes as a group of guys sitting together chatting all turn to look at me. I try to control my breathing as I walk past them to the last seat in the corner of the classroom. As soon as I sit down, I focus on stabilizing my breathing by doing my exercises.

The class is smaller than I expected. I guess this course is uninteresting for most students, but, for me, a course on mental health and wellness seems more than perfect for my first class. Kamila objected, of course, because she thinks school should distract me from my problems, not draw me deeper into them, but Ms. Romes, the counselor, recommended the course and said thinking about these issues might be helpful for me. Besides, I'm curious to know what the other students think about mental health.

From my seat in the back of the room, I assess all the other students. There's a group of four girls, all very pretty, talking animatedly. Two guys sit close together, laughing at something on one of their phones. A couple older women stick together toward the back of the classroom. Close to them is a dark-haired girl sitting alone, reading a book, and behind her, a lovely girl with plump cheeks and wavy hair.

My breathing has normalized. I feel safe in this corner, like I have some shield around me and no one can hurt me. But I realize I spoke too soon when the next students enter the room.

A freckled, red-haired girl enters, chewing gum; she glances at me before taking her seat without a word. After the small classroom is almost filled up, a tall redheaded boy enters with a huge smile. "I have arrived, princesses!" he says to the group of pretty girls.

They laugh and joke back and forth with him for a moment. And then the boy notices me, and I curl up like a snail under my shell. He has beautiful hazel eyes, but the curiosity I see in them frightens me. "Oh, wow, someone new! Why didn't anyone tell me?" he says in a joking tone as he starts walking toward me.

Stay away.

"Good morning." The professor enters, saving me.

The redheaded guy turns around to walk back to his seat.

As I sit in class, paying attention to the lecture, I take a moment to appreciate how much this means to me. I'm in a classroom, surrounded by people I don't know.

This is the first step, Klara. See? It's not so bad.

I take it all in and allow myself to savor this feeling. The world looks a little less scary right now, and as I watch the other students take notes, I realize that maybe I can do this.

The class goes by faster than I expect as the professor lectures the entire time with little to no input required from the students. I'm thankful there's no pairing up in groups, because I don't feel ready for that kind of interaction yet.

Class ends and I'm gathering my things when a screeching sound comes out of the PA system and a voice emerges from the speaker hanging on the wall in the corner of the classroom. "Good morning, Durham Community College."

I stop breathing.

"Welcome to the third week of another great semester."

Kang.

It's Kang.

I would recognize that voice anywhere.

"This is Kang from W-DCC, the Durham Community College station. I'm here to remind everyone that you can tune in to listen to us on Mondays, Wednesdays, and Fridays at seven o'clock, when we'll have news of the week and discussions on important topics that affect us as well as our campus. Happy start of the week and go Panthers!"

"Go Panthers!" the group of boys shout, pumping their fists in the air.

I'm astonished. Kang is here, on the same campus as me, right now. I knew he attended this college, but I stupidly thought the chances of being on campus at the same time would be lower than low. How dumb of me to rely on luck being on my side.

I don't know what I'm feeling—a combination of panic, excitement, and fear, mostly fear. What if I run into him in the hallway?

16

Find Me

KANG'S ON CAMPUS at the same time as my one and only in-person class.

And I need a plan, because it's one thing to be able to attend class after all my efforts, and another one to face the possibility of running into Kang. I only hope it's a one-time thing, a coincidence, and his course schedule doesn't align with mine.

I wait for the classroom to empty out and for enough time to pass for the halls to clear. I'm banking on his classes being on the completely opposite side of campus, or at least in a different building, but I'm beginning to feel like the chances of running into him now are high. Although I don't even know what he looks like, and he doesn't know what *I* look like, so maybe I'm worrying too much.

As I sit here and wait for everyone to leave, I begin to ponder community college life, and I'm amazed by it—seeing so many things I was totally unaware of before, as if I'm suddenly noticing every little detail no matter how small. I guess everything I've been through has made me observant. I feel as if I've acquired some supernatural ability—although there's nothing super about me—to see things so much more clearly. Or maybe I've just totally lost it.

I replay the class and make observations about my new classmates. The older women were the first to leave, saying goodbye to everyone as they walked out. Earlier I saw the redheaded girl explain something to another student who didn't understand, and she has a very warm smile. The group of pretty girls seem nice. The girl with wavy hair and curves to die for exudes a self-confidence that makes me envious. Two guys who sat laughing together walk out teasing each other and exchanging grins... Is it my imagination, or is there a certain chemistry between them? The dark-haired girl seems quiet, but I saw her staring at the redheaded guy who approached me before class started. Does she like him? I guess I shouldn't judge him before getting to know him. The last students to leave are a group of three: one guy with dark purple hair and two girls with glasses and high ponytails. This group is hard to pinpoint. They look somehow quite studious but also unattainably cool at the same time. It's amazing how much you can observe when you have no one to talk to.

I survived the first class, I think to myself, feeling positive, even cheerful. A smile dances on my lips over my small victory.

"Hoodie."

I tense up. It's the redheaded guy. I was so busy celebrating that I didn't notice him return to the classroom. Now we're alone. I look up and see him walking toward me.

No. My breath quickens and I clench my fists.

"Do you have a name?" He sits at the desk in front of me. "Or should I just call you Hoodie?"

I swallow and my throat feels like sandpaper. It's the first time I've spoken face-to-face with someone my age in a very long time. I can't find my voice.

He cocks his head to one side, observing me. I want to disappear into my sweatshirt.

"Are you mute?"

I have the urge to get up and leave. I can't stand his inquisitive gaze. The only reason I haven't darted out of the classroom is that I know Kang is out there somewhere.

The guy's hazel eyes move to my notebook and the sketches I made during class. "Hey, cool."

I cover the drawings.

"Are you really not going to talk to me?"

I shake my head.

He smiles and stands. "Fine, have it your way, Hoodie." He throws up his hands as if surrendering, but there's something in his eyes that says he won't give up.

When he leaves, I let out a breath that I didn't know I was holding. Why was he so insistent on talking to me?

I exit the classroom and walk toward the main doors of the building. I know I could order an Uber and go home now; I'm done with my class for the day. It went smoothly, so maybe I should take this victory and quit while I'm ahead, but the fact that everything went so well motivates me to push a little further. I need to take more risks if I want to get better, and I know the perfect place to do that.

The very notion of the cafeteria horrifies me—so many people in one place, an unfamiliar place at that, and Kang has to eat, too, so he might be there. But I have to remind myself we don't know what each other looks like, and that's enough to settle my nerves, at least about that issue.

I can just barely see the door, and already my heart is pounding in my throat.

You can do it, Klara. You dealt with that redheaded guy; you can handle this.

I think about the fact that it could be worse—it could be a massive dining hall like those in bigger universities, but it's literally the size of my high school's.

With my hands in my sweatshirt pockets and my head down, I

make my way through the cafeteria. I get in the buffet line, tray in hand, and start looking at the food. I need something soft and easy to chew because my anxious brain instantly goes to the possibility of choking here. I choose mashed potatoes, chicken teriyaki, and a banana for dessert.

After I'm done, I quickly move to a desolate table in the corner. I understand why no one sits here. It's right next to the trash cans, which give off an unpleasant odor, but I don't care. I look down at my tray of food and suddenly my eyes fill with tears: I'm living a normal life, eating in the cafeteria after class like a regular college student, not locked away in my room. These are not tears of sadness, but of joy at finally being able to accomplish something I thought I would never be able to. I wipe a rogue tear and blink, blowing out a breath to regain control of my emotions; I don't want to cry in front of everyone here.

"I know the food is bad, but I've never seen anybody cry about it before." I look up to see the curvy girl from class standing in front of my table with a tray in hand. She shakes her head, tossing her wavy hair over her shoulders, and sits down across from me. "I'm Perla," she informs me, unwrapping a plastic spoon and fork.

Up close, I see how beautiful her face is, framed by long wavy hair, with soft features and the brightest dark eyes I've ever seen. Her eyeliner game is on point and looks great. I want to say something, but no words come—I don't know why it's so difficult.

"Don't be scared. I'm not going to hurt you." She starts in on her lunch. "Eat up, it's worse when it's cold."

I start taking bites of my food as we sit together in silence. Perla doesn't push me into conversation, as if giving me my time, and I thank her for it. "My name is Klara, with a K," I finally say after I finish chewing. Hearing my own voice feels refreshing after a morning of silence.

Perla smiles and dimples appear on her cheeks. "Great to meet you, Klara with a K."

I smile back.

"If you're trying not to draw attention to yourself, you might want to lose the hood," she suggests, taking a sip of her soda.

"I'm fine like this, no one has noticed me."

She raises an eyebrow. "Is that what you think?"

I nod.

She shakes her head. "The more you try to hide, the more you'll make everyone curious about you. If you don't want to be easy prey, don't act like you are."

Prey? Am I in college or on Animal Planet?

"I don't think anyone has noticed me," I repeat.

"Yes, they have, Klara. I've seen several people looking at you. You're just too lost in your own world to notice."

I avoid her gaze and look down at my food, suddenly all too aware of where I am and the dozens of other students around me. But I remind myself that I have to push through.

Perla continues, "I'm not trying to make you uncomfortable; I just want to help."

"Why? You don't even know me."

"You remind me of me when I first moved here."

"I don't believe that. You look so . . . so sure of yourself. The complete opposite of me."

"I wasn't always like this." Perla sighs. "We gain strength through struggles."

"You make struggles sound like a good thing."

"Our challenges shape who we are, sure, but they don't define us."

Perla is so positive; she reminds me of my mother. But this conversation is getting too deep, and I want to change the subject. There are so many things I want to know, and now I finally have someone to ask. "Okay, so is this the part where you tell me who's cool and who sucks?"

Perla bursts out laughing. "What? This isn't high school, Klara."

"You're right," I reply, slightly embarrassed—I can feel my

cheeks starting to heat up. Though, to be fair, this cafeteria does remind me of high school.

"I'll humor you, though. Hmmm, who sucks?" She's playful. "Ah, if only it were that simple. I don't like to view people in black and white, but rather in grayscale. A person may have a kind heart but make selfish decisions, and another person, with a cold heart, may be capable of huge sacrifice for others. The human being is an enigma, one big gray area."

"You sound like my therapist," I say without thinking and immediately regret it. *Nice one, Klara, great way to start a friendship! Now I'm the crazy girl who has a therapist.*

Perla doesn't flinch. "My mom's a counselor here. I guess her endless lectures have rubbed off on me."

Her mother is a counselor . . . Something clicks inside my head. "Is your mom Ms. Romes? Did she send you to talk to me?"

I can't hide my disappointment; I thought this girl sat with me because she wanted to be my friend, not because her mother asked her to take pity on me.

Perla looks embarrassed. "Well, I . . ."

I stand up, empty my tray into the trash, then rush out of the cafeteria. *I'm so delusional*, I think as I walk down a long corridor of the Hawthorn Commons Hall, crowded at this time of day, but I'm too upset to let that affect me. I can't believe I thought I'd be able to make a new friend so easily, just like that. How could I buy into the lie that a normal life was something within reach?

"Kang!"

I've never stopped so abruptly in my life. My feet are glued to the ground as I stare at the person in front of me who just called out the name Kang. It's a tall blond guy wearing a leather jacket, looking at someone behind me.

"Dude, Kang, I've been looking all over for you," says the blond guy, shaking his head.

I can't breathe.

Kang's voice behind me sets my heart racing. "I was having lunch."

It's him, that voice . . . but it sounds deeper and huskier in person.

"Let's go." The blond guy gestures for Kang to follow him.

I feel like everything is happening in slow motion: the guy behind me, owner of Kang's voice, passes right beside me in a confident stride. I only catch a glimpse of his back and his messy black hair, the same color as the shirt he's wearing. He's tall . . . very tall.

Kang catches up with the blond guy and they move away down the crowded hallway. People jostle past me, but I don't move an inch. I suddenly notice that I'm clutching my chest with one hand as if my life depends on it. I just saw Kang in person. He just walked right past me. I can't believe it. After following his voice for so long, I was one step away from him.

"Wow, you're completely starstruck." Perla's voice startles me. She has one eyebrow raised.

I clear my throat and begin walking, my heart still threatening to burst out of my chest.

"Klara." Perla follows me as I head out of the building, ready to go home for the day. "Klara, listen. Yes, my mom told me a new girl would be joining my class and suggested I talk to you, but it was never an order. I decided to do it because you really do remind me a lot of myself."

I purse my lips, taking in her words, and sit down on a wooden bench outside. Perla sits next to me, but I don't look at her, I simply stare out into the distance.

"Really, Klara, my interest in talking to you is genuine."

Perla seems sincere. Maybe this was all her mother's plan, but I don't want to close myself off to the only person who has spoken to me so far other than the redheaded dude.

"You're wasting your time with me. I'm very boring," I tell her.

She smiles. "Nah, I don't think so. You can't be—for the third time, you remind me of myself, remember?" She looks at me mischievously. "If you still want the scoop, I can tell you all about the guy who just dazzled you in the hallway."

"Really?" I squeak a little too excitedly.

"Yeah, what do you want to know?"

I open my mouth and close it again, not quite sure what to ask.

"I didn't imagine a guy like Erick would be your type."

I frown and can feel the disappointment taking over me. "Erick?"

"Yeah, that's his name, the tall blond guy you were staring at in the hallway."

It dawns on me then that Perla doesn't realize I was actually interested in the guy Erick was waiting for, the one who walked right past me: Kang.

That must be the same Erick from the radio show I hate, Kang's friend. I try to remember his face, but I was so shocked by Kang that I hardly noticed him. "I'm not interested in Erick."

Perla looks confused.

"Then why were you standing in the middle of the hallway staring at him?"

"No, the other guy, the one Erick was talking to."

The color leaves Perla's face. "Kang?" Perla's expression hardens. "Forget about Kang, Klara."

"Why? What's wrong with him?"

"You don't have to listen to me. You can line up behind everyone else in his fan club if you want, but don't get your hopes up."

"Fan club?"

Perla sighs. "Of course. He's good-looking, people love his radio show, and to top it off, he's the captain of the soccer team. Everyone adores Kang around here."

That makes sense. "And so I shouldn't be interested in him? Just because he's popular? I thought this wasn't high school? There must be something you're not telling me."

She gives me a sad smile. "I'll tell you the story another time, Klara. I have to get to class." Perla stands and walks away, leaving me alone with my thoughts.

All in all, my first day of college wasn't too bad. I'm proud of the fact that I was able to sit through an entire class and even eat in the cafeteria. But there's a couple moments that I know I'll keep replaying in my mind: Kang's voice behind me, his back, the dark hair against his black shirt.

I found you, Kang. But I can't let you find me; not today, not ever.

17

Keep Me Out

"SO, WOULD YOU like to tell us about your first day of college?" I've been expecting this question. Kamila has done a good job of keeping herself from interrogating me; we've just finished dinner and she managed to make it all the way to dessert without grilling me. Andy shoots her a disapproving look, but she blatantly ignores him. "Did you like your class?"

I bury my spoon in my slice of chocolate cake and smile. "I guess so, it was . . ." My mind flashes back to every moment: the pretty girls, the redheaded guy, Perla, Kang . . . I clear my throat. "Yeah. It went well, I think."

Andy beams. "I'm so glad."

Kamila takes Andy's hand and then mine. "We're so proud of you, Klara."

"It's only been one day." I shrug. "It's too soon to make a big fuss about it."

Kamila squeezes my hand, rubbing her thumb against it. "You're wrong. This is a huge accomplishment. Every little achievement counts. You're a fighter, Klara. Don't underestimate any battle, no matter how small, because that's how you win the war."

"You're *such* a psychiatrist."

She laughs and her eyes light up. "And you're so *you*."

We joke, talk, and fight over the last piece of chocolate cake. It's a normal, happy family dinner, and it feels great. Kamila is right: Every step forward, no matter how small, provides a little more reassurance that I can make it, that I will be okay, that I will be able to overcome my fears.

My cell phone vibrates against the table, announcing a new message.

Kamila raises an eyebrow. "Looks like someone made new friends on the first day."

I open the message and my heart races, as usual, when I see Kang's name on the screen.

> **Kang:** You've been strangely quiet today. Have you had enough of this intense radio announcer?

I smile. If he only knew I was just a few steps away from him today. My mind travels back to the moment when I heard his name, how close he was when he walked past me. The black shirt that matched his hair, his jeans, his height. But what I remember most is his voice. Without the radio, telephone, or PA system as a filter, his voice sounded so much deeper, more captivating.

"Klara?"

Kamila's voice pulls me back to reality. She and Andy are watching me with amused expressions.

"What?"

Andy takes a sip of his juice.

"Nothing. It's just been a while since we've seen such a huge smile on your face. It suits you."

I blush. "Oh, it's just . . . I remembered a scene from a movie I saw . . . beautiful."

Andy nods. "Right, right."

I stand up and excuse myself by saying I have homework to get to, then I go into my room and close the door behind me to respond to Kang in private, where no one will notice any unintentional smiles.

Me: Always so over the top. How was your day, Kang?
Kang: Boring. Went to practice, had class, did some homework. How about yours?

It was one of the best days of my life because I started college and because I got to see you. You have no idea how close we were, I want to say, but I opt for a less crazy response:

Me: It was good, very eventful.
Kang: Can I call you?

We've been talking on the phone a lot lately, and it's always Kang who calls me. I guess somehow texting isn't enough anymore. I dial his number and he picks up on the third ring.

"Ms. K."

"Mr. Kang."

I hear him laugh and I love it, it's contagious. Kang is addictive. I'm drawn to everything about him, but most of all I love how comfortable I feel talking to him. It comes so naturally.

"Did you finish watching your Korean drama today?"

"No, I spent all day . . ." I pause. "Out."

"Out? Are you this mysterious with everyone or just with me?"

I shake my head. "I'm not mysterious."

"No? You won't tell me anything about yourself. I don't know where you go to school, you've blocked me on social media . . ."

"What, no . . . I don't have any social media accounts."

I hear him sigh. "Are you afraid of me, Klara?"

"Of course not."

"Then why do I feel like you put up a wall between us? Like you're trying to keep me out?"

It's the only way to keep myself safe, Kang, I think.

"I am doing no such thing," I say. "Besides, I still don't understand why you're so curious about me." I say it without even thinking about it, and I instantly regret it. Before I can panic and take it back, I hear him sigh again.

Kang takes a deep breath. "I told you . . . at first it was because of the quotes you'd sent to the show. It showed me how well-read you were, showed me we liked the same type of literature. I get a lot of my inspiration for the show and the topics I choose from books, so . . . I don't know, I wanted to talk to someone else about them. You know, since it's not something my teammates or Erick and I talk about. But now that we've actually begun talking, to be honest, it's gone past that. I think you remind me of myself, of a time where I put all the walls up and didn't let anyone or anything get to me. I was lost in a dark place, wishing for someone to reach out to me."

His words sound genuine and it takes me a moment to process them.

"So, you think I'm lost in a dark place?" I joke.

"No, I think you need someone reaching out to you, and I want to be that person, if you let me."

"I don't know. There are so many candidates," I say with a nervous chuckle. *What am I doing?*

"Oh, really?" he goes along, "I thought I was your favorite."

"You are." I respond way too quickly and proceed to blush.

A few seconds of silence pass. I hear only his breathing on the other end of the line, until he finally speaks: "I want to see you, Klara."

I bring my free hand to my chest.

"I'm nothing special, Kang."

"Why don't you let me decide that?" I notice a hint of annoyance in his voice. "Klara—"

"Why don't you tell me more about what else you did today?" I interrupt before he can say anything else. I know that once he starts asking about me, he won't stop.

"I don't have much to say, and I have to go now, the show starts soon. Will you be listening?"

"Always."

"Okay, we'll talk after *Follow My Voice*, Klara."

"Okay."

I hang up and immediately reach for my headphones.

"Good evening, thank you for tuning in and being here with me tonight. I want to welcome you to today's evening program, *Follow My Voice*. This is Kang, your friend and companion for this hour."

I drop back onto the bed and stare at the ceiling as I listen to him.

"It was a beautiful sunny day today, but don't get too excited; apparently an unexpected cold front is moving in and, combined with the chance of thunderstorms, it could bring sleet or even snow. Snow in September? I know, sounds impossible, but those of us familiar with North Carolina's crazy weather know that anything can happen. In any case, it's important to always have the essentials at home: drinking water, canned goods, and plenty of blankets, in case of a power outage."

Kang's always worrying about others, which leaves me confused about Perla's tense expression as it flashes in my mind. Why did she warn me against liking him? I've been listening to his show for a long time, and we talk on the phone regularly, so I think I know him fairly well. He's always seemed like a great guy. I've never gotten any bad vibes from him. Am I being naive? I don't think so. Kang has given me no reason to think badly of him, so I won't let other people's opinions affect how I see him. But that doesn't mean I won't keep bugging Perla until she finishes telling me what she started to say about him today.

When Kang's show ends, I take off my headphones and stare into space for a few minutes, my mind wandering. I wonder if I will run into Kang again the next time I go to class. Just thinking about it produces a mixture of excitement and fear.

I stand up and walk over to the mirror. I still look so pale and thin. I've had more of an appetite lately, but I'm well below my ideal weight. At least my bones don't jut out so prominently anymore. My brown eyes have a new sparkle to them that I like. I smooth down my hair and look over at the shelf where my wigs hang. I stare at the pink one and recall Andy's words: *"Pink looks good on you."* Next to the pink wig is the purple one, my neighbor's favorite. *"I love the purple, it's your color."*

I glance back at my reflection. Today I'm wearing my short black wig, and I remember Andy's words again. *"Black, huh? I liked the pink."* Personally, I feel most comfortable in the black wig because it's the closest to my natural hair before I lost it completely to chemotherapy. Carefully, I remove the wig and run my hands through my short hair. It's growing in fast, which makes me happy. I miss the bouncy curls that used to brush my shoulders.

Cancer...

When my mother died, I thought the nightmare of that disease was gone from my life; it had already taken enough from me. I was wrong. My own cancer diagnosis, almost immediately after my mother's passing, kept me from processing the pain of that great loss. It was an abnormally sunny January afternoon when I felt the hard lump in one of my breasts. I told myself I was being paranoid after my mother's death, but then Kamila examined me, and I saw the concern in her eyes.

Tests, analyses, hours of waiting; returning to the hospital was terrifying. *"We need to do a biopsy,"* the doctor said, and his tone conveyed everything. I knew what it was, but that didn't make it any more bearable when the biopsy came back positive. I had breast cancer.

Chemotherapy, hormone therapy, and an operation to remove both my breasts. The other one was healthy, but a DNA test revealed that I carry a BRCA1 gene mutation, which makes me more prone to breast and ovarian cancer. My mother and grandmother probably had the same gene, but, fortunately, Kamila does not. There's a fifty-fifty chance of inheriting it, and I'm glad that my sister is safe, at least.

It was not easy to make the decision to remove the other breast after chemotherapy, but I had to do it. My mental health was already destroyed, so living in constant fear that I might have to face that nightmare all over again was not an option for me.

I take off my shirt and sports bra to examine my breasts. I was never large-chested, but the mastectomy still made me feel like I'd lost my femininity, the proof that I was a woman. I had both breasts reconstructed, but it's not the same; there are scars. I run my finger over them and the skin is sensitive to the touch.

Fortunately, after almost a year of treatment, I was declared cancer-free, but I still have to go in for checkups every three months. Because this relentless disease could come back, especially in my case, due to the BRCA1 gene mutation I carry.

My depression and anxiety went through the roof during all this; my fear of death intensified. But I don't want to live like that anymore. I want to move forward, without fear.

I look at myself in the mirror and smile sadly. *How could I ever let you see me, Kang? I'm not good enough for you. My body is too full of scars and imperfections.*

18

Hide from Me

THIS IS NOT going to work.

It's been over two weeks of class, and I have realized I can't go on hiding from Kang every time I come to campus. This constant state of anxiety and fear whenever I turn a corner or pass a classroom is not healthy. My plan to get through my first semester of college wholly unnoticed is not working, either, since my new friend Perla is one of those people who attracts attention wherever she goes. She is the complete opposite of me: loud, cheerful, outgoing, talking to everyone and laughing easily with a cackle that can be heard miles away. The redheaded guy from my class won't let me pass unnoticed, either. Diego, Perla said his name was. He takes every opportunity to try to talk to me. I have blatantly ignored him because I don't need another friend who draws so much attention to themselves, and, with his loud voice and huge laugh, everyone notices Diego wherever he goes.

And now, like a cruel joke fate is playing on me, the storm hits earlier than expected and I find myself stranded on campus. There was talk of classes being suspended, but since the storm was not forecast to hit until much later in the evening, the dean kept classes as scheduled.

I tried to convince Kamila that I should stay home, but she insisted that I should try to keep my momentum going. She promised to come for me if anything happened, and I agreed, despite the fact that her hospital is on the other side of town and so is Andy's office. So now I'm one of the many students stuck on campus and—more proof of fate's cruelty—Diego is here, across from me in the hallway where we're clustered since the wind gusts are so strong we can't sit near any windows or doors.

"I told my mom we should've stayed home today," Perla grumbles beside me.

"I said the same thing to my sister." I sigh.

"Hey, Hoodie," Diego says.

Perla shoots him a murderous look. "Leave her alone, Diego."

He rolls his eyes. "I'm not talking to you."

We hear the sound of voices, and I glance down the hall. Ms. Romes, Perla's mother, is leading a group of students toward us and asks them to sit down along the wall.

"Everything good?" asks Ms. Romes, looking at her daughter.

"Yeah, good and boring. When can we go home?"

Everyone in the hallway is listening attentively.

Perla's mother sighs. "We can't leave until they lift the extreme wind and tornado warnings; it's too dangerous. If anyone has asked a family member to come get them, I'd recommend you cancel the ride. No one should be out in these conditions. We'll keep you safe here, don't worry."

But the grim expression on Ms. Romes's face awakens my latent fear. How have I been so calm up till now? My breathing quickens, but I try to relax, glancing around at the other students. We're all here together and no one else is panicking. We'll be fine. Won't we? I look to the end of the hallway as I see more students filing in and sitting down.

I frown. "What are they all doing here?" I ask as the hallway quickly fills up.

Perla glances down the hall. "This is a designated 'safe corridor' in the event of a tornado warning."

"Does that mean all the students are going to be crammed into this tiny space?"

Perla nods. "The ones who have class in this building, yes."

Please don't let Kang have class in this building, or at least let him have been smart enough to stay home today.

I scan each new group of students as they arrive, examining them carefully, hidden beneath my hood with my heart in my throat. Somehow, the prospect of sharing physical space with Kang terrifies me more than the fury of the storm outside. I must be totally insane.

After a while, students stop trickling in and I lean back against the wall, relieved.

Thank you, fate.

But I called it too soon.

As always, I hear him before I see him. His laughter echoes down the hall as he says hello to several people sitting against the walls. It's that voice that haunts my dreams, that makes my heart race and my brain run wild. And it's coming from mere feet away. I'm dying to get a look at him.

"Hey, Kang!" a guy calls out to him. "You really think there's a storm coming? Last time you talked about one on your show, it barely drizzled."

Kang laughs. "I don't know, dude. Can't trust the meteorologists after that."

I feel eyes on me, and when I look up, I see that Diego is watching me with curiosity. Oh, no, the last thing I need is for him to notice my weakness for Kang.

"Let's find a place to sit down." Erick's voice sounds very close.

I look away from Diego and fix my eyes on the ground in front of me. Two pairs of shoes walk past, and I shrink into my hood to hide my face. Erick and Kang sit down along the opposite wall, diagonally across from me; if I turned my head, I would be able to see them. They are close, too close.

It wouldn't hurt to take a peek at him, Klara.

Cautiously, I glance up and try to get a look at him out of the corner of my eye, but Erick is blocking Kang, animatedly telling some story. I'm about to give up when Kang leans forward, past Erick, and I see his face.

I feel as if the wind is knocked out of me. He's good-looking, much more handsome than I expected—not in a conventional way, but in a different, unique way. His black hair falls across his forehead over his deep black eyes. His skin is smooth and his cheeks are slightly flushed from the hustle and bustle of this whole affair. What strikes me most, however, are his smile and the two dimples that appear in his cheeks as he laughs; they're adorable. I stare at him, awestruck, until his black eyes meet mine. Immediately, I turn away from him, hiding behind my hood. *What was I thinking? Did he see me? No, no; I was quick enough,* I think.

Perla leans over with a raised eyebrow. "Kla—"

I cover her mouth. "Shh! Whatever you do, *do not* say my name."

I move my hand away and she gives me a *What the hell!* look.

"It's a long story, I'll tell you later," I whisper, using her words against her.

Perla is about to object, but, suddenly, the lights go out. Shrieks and gasps echo down the darkened hallway. I hear Mrs. Leach's voice. "Everyone, please remain calm—the emergency generator will kick on soon."

I lean closer to Perla. Between the storm and the nerves of having Kang so close, my poor heart feels like it might burst. At least I can hide from him better in the dark. But fate is truly not on my side today. Out of the silence and darkness, my cell phone dings twice, alerting me that I have new messages.

I don't think anything of it until I hear Kang speak. "What the . . . Did you hear that?" he says to Erick. "I just sent a couple messages and a phone alert sounded at the exact second."

Crap. Kang messaged me.

Erick snorts. "Dude, shut up. You're imagining things."

"Could be, but it seems too coincidental. I'm going to send another one to check."

Shit, shit! I fumble in my pocket for my phone, but I'm not fast enough and it dings again.

"Hear that?" Kang asks.

I can feel his eyes probing the darkness of the hallway. Sitting on my phone to muffle it, I press the button to silence it.

"It's a coincidence." Erick chuckles. "There are a hundred cell phones in this hallway. Look around you—everyone's using their phone."

Kang sends another message. This time my phone doesn't ding but the sound of the vibration is clearly audible in this narrow, enclosed space. I should've turned the phone off.

Kang stands up.

"Hey, come on, sit down, man, it's a coincidence." Erick sighs. "Dude, Kang!"

Kang puts his phone to his ear and my phone starts vibrating in my pocket. It's an incoming call. He stands up, trying to figure out where the vibration sound is coming from. If I pull out my phone, he'll see the light from the screen.

He begins to move toward me and I panic. *What should I do?* Without thinking, I get up and rush in the opposite direction, to the end of the hall.

"Hey!"

I hear Kang behind me, and I run even faster.

"Stop! Hey!"

"Excuse me . . ." I hear Mrs. Leach say as I rush past her into the main hallway.

Please don't follow me, Kang, please.

To one side of the hallway is the main entrance to the Blue Ridge Health Sciences Center and on the other are bathrooms. There's a staircase that leads to other classrooms upstairs, but I'm unfamiliar with that part of the building. I can't go out into the storm—besides, I'm sure the door is locked—so I run for the women's bathroom, the sound of footsteps trailing behind me.

"Hey, stop!" Kang's voice is close; I know it won't be long before he reaches me.

I grab the edge of the doorframe and slide into the ladies' room. The door swings shut behind me but there's no lock. I press my back to the wall, trying to hide. My chest is rising and falling. Kang wouldn't come into the girls' bathroom, would he?

"It's you." Kang's voice on the other side of the door destroys me. "I'm not moving from this spot until you come out, Klara."

I slide down the wall and sit on the floor. I turn my face to the entrance and catch a glimpse of Kang sitting against the wall as lightning strikes and the strong winds outside make the door sway gently open and shut. A smile plays on his lips.

"I can't believe I found you. You don't know how many times I've imagined seeing you, pictured your expressions. I've been dying to put a face to your name, Klara with a K—the girl I haven't stopped thinking about since the first time I talked to her."

More lightning, followed by a gust of wind that causes the door to slam shut, but not before giving me a brief look of the excited expression on Kang's face. I've followed his voice for so long and now he's only a few steps away. But I'm afraid of his reaction if he sees me.

19

Face Me

I DON'T KNOW what to do.

I pace back and forth across the bathroom, trying not to panic, though I'm not sure I'm succeeding. Kang is out there, waiting for me, and this bathroom doesn't even have a window I can use to escape like in the movies. I can't let him see me. From everything he just said, it's clear that he has very high expectations of me and I don't want to let him down. I want him to go on thinking I'm worth talking to; I want him to keep being interested in me. I don't want him to see the reality of what I am and be disappointed.

Think, Klara, think.

I'm still trying to decide what to do when I hear Ms. Romes's voice outside the bathroom. "You can't be here, Kang. For safety reasons, all students must remain in the interior hallway."

"Okay, but there's a girl in the bathroom—she needs to come back, too, doesn't she?" he replies.

"Well, a moment ago it seemed to me that she was running away from you. Can you tell me what's going on?"

"She wasn't running away from me."

"That's not what it looked like. Klara is new here and she might need a little time to adjust. Why don't you go back to the hall by yourself for now?"

"No."

"Kang, I'm not asking, I'm telling you. Go."

"Fine."

I hear what I assume to be Kang's footsteps walking away, and then Ms. Romes's voice. "Klara, you can come out now; he's gone."

I poke my head through the doorway to make sure she's alone before I step out of the bathroom. "Thank you."

"Don't thank me. You have to return to the hallway, too."

"I can't."

"I don't understand what's going on, but I need you to go back with the rest of the students; student safety is my priority right now."

The wind howls outside as incredible amounts of rain lash the roof. With my heart in my throat and my hood pulled as low as it will go to hide my face, I return to the hallway, trying to stay behind Ms. Romes. The lights are still out and I'm grateful for the cover of darkness. I know that, if I sit back down next to Perla, Kang will find me. So, instead, I take a seat toward the front end of the hall, far from Perla and Kang. Ms. Romes says nothing and moves on.

Taking a deep breath, I relax my tensed-up shoulders. I know I'm being a coward, but I can't let him see me, at least not today. I'm not ready; I'm not brave enough yet.

I try to distract myself from these impeding thoughts by focusing on breathing exercises, when my phone alerts me to an incoming text, and I'm grateful to be sitting so far away from Kang.

Kang: Why did you run away from me?

I sigh and respond.

Me: I didn't run away, it's complicated.

I get another message, expecting it to be Kang's reply, but it's from Perla.

Perla: What happened to you? Where did you go?

I turn around, dim the brightness on my phone's screen to be cautious, and strain my eyes through the darkness to see where Perla's sitting, still in the same place as before. I reply, saying that I'll explain later, and read the new message from Kang that just came in.

Kang: You don't want to meet me, Klara?
Me: It's not that.
Kang: So, what is it then? I'm dying to meet you but I feel like I'm the only one.
Me: No, it's not like that. I want to meet you, too.
Kang: I'm right here, Klara, within reach.
Me: It's just unexpected, Kang, that's all.
Kang: You never intended for us to meet in person, did you?

He's right, but not for the reasons he thinks. I stare at the screen, unsure how to respond, but Kang sends another text before I have the chance.

Kang: It's crystal clear. Don't worry. I won't bother you anymore.

I feel a tightness in my chest. His words sound like a goodbye and I don't want that, but I also don't know if I'm ready to let him see me. I've handled starting college pretty well, but I'm not sure I'm prepared to deal with much more than that right now.

As I'm contemplating what to do, I hear footsteps and see Kang and Erick coming down my way, toward the exit.

"Let's sit somewhere else—I'm over this bullshit," Kang says as they walk past me without even looking in my direction.

His words are so cold they burn. He sounds angry, and I understand. I replay what he said in my mind: *"I can't believe I found you. You don't know how many times I've imagined seeing you, pictured your expressions. I've been dying to put a face to your name, Klara with a K—the girl I haven't stopped thinking about since the first time I talked to her."* He seemed so excited and now he's so disappointed that I didn't react the way he expected, that I don't seem as interested in him as he is in me.

I am, Kang, but I don't know how to prove it to you without agreeing to meet.

I know that if Kang knew my situation, what I've been through, he would understand my reluctance. But I haven't told him, so of course he feels rejected.

I look down the hall and see that he and Erick have stopped at the end.

You have to face him, Klara. Once he meets you, he'll understand that you're not good enough for him and he'll move on. It'll be better that way. It will hurt, but you can handle the pain; you've been through worse.

I stand up and walk to the opposite side to where Kang just sat down. I follow the campus map I received on day one and head to the door that connects to the Harold Collins Building, then stop outside the auditorium. With my back against the wall, I take out my phone and, before I have a chance to regret it, I text Kang.

Me: Come to the auditorium.

I'm shaking. I slip my phone back in my pocket and try to slow my breathing. I don't know if I'm doing the right thing, but I can't let Kang think that I don't care about him at all. It's better to get it over with, to just let him meet me and be disappointed.

A couple minutes later, Kang appears, standing a few feet away from me, and I stop breathing. His black eyes meet mine as he walks toward me with his hands in his pockets. His expression is neutral as he stops in front of me, openly searching my face. I want to say something, but no words come. Kang is here, standing in front of me, and suddenly I remember all the times I've heard him on the radio. His usual greeting: *"Good evening, folks. This is Kang, your friend and companion for this evening's radio program, Follow My Voice."* I remember the sound of his laughter, his messages, his voice, the entire journey that has brought us together in this moment.

"Hello," I murmur, so softly that I doubt he can hear me.

Kang smiles and those dimples appear on his cheeks. "Hello, Klara."

20

Smile at Me

MY POOR HEART beats as desperately as if I've just run a marathon and I silently thank it for not failing me in this moment. I don't say a word as Kang stares at me, putting a face to the voice he's been talking to all this time.

I would like to say that his expression reveals some hint of what he thinks, but his dazzling smile doesn't falter for an instant. Unable to stand the intensity of his gaze any longer, I look down at his black shirt with the mascot and blue lettering that reads DURHAM COMMUNITY COLLEGE. I notice his biceps, more defined than I remember from the last time I saw him, however fleetingly. At first glance he seemed very thin, but now, up close, I see that he has an athletic build, like someone who plays sports, which he does.

"So we finally meet, Klara." He says my name slowly, as if testing it out.

I swallow but keep my eyes on his shirt. "Um . . . yeah." I can't get out more than two words.

Kang takes his right hand out of his pocket and offers it to me. "Nice to meet you, Klara."

I stare at his hand like an idiot. I don't want him to feel how sweaty my palms are. I subtly wipe them off on the inside of my sweatshirt pocket and shake his hand. My stomach tingles instantly at his touch.

He squeezes my hand lightly. "It's an honor to finally meet the mysterious K."

I let go of his hand as fast as I can. I don't know what to do or say. Having him so close is too much.

"Hey, it's just me," Kang says.

I look up and try to find calm in his eyes.

"It's me, Kang, the guy you've been talking to nonstop for weeks. I'm not a stranger, there's no reason to be afraid."

"I'm not afraid."

He chuckles. "Really? Because you look terrified. I promise I'm not a serial killer."

"That's exactly what a serial killer would say." My lips tremble as I speak. God, I'm so nervous.

Kang purses his lips to suppress a smile. What beautiful lips!

He raises his right hand. "I solemnly swear that I will not murder you and bury your body in the mountains."

"Wow, that really makes me feel so much safer."

"I'm glad. So"—he pauses to lean a shoulder against the wall—"you've been right here on campus all this time?"

"Um, not exactly, I just started recently."

I expect him to ask me a thousand questions, but he doesn't, as if he knows it would make me too uncomfortable. He peels his shoulder away from the wall and takes off his backpack. "Well then, I guess a welcome celebration is in order." He slides to the floor and places his backpack between his knees before patting the spot beside him. "Will you sit with me?"

I don't budge.

He sighs. "I think I've made it clear that I'm not a murderer."

Uneasy, I sit down next to him, leaving a safe distance between us. I watch out of the corner of my eye as he opens his backpack and takes out a bag of candy and then continues to pull snacks out of his bag.

Somehow, I feel more relaxed now that we're not standing face-to-face. "Sheesh, why do you have so much food in your backpack? Did you know we were going to get stranded here?" I say, looking at the bags of potato chips, boxes of chocolates, and so on.

"No . . . they're gifts."

I raise an eyebrow. "Gifts?"

"Yeah, listeners send stuff to the show, or bring it to me in person."

"So, like, you have some sort of fan club?"

"Nah, I wouldn't call it that." He blushes and I feel like I'm going to faint. He's so handsome. "I just have *very* dedicated listeners." He winks.

I totally understand; I love his show. And his voice. "I guess you're super popular around here."

I'm surprised at how easy it is to make him blush again. "You could say that. So, what'll it be?" he says, gesturing to the display of sweets and snacks.

I evaluate all the options, overanalyzing as usual: The chips will give me bad breath, but it would be awkward to lick a strawberry lollipop while I talk to him . . . Urgh, I hate my brain!

Kang waves a hand in front of my face. "Hello, Klara? Take whatever you want. You like chocolate, right?" He offers me a bar of white chocolate. "Didn't you say this was your favorite?"

"Yes, thank you." I nod.

He grabs a Snickers and I roll my eyes.

"What? We've had this conversation before, white chocolate is no match for milk chocolate. Plus, you love hot chocolate . . . and I doubt the one you drink is white."

"What? Those are two entirely different things. Either way, white chocolate is a more elegant and refined chocolate," I say, feeling slightly more at ease.

"So, you're fancy and I'm basic."

I shrug, smiling. "You said it, not me."

I glance up at him and the look on his face almost makes me choke on the square of white chocolate. Kang is staring at me so intently that I forget to chew. "What?"

"You smiled."

I swallow. "And that's noteworthy?"

He shakes his head. "No, I just . . . I hadn't seen you smile before. It's . . ." He furrows his brow. "Nothing. I guess you're starting to trust the serial killer."

"I guess white chocolate is the way to my heart." I smile again.

He looks away and clears his throat. "Well . . ." He reaches into his backpack. "Do you want something to drink?"

"Don't tell me you have drinks in there, too? What kind of backpack is that?"

"I just have a Coke and a Sprite, so fewer choices than with the food."

"Do you come to campus to study, too, or just eat?"

"I told you already, I got all this for free. Besides, who says I can't do both?"

"You don't look like the kind of guy who sits around eating and studying all day."

Kang turns to face me, a twinkle in his eye. "What kind of guy do I look like?"

"Ummm . . ." *Think, Klara, keep the banter going.* "You look . . . very . . ." *Handsome, hot, ripped, sexy.* "Uh . . . healthy."

A mischievous grin forms on his lips. "Healthy?"

I nod.

"That's a new one."

"You know me, very innovative." *Shut up, Klara, shut up.*

"I'll take healthy," he says. Then he raises a hand to my hood and the movement is so sudden that I don't have time to pull away. Kang pushes it back to reveal my fake black hair. His fingers lightly brush my cheek as he lowers his hand. "You don't have to hide, Klara—you're very . . . hot."

I stop breathing and I feel heat rise in my face. I must be bright red. "Thank you," I whisper, looking away. Is he . . . flirting with me? *No, Klara, you're imagining things. You've only just met.* I'm hyperaware of his presence so close beside me, and I can't help but chance a glance at him. His hair looks so soft as it gently falls over his forehead; his eyes are the deepest black; his lower lip is so full, and those dimples . . . God, those dimples when he laughs!

Silence falls between us. I can feel his eyes on me, so I keep my gaze fixed on the doors at the end of the hallway, where rain is sliding down the glass.

"It's beautiful, isn't it?" says Kang, seeming to read my mind.

I say nothing and continue to watch the rain fall.

Kang sighs loudly. "I don't know if we'll be able to get out of here today."

"Caught in a storm—sounds like the premise of some bad romance movie."

"Romance, huh?"

I cough and clear my throat. "Well, yeah, because . . . you know . . . I just meant . . . Not because of you and me . . . I mean, well, nobody can leave . . . a bunch of college kids, stranded, and, you know, the hormones . . ."—*Shut up, Klara*—"stuck here all together, it's . . ."

Kang sounds amused. "I understood you, Klara."

We look at each other for a second before we both burst out laughing. This isn't so bad; I feel much more comfortable than I expected. Maybe it's the fact that we've talked on the phone so many times before.

"There you are," Erick says, turning the corner and stopping in front of us.

I'm surprised I don't immediately retreat back into hiding behind my hoodie, or avoiding Erick's gaze, and I conclude it has to do with the fact that I have Kang sitting next me and how safe he makes me feel.

Erick looks exactly like I imagined he would from hearing him on the radio. I can only hope he's not as annoying as he sounds; I'll give him the benefit of the doubt since he's Kang's friend.

"What's up?" Kang asks.

Erick shamelessly looks me up and down. "Is this the famous K?" He crosses his arms.

"And you must be Erick."

"Yeah, the one you kicked off Kang's show because 'Kang's *show* is perfect on its own.'"

I feel like dying of embarrassment as he quotes my text message. "I was only telling the truth."

"Ooh, she got you there, didn't she? To be fair, she's only spitting facts," Kang says.

"For your information, my show is just as popular as Kang's."

"Oh, really? Then I guess your backpack must be full of gifts from listeners, too. Are you going to share?"

Erick narrows his eyes. "I don't need snacks to prove my worth."

Kang applauds. "Wow, Klara, I didn't know you had this side to you."

Erick sighs and sits down across from us. "I'm so over this; it's so boring being stuck here. I tried to sneak out but that counselor lady says no one's allowed to leave until the tornado warning is lifted."

Erick picks up the other white chocolate bar and, instinctively, I reach out and grab it from him.

"Hey," he objects.

"Sorry, that's mine. It's my favorite."

"Mine, too."

"I was here first," I argue.

"And I picked it up first."

"But I took it away from you, so . . . too bad."

Kang laughs and Erick shoots him a murderous look. "Thanks for your support, bro. So quick to screw me over for a girl!"

Kang holds up his hands. "She took it from you fair and square."

Erick gives us the middle finger and I laugh. He looks like a kid who just had a piece of candy taken away. Well, that's literally what happened.

And so the afternoon flies by over candy, playful arguments with Erick, and witty banter with Kang. For the first time in a long time, I'm hanging out with people my own age and I don't feel at all out of place. My eyes meet Kang's as he laughs at something I've just said.

I feel . . . normal.

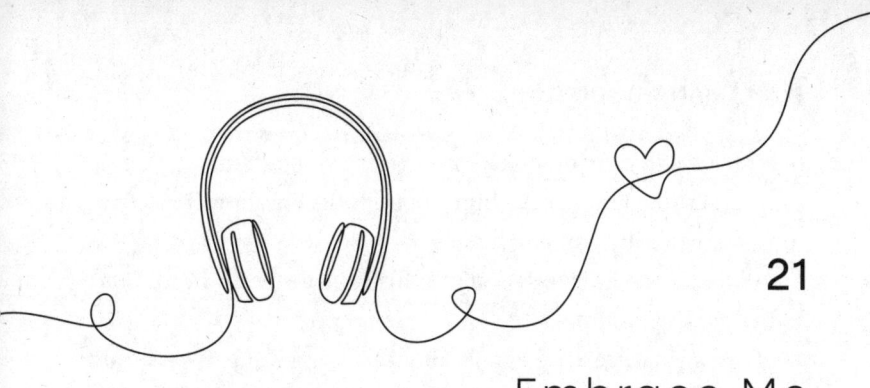

21

Embrace Me

ERICK IS NOT as much of an idiot as he seems on the radio; maybe he's just playing a part for his show. Not once has he made an even slightly sexist or inappropriate comment. It may be too early to be completely sure, but for now I'll trust my instincts.

Kang, however, is the exact same guy I hear every other night on the radio: warm, calm, and confident in who he is and what he says. Every time I look at him, I feel like my heart is going to burst out of my chest and my stomach flutters in a way I've never felt.

All these feelings are new and exciting to me. Before the whole journey of my mother's illness began, I hadn't given boys much thought. Then, after my mom died almost two years ago, I got tapped in for the battle with cancer. Boys haven't been a priority for me; I've been too focused on surviving.

So Kang is my first, for everything. The first guy I've had a crush on that I've started texting and talking to. I'm enjoying discovering so many sensations and reactions in my body. Now that I've met him, I wonder what it would feel like to kiss him, to touch him. This is unknown territory, but there's a longing in me that wasn't there before. I watch him jokingly punch Erick on the shoulder after he says something that annoys him. I stare at his lips, how they curve into that beautiful smile of his.

Will you be my first kiss, Kang? I blush and lower my head. *Don't flatter yourself, Klara.*

This is what scared me most about meeting Kang. I was afraid of his reaction when he saw what I looked like, but I was also terrified because I knew I would get my hopes up. Having him within reach only makes me like him more and want more from him, when he probably just wants to be friends. I'd like to say I can control my feelings, but that would be like saying I can control my panic attacks.

Ha! Dark humor is definitely back, Klara.

"Oh, by the way, dude . . ." Erick pulls a crumpled paper out of his pocket and straightens it in front of Kang. "Did you see this?"

My curiosity gets the best of me and I read the advertisement with a QR code at the corner to sign up. It's a talent show in Charlotte in a few months.

Kang doesn't seem surprised or excited. "Yeah, I heard."

"And?" Erick puts the paper down. "Are you signing up for it?"

Kang shakes his head. "No."

"Why not?" I look at Kang, and his expression has soured.

"I'm not interested."

"Come on, man. This may be your shot to be a famous singer or something," Erick whines.

"Dude, drop it. I said I'm not interested." Kang's voice sharpens, surprising us both.

Erick and I exchange a glance, and he sighs.

"Fine. Whatever. We need to go back with the rest of the students either way," Erick says after taking a swig from the can of Sprite Kang has passed him. "Ms. Romes sent me to get you guys. We should probably go back before she comes for us herself."

I look at him in disbelief. "You've been sitting here almost an hour and you forgot to mention that little detail?"

Erick shrugs. "There were snacks, I got distracted."

We stand up and I feel like an elf walking between the two of them. I grab my hood with both hands and flip it over my head. Kang gives me a disapproving look but doesn't say anything.

Erick leans down and I take a step back. "Are you going to sit with us in the hall?"

I would like to spend more time with them, but I don't want to draw everyone else's attention.

"Let her breathe, Erick," Kang says, seeming to notice my hesitation. "Come and sit with us whenever, if you want." He offers me a smile.

"Okay."

I wave to Erick as he walks ahead of us. Kang just stands there, looking at me, and I'm short of breath again, but I manage to speak. "See you later, Batman," I say, remembering how he told me he wears a Batman mask when he sings.

He crosses his arms and takes two steps toward me. "So you remember that?"

"I remember everything you tell me." *Ahh, Klara, don't say things like that!*

Kang raises an eyebrow and bites his lower lip. "And why do you remember everything I tell you?"

"I have a good memory." *Good answer!*

"Well, I don't have a good memory"—he steps a little closer—"but I remember what matters to me."

My heart is on the verge of collapse.

"So I remember absolutely *everything* about you."

I forget how to form words. He is so close, his dark eyes are so deep. I take a cowardly step back, but he takes a step forward and holds out his hand. "Again, a pleasure to meet you, Klara with a K."

I grin like a fool as I shake his hand.

Kang's cheeks flush; he looks away and releases my hand to scratch the back of his neck. "Damn, you've got such a nice smile."

It's my turn to blush, warmth creeping up my cheeks then settling in my stomach. "Thank you."

Kang clears his throat and extends his arm for me to walk ahead of him. "Shall we go?"

"You go first. I'll be there in a minute."

"Are you ashamed to be seen with me?" He gasps, as if in horror. "Am I your little secret, Klara?"

I play along. "Something like that."

He places both hands over his heart as he walks backward down the hall. "That hurts, Klara, that hurts."

"You'll survive."

"Oh, yeah?"

"Of course. You're Batman, after all."

Kang stops and lowers his hands, but before he disappears around the corner, he flashes those adorable dimples.

I don't know how long I stand there, staring at the spot where he stood, trying to process everything that just happened to me.

I met Kang.

I talked to him in person, just inches away.

He called me pretty—well, "hot," technically—and said I have a beautiful smile.

I met his friend Erick and he wasn't a jerk.

I chatted with my crush and I didn't die!

I pat myself on the back. *Good job, me. You did well today.*

When I return to the Blue Ridge Health Sciences Center and sit back down next to Perla, I can't help but notice the confusion on her face and the thousands of questions in her eyes. I don't know what she's thinking, but I do know that she saw me run away from Kang earlier. My eyes meet Diego's, who's staring at me with a smirk plastered on his face. I'm imagining things.

"What did I miss?" I ask, trying to make things normal between Perla and me.

"Nothing interesting," she replies.

All of a sudden, the power comes back on and the building lights up. There is cheering and laughter all around as Ms. Romes appears at the end of the hallway.

"The storm has died down for now, so we'll wait a bit for everyone to either go home or continue with your regular schedules."

Diego frowns and raises his voice for everyone to hear. "Regular schedules? I think we should have the afternoon off."

She gives him an annoyed look. "That's for the dean to decide."

Kang and Erick are sitting near Ms. Romes. Kang's eyes meet mine and he subtly waves at me. I press my lips together to keep from smiling and wave back. I look down and when I look back up, Diego is watching me, again with that same smirk. Doesn't he have anything better to do?

I spend the next few minutes chatting with Perla. Surprisingly, she doesn't ask me about Kang. Maybe she doesn't want to bring him up because she knows I have a lot of questions for her, too. I still want to know why she warned me about him.

One by one, the students begin to disperse. Perla sighs. "Well, this adventure was fun while it lasted. See you next class, Klara."

"See you."

Kamila texts to let me know it will still be a while before she or Andy will be able to get across town to pick me up, and I feel a little anxious as I watch the hallway emptying out. There's no one seated nearby except for Diego, who is on his phone. A few other students linger around, including Kang, chatting with another guy now that Erick has left.

"Hoodie," Diego whispers.

I shoot an exhausted look at him but say nothing.

"Seems like it's just you and me. Destiny keeps throwing us

together, but you won't cooperate." He runs a hand through his red hair. "Do you have something against redheads?"

I shake my head.

"So it's just that I'm not worthy of being spoken to?"

I shake my head again. *It's just that you're so loud and you like to draw attention to yourself, and I want to go unnoticed.*

Diego sighs, almost as if pretending to feel defeated. "Hoodie?"

I feel bad for ignoring him. So, against my better judgment, I engage. "I know you know my name, so why do you keep calling me Hoodie?"

The wide grin that spreads across his face is almost contagious. "Because I like to be original."

"Well, Mr. Original, why are you so insistent on talking to me?"

Diego presses his back against the wall, his elbows resting on his knees. "Why are you so mysterious?"

"You can't answer a question with another question."

"I'll tell you why I'm so insistent if you tell me something that has me curious."

"What is it?"

"Well, my darling Hoodie, more elusive than my ex after I begged her to take me back—how is it that you've gotten so close with the radio host?"

"It's complicated."

"That's what my ex said, too."

I can't help but chuckle. Diego's funny, I have to admit. "I don't have to explain myself to you, Diego."

"Oh, so you know my name." He winks at me.

"How could I not? You haven't stopped messing with me since I started here."

"I wouldn't say I've been messing with you; more like I've been fighting for acknowledgment."

"Why all the effort? You seem to have plenty of friends already."

His features soften, and he bites his lips as if thinking very carefully about his next words. "This isn't the first time I've seen you, Hoodie."

I frown. "What are you talking about?"

"It was a while ago, at the hospital. I saw you in the chemotherapy room, many times."

A bolt of icy electricity runs through my body at the possibility of Diego knowing my secret. I swallow. "I don't know what you're talking about."

Diego approaches me and gives me a friendly pat on the shoulder. "I'm glad you made it, Hoodie." He smooths out his pants. "Well, this exotic redheaded beauty has to go now."

"Diego . . ." I don't know what to say. "How . . . ?"

Sadness settles into his features, an expression I've never seen on him, always so cheerful, joking around. "My father." He answers the question he can see written on my face. "He always talked about you, the girl who made him laugh in the chemo room with her dark sense of humor."

My mind travels back to Dario, a man in his forties who was fighting an aggressive colon cancer, with whom I shared my chemo sessions several times.

"How do you manage to keep your sense of humor under these circumstances?" He runs his hand over his bald head. "I admire you, Klarita."

"Cancer has taken too much from me already. My mother, my hair, my energy . . . If I let it take away my sense of humor, I'll have lost everything."

The reality was that I was very depressed; I hadn't even been able to grieve my mother's passing before I started my own battle with cancer. But somehow Dario looked even more depressed than me. The first time I saw him, he didn't speak or interact with anyone. That made me want to cheer him up and be a source of laughter for him, even though I was dying inside. Trying to make him smile was my motivation to be strong during chemo.

We sit together as the medication, hanging from a metal rack between us, enters our veins. Dario motions for me to lean closer, and he whispers, "Wanna hear a secret?"

I nod.

"If you say you feel nauseous, they'll bring you Jell-O. Any flavor you want."

"Really?"

He nods. "Ask for strawberry, the other ones taste like medicine."

I try it out and, sure enough, the nurse brings me a cup of Jell-O. Dario and I high-five, giggling.

After I'd recovered from my mastectomy, I wanted to stop by and visit with him; I hated the idea of him sitting there alone during chemo. Very rarely did they let family members in, and Dario didn't want his relatives to see him like that anyway, so he always asked them to wait outside. I thought he might get depressed being there alone, so I bought some strawberry Jell-O and went to see him. But I was told he had passed away.

I was devastated by his death in many ways that I cannot explain.

I sent a letter to his family, offering my condolences and telling them how wonderful it had been to get to know Dario—how he had made me feel stronger and made the treatments more bearable. Dario had talked about his son, but it would've never occurred to me that it was the same Diego. What a small world we live in.

Diego holds out a hand to help me up, bringing me back to the present.

"I'm sorry, Diego. I didn't know."

He pulls me into a hug. "Thank you so much, Klara," he whispers. "In the name of my father, may he rest in peace."

Tears spring to my eyes and I try to hold them in. It's been a long time since I've thought about Dario and it's as if the pain is now revived with the memory of him.

Diego's eyes are red. "Your letter was a comfort to my mother and me. Thank you."

I don't know what to say. I have no words.

Diego takes a step back. "I gotta go, but I'm going to take you out for the best strawberry Jell-O in the world, and you can't say no."

I smile, my vision blurred by tears. "Okay."

Diego feigns a smile in return as he walks away. "I'm sorry, but you're going to have to get to know me, whether you like it or not." He shrugs. "You don't have a choice."

"If you're anything like your father, then it would be my honor, Diego."

He gives me a thumbs-up before turning to leave. Even after his death, Dario has found a way to brighten my day, to encourage me to stay strong. He helped bring someone new into my life today.

Thank you, Dario.

22

Understand Me

I'M GRATEFUL FOR the upcoming weekend; it will provide time for well-deserved rest. I consider the days I've managed to attend in-person classes a small victory, as well as my online class, since I have to leave my camera on. Now I can once again enjoy the comfort and safety of my room. I won't have to see Kang, which is a relief for my anxiety, but it also makes me sad. Now that I've met him, I want to continue seeing him.

It's dark out and I'm sitting by the window, remembering my last panic attack and how Kang stayed on the phone with me until it passed, distracting me with thoughts of autumn. He's been so kind, so understanding.

Part of me still can't believe what happened today. I had face-to-face conversations with Kang, Erick, and Diego, three guys my age, and I didn't die trying. A few weeks ago, if someone had told me that I would do what I did today, I wouldn't have believed them. I didn't think I was capable of talking to anyone my age. Let alone a guy I like.

I guess Dr. B. is right: Every breakthrough, no matter how small, propels me further down my path to a normal life. Today felt pretty normal. *I* felt normal.

For the first time I truly begin to believe that I can do this. I feel even more motivated, especially after the conversation I had with Diego. The fact that my words had a positive effect on Dario's family feels gratifying.

I breathe on the window, fogging up the glass, and trace the letter *K* with my finger. It reminds me of finger painting, which was one of my favorite techniques.

I hear someone clear their throat and I turn around. Kamila is at my bedroom door in her pajamas with two steaming mugs in her hands.

"Hot chocolate?"

I beam. "Is there anyone alive who can say no to hot chocolate?"

She nods. "Andy."

"Andy doesn't count."

She comes into the room and sits beside me at the window, handing me a cup. For a moment we don't say anything. It's not awkward—it's just us, two sisters enjoying a nice cup of hot chocolate. I take several sips before breaking the silence. "I know what you want to ask."

She raises an eyebrow. "I don't know what you're talking about."

"Kamila . . ."

"What?"

"You don't have to pretend. I know you."

She takes a sip from her cup. "I'm a new person. I'm trying to be less . . . invasive."

"Asking people questions and analyzing their answers is part of who you are. That's why you studied psychiatry. So go ahead and ask."

"I don't want to pester you, Klara."

"Kamila, I admit that your constant questions can be annoying at times, but I'm used to it. I love you just the way you are; I wouldn't change anything about you."

Her eyes redden and she lets out a long breath of air. "Don't say things like that, you'll make me cry."

I take her free hand and squeeze it.

"But, since you've given me the green light, I'm dying to know how your day went. You have no idea how worried I was when the storm suddenly hit, with you stuck on campus."

"I did so well, Kami. I had a normal day—can you believe it? I can't. I talked to people my age, made friends."

"I'm so glad, K. I can believe it. You've fought hard to get where you are. It's time to reap some rewards, like today."

"Hey."

Kamila and I turn to see Andy in the doorway.

"You're having a pajama party and you didn't invite me?"

"No, come on in. The entrance fee is a cup of hot chocolate."

He opens his mouth to protest, but Kamila cuts him off. "No exceptions."

Andy leaves and comes back a few minutes later with a cup in his hand. Kamila and I share an amused look as he sits on the bed since there's no more room at the window.

"What? I wanted to join the PJ party."

Kamila narrows her eyes at him. "We know that's tea in there."

I smile and the three of us sit enjoying our hot drinks.

"So, what did I miss?"

"Klara was telling me how well she did today, despite the storm."

"We're so proud of you, Klara." Andy fist-bumps me.

I thank him, and we continue to chat about my first couple weeks of college until eventually Andy looks at his watch and asks, "Isn't it time for that radio show you like?"

I sigh. "There's no show today because of the storm."

"Don't worry," Andy says. "I'm sure it'll only be for today."

I glance at my phone: zero messages. I haven't heard from Kang since I left campus this afternoon, and I can't deny that it has me feeling a little anxious. We've never gone this many hours without texting. My insecurities return: *He's met me now and I'm not what he expected, so he doesn't want to talk to me anymore.*

I consider sending him a message, but I don't want to seem desperate or intense. But then again, he's always the one who reaches out first. Maybe it's time for me to take the initiative.

Andy and Kamila leave and I get in bed, but I can't fall asleep. Every time I close my eyes, I see Kang—his smile, his eyes, his expressions . . . those dimples that just disarm me.

I could get started on my reading assignment for my American Literature course or look over my slides for the presentation we have coming up—that will definitely make me tired. But I'm not sure I'd be able to concentrate, especially when I know the cause of my restlessness: Kang not having texted me.

I give in. I pick up my phone and send him a message.

Me: Awake?

He doesn't answer. He can't be asleep. It's barely ten o'clock and Kang is a night owl, as he's told me many times. Well, at least I tried; now maybe I can fall asleep.

My phone buzzes with a new message and I sit up to check it.

Kang: Yes.

Something's not right. Kang has never been one for dry, one-word responses.

Me: What are you doing?
Kang: Nothing.

His message seems to confirm my greatest fear: Now that he's met me, he no longer wants to talk to me. Why would he? He's seen what I look like: a skeleton in a wig.

Did you really think a guy like him would ever be attracted to you? He clearly only said you're hot to be nice. Again, that cruel voice inside my head.

I don't bother to respond, because I get it, I'm not stupid. I put my phone under my pillow and stare up at the dark ceiling. My chest burns and my stomach aches; this hurts, a lot. These feelings of rejection and disappointment are much more heartbreaking than I thought they would be. Even though I've tried to keep my expectations in check, I couldn't help but get my hopes up, especially after how much fun we had today. I'm such an idiot!

My phone buzzes under my pillow, and I check the screen. It's an incoming call from Kang. My broken heart wakes up and beats with hope once again.

"Hello?"

"Hey."

How is it that he can make me melt with just one word? I don't know what to say. He sighs and I begin to chew on a fingernail. "What's wrong, Kang?" I ask. Ignoring the fact that he's acting different won't get us anywhere.

"Nothing, just . . ." He pauses, and his voice sounds off. "I'm sorry, Klara, I was being an idiot."

"What are you talking about?"

"I was dying to text you, and I shouldn't have responded like that. I just got carried away by my emotions."

"Emotions?"

"I was a bit hurt by you."

I'm even more confused now. "Why? What did I do?"

"It doesn't matter, Klara. Let's pretend it didn't happen and talk like normal, okay?"

"I'm so confused, Kang."

He lets out a long sigh. "I know, it's my fault . . . What are you doing? How did the rest of your afternoon go?"

I hesitate. I know he wants to move past this, but how can he expect me not to ask what I've done to upset him? But he's always been so patient with me, never pressuring me to explain things even when he's dying to know. I can return the favor; I can be understanding with him.

"Well, I had a hot chocolate with my sister and brother-in-law," I say, making myself comfortable.

"Would you believe me if I told you I did exactly the same thing tonight?" His voice has recovered its usual charisma. "Not with my sister, of course—she's not good at sharing when it comes to chocolate."

"I believe you," I say, smiling. "I missed your show today."

He laughs and it makes me smile once more. "Yeah, I wish I could go on every weekday—days without my show are strange for me, especially when I'm supposed to be on."

"For me, too. I hate not being able to hear you on *Follow My Voice*."

"I'm curious, Klara: How long have you been listening to the show?"

I stay silent a moment, deciding whether to tell him the truth. That I have been listening to him every other night for a year now because his voice gives me peace and helps me forget my fears, my negative thoughts, my sadness. That his show has saved me.

"A little over a year."

"A year? Really?"

"Yes..." I pause. "And I can't thank you enough for... this whole year. You have no idea how much you help people with your show."

"That means a lot to me, Klara. I started *Follow My Voice* with that intention, to help people, and if I've affected your life in a positive way, I'm glad."

"Well, you have." *You've done so much more than help me. You've made me feel things that no one has ever been able to make me feel. I had a hard time feeling anything for so long after what I went through. But it's so easy with you, Kang.*

"Wow, but a year is a long time . . . Why didn't you ever send any messages to the show before?"

"Well, I figured they would just get buried under so many others. That's the only reason I even got the courage to finally message you; I never imagined you would actually read it."

"I read all your messages, Klara, until I finally got the courage to get your phone number from the station and text you directly. Honestly, I expected you to call me a stalker and block my number."

I smile. "I considered it."

"Really? Then why go through the trouble of getting me to read a quote on the air? Erick teased me for days afterward, by the way—said I started incorporating more quotes into the show because of you without even knowing you."

"Sorry not sorry about Erick, but I needed to make sure it was you."

"Why?"

"What do you mean, *why*? I didn't want to talk to someone pretending to be you."

"Well, it's me. Just plain, boring me."

"You're not boring," I respond. "How can you say that when you have a radio show that dozens upon dozens of people listen to? You've even got a little fanbase going on."

"Fair point."

"Someone's cocky."

He lets out a gasp. "Ouch. You wound me, Klara. Not cocky, I just happen to think you made a fair point, seeing as we did share some of those snacks today."

I'm about to respond, but a yawn comes out instead, and he seems to hear it.

"I'll let you sleep. Talk tomorrow?" he says softly.

"Talk tomorrow, Kang."

"Goodnight, gorgeous."

He hangs up and my heart skips a beat at that last word. Kang just called me "gorgeous." I must be hallucinating. And even though I want to know why he was upset with me, I can't help but fall asleep with a smile on my lips. I'm so tired after this long, normal day.

23

Touch Me

EVERY STEP I take is slow and measured as I observe the hallway filled with college students chatting in groups or absorbed by their phones. I wonder if they're at all aware how lucky they are to be young and healthy, to not have to worry about their health every day.

Fear of death continues to fuel my anxiety, but I've reached a point of calm; after everything I've been through, I feel that I am able to have a different perspective on life and empathize with others more readily. Surviving cancer has given me skills that I would never have gained if I'd lived a normal life.

I am Klara, the girl who lost her mother to cancer and couldn't even mourn her loss because she immediately began fighting her own battle with the disease. The girl who has suffered from anxiety, depression, panic attacks, agoraphobia, and low self-esteem. The girl who smiles to herself now in a crowded hallway because she has won a small battle and is fighting to live life and enjoy it to the best of her abilities. The mere fact that I was able to leave the house today without going over all the negative things that could happen to me, that I was able to focus on the feeling of the morning breeze on my skin, is an accomplishment.

As I enter the classroom, I freeze in the doorway. The two guys who are always together, Ben and Adrian, are standing in the corner. Ben rests his hand on the wall above Adrian's shoulder, cornering him. Adrian sees me and goes red. Uh-oh. I consider turning around to give them privacy, but they quickly step apart.

"Hey..." Adrian says, scratching his head. "What's your name? I can't remember."

"Klara," I say as I walk to my seat.

"Klara, I'm Adrian and this is Ben."

Ben doesn't even look at me.

I know; I've been cheering them on from afar. They make a cute couple. "Nice to meet you guys."

Adrian smiles. "We were just messing around."

I nod.

Emma, the redhead, enters, chewing gum as usual, and behind her Perla appears with dark circles under her eyes. She sits down next to me, sighing. She turns to meet my gaze. "I know, I look like death warmed over."

"Actually, I was just going to say hi." I wave with a smile. "Hi, Perla."

She laughs. "You look . . ." Perla searches for the word. "Less pale."

"I feel good today."

"I'm glad. Any specific reason?"

"No."

Perla raises an eyebrow. "You are very strange, do you know that, Klara? In a good way."

"Thank you."

The classroom quickly fills up and Diego comes in, greeting everyone in his overly loud voice. "Here I am, you don't have to miss me anymore," he shouts as he slides across the floor in front of the whole class.

Perla rolls her eyes.

Diego winks at me and I smile. I feel bad for avoiding him for so long. I'm not perfect, but I will try to learn from my mistakes. I plan to apologize for openly ignoring him before. I realize now that I've had my guard up because I was afraid people would reject me.

Diego sits down in front of me, and Perla again raises an eyebrow. This is not his usual seat. I know it will be impossible not to engage with him.

Diego turns around in his chair to look at me. "Hoodie."

"Are you going to call me that forever?" I joke.

He nods. "I told you I like to be original. So, how was your weekend? It must've been a good one—you look refreshed, relaxed."

It's nice to have people other than Andy or Kamila ask me about my life. "Yeah, it was great. I slept a lot."

"Would someone mind telling me what I missed?" Perla interrupts. She doesn't sound angry, just shocked and confused. "Last week you refused to speak to this dude and now you're telling him about your weekend? Did something happen the day of the storm, after I left?"

You have no idea, Perla.

Diego clears his throat and puts on a serious expression. "The truth, Perla, is that, after you left, Klara declared her burning feelings of unrequited love for me."

"Diego!" I protest.

Perla laughs. "Yeah, sure, right."

"You don't believe me?" Diego gives her a wounded look.

"Nope."

I smile as I watch them argue jokingly, when I suddenly feel someone watching us and look up to see who it is. It's the girl with glasses who's always reading. She seems . . . sad? She can't take her eyes off Diego.

Oh, I get it!

I look back at Diego; he's very handsome. The red hair, freckles, and his charismatic personality and self-confidence attract people to him. I understand why he would be popular with the girls.

Diego pauses his conversation with Perla and looks at me. "What?"

"Nothing, I just like watching you two argue."

Perla grunts and makes a face. "Well, we should be talking about the presentation. How come I have to be the one presenting from the two of us?" she directs at me.

"You're the chosen one." Diego winks at her. "Plus, Klara told me she worked really hard on the PowerPoint. All you have to do is get up there and read it."

Diego is lying, of course; I never told him such a thing.

"Right, because talking about the high rates of STIs and STDs on campus is so much fun." Perla rolls her eyes.

"I added pictures," I say with a smile, grateful that she agreed to present in front of the class. Regardless of how much progress I've made, I'm still not quite there yet.

Perla grimaces.

"I hate you, guys. I do."

◆ ◆ ◆

After class, Perla and I go into the cafeteria to pass the time before Kamila can pick me up. I'm not that hungry, so I settle on a small turkey sandwich before we choose a table facing the entrance. My heart skips a beat when I see Kang enter wearing a white T-shirt and jeans, followed by Erick and a bunch of guys wearing soccer team sweatshirts. Kang looks so cute laughing at something Erick has said. How could a guy like him be interested in me? It seems so illogical.

Stop it, Klara. What have we said about thoughts that belittle you? You are worth as much as anyone else. I'm practicing positive thinking.

Kang's eyes dance over the crowd in the cafeteria, and when

they land on me, the whole room seems to fade away and it feels as if it's just us two, alone, with no one else around. He smiles and starts walking toward me, but then he sees Perla and stops. I furrow my brow in confusion as he goes to sit with his teammates. Okay, that was really weird. What could have happened between these two for them to avoid each other like that? I hear a text notification and I take a bite of my sandwich, then look at my phone.

> **Kang:** Hey, gorgeous. Can I see you after lunch? I have some time before my next class.

I feel butterflies in my stomach and grin widely.

> **Me:** Yes. Auditorium hallway?
> **Kang:** Is that your favorite hiding place?
> **Me:** Do you have somewhere else in mind?
> **Kang:** No. See you there.

I've never eaten so fast in my life, the excitement making my hands so clammy that I have to constantly wipe them on my sweatshirt. I glance over at Kang and catch him already looking at me. Our eyes communicate but no one around us has any idea that we know each other and talk all the time on the phone. It's our secret.

I give Kang a head start to avoid suspicions from Perla, then I leave the cafeteria a few minutes later, feeling nervous as I make my way to the auditorium. And there's Kang, leaning against the wall, his hands in his pockets. When he sees me, he pushes himself away from the wall and stands to face me.

Breathe, Klara.

"Hello, Klara with a K."

"Hello, Batman."

He smiles. I think the dimples in his cheeks might do me in.

"Again with that?"

I shrug. "I'm not going to leave you alone until you tell me the story behind the mask *and* let me see you play."

He purses his lips. "Are you twenty-one all of a sudden?" he asks, pointing out the obvious.

"I will be . . . soonish."

"Okay, we'll just explain that to the doorman when he asks for ID."

"You're annoying."

Kang bites his lower lip and takes a step toward me. "Oh, yeah?"

I swallow and lift my face to look up at him. Having him so close is hard to handle. Did I mention how good Kang smells? It's soothing, like a mix of gentle laundry detergent and something sweet.

Calm down, Klara, you're almost salivating.

He reaches toward me cautiously, as if afraid of scaring me away. With his eyes fixed on mine, he places his hand on my cheek and caresses it with his thumb. His touch sends shivers through my body, and my knees threaten to give way beneath me. How can such a simple gesture feel so intimate, so consuming, as if he's unraveling me with just his fingertips? *How can I have missed you so much when we've only met once?* I open my mouth to say something, but just then a group of girls walks by, laughing, and I quickly step back, breaking off all contact.

Kang blushes and clears his throat. "Hey, so, it's almost time for my next class. If you're going to be on campus for a while, I could drive you home after."

Surprisingly, my first thought isn't about staying on campus longer than I need to. Instead, it's about how I explain that to Kamila. "Um, let me check with my sister. I'll text you."

"Okay."

We part ways, grinning at each other as we wave goodbye. I'm smiling so hard my face hurts when I open the entrance door and run straight into Diego.

"You might want to look a little less in love, Hoodie," he says.

"I don't know what you're talking about."

Diego smirks, shaking his head, as he continues on his way.

I make an effort to keep my smile in check when I receive Kamila's response saying she doesn't mind if I ride home with a friend.

I'm going to be alone with Kang . . .

24

Destroy Me

I NEVER IMAGINED I could go from feeling so excited and happy to being so completely knocked down to size in a matter of minutes. Over all the months I stayed locked up inside my room, I never experienced such abrupt changes in mood. I guess it's because there are fewer variables at home; I can control things. But in the outside world I'm at the mercy of other people. I learned this in the worst way possible.

"Hey there." It's the tall, gorgeous, black-haired girl from my class blocking my path, her two friends lingering close by. She's even prettier up close, with full lips and a thin nose. Her face is contoured to highlight her striking features, but I'm sure she's just as beautiful without any makeup.

"Yes?" I answer politely, a little nervous since socializing with strangers is something I haven't quite mastered.

She gives me a warm smile. "We haven't been introduced. I'm Liliana, but everyone calls me Yana for short." She takes my hand and I tense, but I don't pull away. I don't want to seem unfriendly.

Wait... Liliana? As in the girl who always messages Kang's radio show? No, it can't be.

"I'm Klara."

"Are you on social media, Klara? We've set up a TikTok for the school, and we're trying to get students to follow the account."

"Oh . . ." I swallow. "No . . . I'm not on any social networks."

"Really?" The surprise on her face is evident. I feel dumb. Everyone is on the internet; it's weird not to be. *You're weird, Klara.* This thought makes me feel even more nervous.

"Well, come on, we'll help you set up an account."

Yana guides me through a wooden door with a frosted glass window. We're inside a classroom that looks like it's being used for storage for the theater department. There are racks full of costumes, props, made-up sets. There's even old, cracked mirrors lined up against one wall.

Her two friends follow us inside and introduce themselves: Kayla and Andrea. I'm not at all comfortable in this situation, but I don't know how to get out of it without being rude. Besides, these girls are just being nice, right?

Yana takes my phone and starts downloading the app, asking me the required questions.

"Sorry, but I have to ask: Is that your real hair or a wig?" Kayla says, smiling kindly.

The comment stings since one of my fears about starting college was that people would notice my wig and say something about it. Kayla's question sends my thoughts spiraling: *Is it that obvious? Has everyone noticed? Perla? Diego? Kang?*

"It's . . . a wig," I admit, embarrassed.

"Oh, it looks great on you."

"There, now you can follow the college's official TikTok account, and all of us, too," Yana says. She's about to hand my phone back when a message from Kang comes in. "Oh, you know Kang?"

"You know him, too?" I ask, taking my phone back.

"Yeah, everyone does—he's our favorite radio host," she says, leaning against a table.

"Yeah, his show's great," I say.

Yana has left the school's TikTok account open on my phone and a video is paused on a photo of Kang in his soccer uniform next to Yana in cheerleading attire. The photo is captioned *Goals* and there are a bunch of comments from people saying they make a cute couple. And it's true—they look perfect together, made for each other. I try to speak, but the words are stuck in my throat.

"Kang's going to be such a great therapist," Kayla says, sighing.

"Therapist?" I thought Kang was studying something related to radio broadcasting or communications. He's never mentioned therapy to me.

"Oh, yeah, I thought everyone knew. He volunteers as a peer counselor once a month," Yana says. "I think he helped out your friend Perla, too."

"Oh."

I'm left speechless, processing this bizarre encounter, as the girls say goodbye and leave the room. They were friendly enough, but there was something about them that intimidated me, as if they had some underlying intentions. *You knew this would happen*, I tell myself. *You thought you could have a normal life, that a guy like Kang could be into you.*

Stop, Klara. You're ruminating, as Dr. B. would call it—the pattern of negative and repetitive thinking that is difficult to stop.

It's just hard to fight these thoughts when everything makes more sense with all this new information. Kang wants to be a therapist; he volunteers to counsel messed-up kids like me; he's only talking to me to help me adjust, probably because Ms. Romes asked him to. I glance back at the picture of Kang and Yana. She looks like the kind of girl who deserves to be by his side. The two of them together make perfect sense.

I suddenly feel that the outside world is too terrifying. This is why I didn't want to get my hopes up, this is why I didn't want to expose myself to him. I knew everything was too good to be true . . . Kang was too good to be true. That, sooner rather than later, everything would fall apart and reality would set in.

I see my depressing reflection in one of the cracked mirrors, face flushed, tears in my eyes. I raise a hand and trace my reflection with trembling fingers.

I close my eyes. I don't want to leave this room; I don't want to see anyone now that I know how they truly view me. Everyone has been so friendly because they pity me, because they see me as weak, because society requires them to be nice to sick people to keep from appearing cruel. None of it was real.

I sit down with my back against the wall, hug my knees, and cry until I run out of tears. I don't know how to handle this sudden emotional low. I ignore my cell phone, which vibrates repeatedly. I just want to stay here, safe, where no one can see me, no one can hurt me. *I'll be fine as long as I stay here.*

I'm not sure how many minutes have passed, but the tears have dried and my eyes trace the dusty cobwebs along the walls. My mind is foggy and I have the feeling of being left adrift, alone in an immense and unscrupulous world.

A tapping sound at the window causes me to turn my head: It's raining. A bitter smile forms on my lips; of course it's raining! Life constantly reminds me of everything I've lost, like salt in the wound left by my mother's death. Life wants to sink me.

But I'm already sunk.

You can end it, Klara. You can stop all this pain, all this suffering. Aren't you tired of fighting every day? What for? Just so you can have another relapse? You'll never be completely well. Something will always send you back into the corner, cowering in fear. Imagine no more sadness, no more deathly fears every time you go for your quarterly checkup with the oncologist, no more constantly picturing your death by cancer . . . You don't want to leave this world like your mother did, slowly and painfully.

Fresh tears retrace the well-laid path down my cheeks as the rain becomes heavier against the glass.

Suicide.

That forbidden word that people avoid like the plague. *How could anyone want to end their life? It doesn't make sense,* they say. Sure, it doesn't make sense for a psychologically stable person. But for those of us with major depression, it's an option that's always there in the backs of our minds. I'm not justifying it, I'm not promoting it, but I understand why it's a thought. That doesn't mean I'm going to do it, but I can admit to thinking about it.

Why?

That's the big question, isn't it?

Why would I do such a thing?

Because living hurts—trudging through days with the feeling of drowning because I don't see the point of anything. *Why am I alive? Why should I go on? If I often struggle to find meaning in anything I do, why keep doing it?* I'm exhausted by so many monotonous, colorless days without any feeling besides pain. *What's the point of staying here?*

Emotional fatigue. It's led me to think about suicide several times during my periods of depression. When you feel like you can't take it anymore, like you just want the pain to stop, for it all to end, suicide can seem like the only option. The silence and peace only death can offer are tempting in the midst of the chaos caused by depression. But, if there's one thing I've learned from Kamila, it's a coping mechanism to deal with these thoughts.

"I want you to imagine a spectacular landscape with lush green trees, a cool breeze, green grass, flowers everywhere, clear skies," my sister says in a soothing voice. "It's a beautiful view, isn't it?"

"Yes," I say, my eyes closed.

"Now, suddenly, the sky clouds over, the flowers lose their color, torrential rain begins to fall, flooding everything... Hurricane-force winds whip through the trees, stripping them of their leaves. How does it look now?"

"Very bad."

"That storm is depression, Klara, and with it comes suicidal thoughts, asking why not end it all. But even if the landscape is damaged by the storm, you need to remember how beautiful the view will be again... Why?"

"Because the storm will pass."

"Exactly. Because even if something is damaged, it can be repaired. When the clouds disperse and the sun comes out again to dry the grass and flowers, when new leaves sprout on the trees, the landscape will be beautiful again, even more than before because it will have survived a storm."

"I understand."

"So when you feel overwhelmed, remember what I just told you, okay? Your life is a beautiful landscape, Klara. Admitting that you are in the midst of the storm will help you remember that it has an end, and that you will survive."

I gently wipe the tears from my face.

"I'm in the midst of the storm," I say in a broken voice, "but it's going to pass. I'm going to be okay. I've survived so many storms..." My voice breaks. "When I come out of this one, I'm going to enjoy the hell out of that beautiful fucking view."

25

Visit Me

Me: Hey, don't need that ride today after all.

It's hard for me to send this message, but I can't talk to Kang right now. I don't plan to avoid him forever, but I don't want him to see me in this mess of a state I'm in.

I have been doing breathing exercises to calm my mind, which seems to be at war with itself. Now, after crying so hard, I'm too exhausted to feel anything, like I'm stuck in some sort of limbo, floating endlessly in the nothingness without thinking, just being.

I need to get back to the real world, and the afternoon sunlight I now see filtering through the window gives me a clue as to how late it is. I just have to make sure there's no one around before I leave this room.

My phone vibrates with Kang's reply.

Kang: Everything OK?

No, nothing is okay, Kang, I can't see you right now . . . I don't know how I would feel.

There are so many things I want to ask him, especially about Perla. She warned me about him; maybe she knew I would get my hopes up only to find out that he was simply trying to help me.

Me: All good.

I send the text and sit staring at my phone, thinking about what I'm going to do now. I told Kamila that I was going to ride home with friends; she'll worry if I ask her to come get me now. Besides, the hospital is not close; it would take her a while to get here.

Would Perla be able to give me a ride?

I quickly brush that idea aside. I don't feel like seeing Perla right now, either. We're just starting to establish a friendship and I don't want her to see my face all red from crying.

Maybe I should just get an Uber. But somehow the idea of a stranger seeing the state I'm in is even more terrifying than being stuck on campus.

Diego.

For some reason I don't mind him seeing me so vulnerable; maybe because he saw me at my worst when I was receiving my chemo alongside his father.

I scroll through the group chat for our class and find his number. I'll deal with the consequences later.

Me: Have you left yet?

I pray he hasn't, because otherwise I'll have no choice but to ask Kamila to come get me, or Andy, who always leaves the law firm late. A few minutes go by with no response and I start to lose hope, until, finally:

Diego: Still here, picking up the paintings from last Friday's exhibit.
Me: Where are you? Are there people with you?

I don't want anyone else to see my red, swollen face.

Diego: Just me, in the auditorium.

And then I get another text from him:

Diego: Why so many questions? Are you okay?
Me: I'm fine, I was just wondering if you could give me a ride home. If you can't, don't worry.
Diego: Of course, on the way we can stop for the best strawberry Jell-O in the world.

And right there, I smile.

Diego: Come to the auditorium, I'm almost finished. I'll wait here.

I tell him I'm on my way and stand up, rubbing my cheeks in a futile attempt to disguise the fact that I've been crying. I take a deep breath and open the door, then poke my head out to make sure the hallway is empty.

As I make my way to Diego, memories of Kang flash in my mind. I can almost see him standing there smiling at me, waving goodbye.

"*It's an honor to finally meet the mysterious K.*"
"*You don't have to hide, Klara—you're very . . . hot.*"
"*Hello, Klara with a K.*"
"*Damn, you've got such a nice smile.*"

What am I to you, Kang? I can't help but ask myself this question as I walk through the entrance to the auditorium. Inside, it's bigger than I expected, with three sections of seating. I walk down one of the aisles toward the stage, where I see Diego moving paintings around behind the open curtains in the back. He's slightly sweaty and has a few strands of red hair stuck to his forehead. He smiles when he notices me and carefully lowers the canvas he's holding. His smile fades, however, as I step closer and he gets a look at my face.

"Are you okay?" he asks, stepping forward. The concern in his voice is obvious. "Klara?"

He used my name—a first. Another obvious sign he's concerned.

"I'm fine. Do you have much longer?" I ask.

"No, I just have to put away a few more paintings."

"I'll wait here."

Diego hesitates for a second, as if he doesn't know whether to probe further or leave it at that. I hope my expression lets him know that I don't feel like explaining myself. I'm not ready to talk about my little meltdown.

"Okay." He smiles and turns to go back to the stage.

I follow him, drawn to a corner where ten paintings are lined up against the wall. They are lovely and I have no idea why my heart begins racing as I approach them. I stop in front of a brightly colored portrait of a girl: Her face is a rainbow. Instinctively, my hand moves to feel the texture of the paint, each brushstroke. I gently run a finger along the contour of her face. It's been so long. I still remember my second-grade teacher telling me that I had an innate talent for drawing. She said the same thing to my mother at the parent-teacher conference.

"Whenever we do drawing activities, Klara leaves us all amazed. She has talent. I recommend you enroll her in private drawing lessons."

My mother gives her a warm smile. "That's a great idea."

That night, when we get home, my mother bends down to look me in the eye. "Klara, do you like to draw?"

I shrug.

"Your teacher says you're good at drawing, but I'm not going to put you in private art classes unless it's something you want to do. Would you like to take drawing lessons?"

I shake my head.

"Okay, that's fine."

"I want to paint, Mom."

"Paint?"

I nod energetically. "Yes, that's what I want to do."

And that's how I began taking art classes. Being good at drawing is helpful when it comes to painting, but it's not a requirement. I'm a good sketcher, but painting is my passion—experimenting with brush techniques, mixing different colors. My second-grade teacher found it strange that I preferred painting over drawing, but I'm grateful to my mother for taking the time to ask me what I wanted instead of just listening to the teacher. I was lucky to have a mom like her.

I remember the tears of joy in my mother's eyes when my paintings won a district-wide art award and were exhibited at several schools.

I step back from the painting and stare at it. The more I look at it, the more I feel like I can see the mood and emotions of the person who painted it. At first glance, the face looks cheerful, full of color, but looking closer there are colorful tears under the girl's eyes. That's what I like about art: It's so subjective and lends itself to so many interpretations. A painting might make me feel one way and make someone else feel completely different.

"Do you like it?"

I jump at the sound of Diego's voice behind me. I turn to him. "Yes, it's . . . It has a lot of feeling."

"My father told me you liked to paint. Are you taking any art classes?"

I shake my head.

"No, I can't . . . not yet."

"Why not? The way you were looking at that painting—"

"I was just enjoying it; that's all," I say, cutting him off.

"Okay . . . Well, are you ready to go?"

I nod, and we begin to head toward the student parking lot.

Diego's car is two-toned black and white. It looks new and classy. We get in and the scent of his cologne permeates the air; it smells great. It's the first time in a long time I've ridden in a car belonging to someone other than Kamila, Andy, or an Uber driver. I feel a bit anxious, imagining a variety of horrible accidents, but I'm not as scared as I would've expected.

Diego sighs and I hold on to my seatbelt as he pulls out of the parking lot. We stop at a local drive-thru, where Diego orders two cups of strawberry Jell-O with vanilla ice cream. Then he drives to the cemetery, and I immediately tense up. I haven't been back to the cemetery since the one time I was able to visit my mother's grave before I was diagnosed with cancer.

Diego cuts off the engine, then turns his hazel eyes on me. "We can leave if you don't want to be here."

"No, it's okay."

He doesn't question me further, and instead guides me along lines of gravestones until he finally stops in front of one.

DARIO ANDRADE
(JUNE 5, 1978 – NOVEMBER 19, 2023)

BELOVED HUSBAND AND FATHER.

"DON'T LET FEAR OF DEATH STOP YOU FROM LIVING LIFE."

P.S. IF YOU CAN'T CLOSE YOUR EYES AND ENJOY THE TASTE OF YOUR FAVORITE FOOD, YOU'RE NOT LIVING.

I feel a tightness in my chest as I remember Dario's smile and how he changed as we got to know each other better.

We sit to one side of the grave. Diego hands me my cup of Jell-O with ice cream and uncovers his.

"Hey, Dad, I've brought a very special visitor today," he says, glancing at me.

I smile. "Hello, Dario. I've come to share this strawberry Jell-O with you. According to Diego, it's the best in the world—we'll see about that."

Diego and I each take a spoonful of Jell-O, closing our eyes to savor the taste and enjoy the texture. *If you can't close your eyes and enjoy the taste of your favorite food, you're not living.* The Jell-O is delicious. I didn't expect it to be so good with ice cream, but it is. When I open my eyes, I see that Diego is watching me intently. He smiles, lips bright red.

"What?" I ask.

"I thought you were going to ask to leave when you saw where I'd brought you. I'm glad you didn't."

"How could I say no to such wonderful company"—I point to his father's grave—"and such delicious Jell-O?"

"Hey, what about me?"

I rub my chin, as if thinking about it. "Hmmm . . . You're ten percent of the reason I'm here."

"Ten percent?"

"Keep complaining and I'll have to drop it down to nine."

Diego laughs. He looks so sweet that I can't help but laugh along with him. "I can live with ten percent if I can keep hearing you laugh like that."

I shake my head, still smiling. "You're crazy."

We continue joking and eating. When we finish, I look to Dario's grave. "I think I have to agree with your son. This is some of the best strawberry Jell-O I've ever tasted."

I glance at Diego, who seems lost in thought, his eyes on his father's tombstone. The sad look on his face makes it clear that he misses him very much. I'm grateful to Diego for bringing me here;

somehow, remembering Dario, a person who always encouraged me to stay strong, has lifted my spirits.

"Diego."

He looks at me, coming back to reality. "Yes?"

"Thank you."

He smiles sadly. "You're welcome, Hoodie."

I stand up and offer him my hand. "Let's go."

"Are we leaving already?"

"No, I want to introduce you to someone very special to me."

Mourn Me

KATIA RODRÍGUEZ
(MARCH 12, 1965 – OCTOBER 10, 2022)

"EVERY DEFEAT IS A STEP TOWARD VICTORY."

My mother's grave.

Standing before it, my heart cracks. It's still hard to believe she's no longer with us. Seeing her grave makes that fact all the more real, and it hurts. There are two little vases on the sides of her headstone with close-to-wilted flowers inside. Kamila comes every Saturday to change them, but it's impossible for the flowers to survive the damp autumn weather very long. I can't believe I'm here. Not being able to visit her because of my crippling anxiety has been a major source of guilt. *I'm here now, Mom.*

Diego stands behind me, not saying a word. I brush the dry leaves off a rock beside the grave and sit down, then proceed to run my hands over my mother's name.

"It's been a long time, Mami."

Diego sits down on the other side of the headstone, studying me. I clear my throat and exhale, fighting the urge to cry, feeling like I've all but run out of tears.

"Mom, I didn't come alone . . ." I exchange a glance with Diego. "I brought a . . . friend. He's a little crazy, but I know you'll like him."

Diego pretends to be insulted, but not at the friend part, which I surprisingly find to be a relief. "It's a pleasure, Ms. Rodríguez. In my defense, I have to say that Klara is not entirely sane, either."

Our eyes meet and we both give each other a lopsided smile. We sit there for a while, talking, telling my mother everything that has happened since I started college. Time seems to fly by, and soon the sky begins to cloud and darken, lending the cemetery an air of melancholy with its leafless trees and the ground still damp from the recent storm. Then, as if nature is telling us it's time to leave, it begins to drizzle.

"Time to go." Diego stands up but I remain seated. "I'll go on ahead. Take as long as you need."

He walks away and waits under a tree as I say goodbye to my mother. Tiny raindrops fall on her silent, frozen grave.

"Mami"—my voice breaks—"I'm so sorry I couldn't come visit you sooner. It's been . . ." I take a deep breath. "It's been . . . hard, very . . ." Two thick tears roll down my cheeks. "But here I am. Forgive me for leaving you alone for so long. I might not have been able to visit, but I carry you in my heart always. Every time I've given up, you've been there with your vegetable soup to make me all better." A sob escapes my throat. "It'll soon be exactly two years since you've been gone, ten days from today. I miss you so much, Mami . . . I love you so much. You can rest easy now; I will survive. I will somehow manage to go on without you. I know it couldn't have made you proud to see me waste so much time hiding, living in fear. But I'm trying, Mom, hard, to make you proud of me again."

I stand up, wiping away my tears. I head over to where Diego waits, forcing a smile. "That's it, we can go," I say, walking past him without stopping.

Diego takes my arm and turns me to face him. Before I can say anything, he pulls me into a huge bear hug. The smell of his cologne is calming. "It's okay, you can cry," he says, rubbing the back of my head. I try to pull away, but he hugs me even tighter. "You know I won't judge you; I won't even say anything. You can cry, vent, and then we'll go."

I stop struggling and allow myself to sob openly. I cling to him, my arms around his waist. Diego says nothing, as promised, and lets me cry against his chest. There's something very comforting about crying in someone's arms, as if that person is helping to contain your sadness. I'm so used to crying all alone; this is the first time in a long time that I've let anyone comfort me. And Diego transmits so much acceptance, so much warmth in the midst of this cold.

I don't know how much time passes, but I let it all out, releasing the sadness I feel after seeing my mother's grave—this vivid reminder that she's gone. We stand there, holding each other, as heavier rain begins to fall around us.

When I finally stop crying and pull away, I look up to meet Diego's eyes, my hands still around his waist. He smiles and wipes the tears from my cheeks with his thumbs.

"Better?"

I nod. We're so close that I can see the tiny freckles on his face, which is bright red from the cold. I step back and drop my hands to my sides.

"Let's go. I can't feel my fingers anymore," he says.

We drive home through the chilly night. Diego turns on the radio and a soft song plays. I glance at the time. *Follow My Voice* is already over and I regret having missed the show. I check my phone and see that Kang hasn't sent any messages. His lack of communication reminds me of the day of the storm, when he didn't text and then hinted that I had done something to upset him. Is he mad that I didn't ride home with him?

I show Diego where to turn and point out my house. He parks in front of it.

I take off my seatbelt and turn to him. "Thank you so much, Diego, from the bottom of my heart."

"I'm here to serve, Hoodie," he says, one hand on the steering wheel and the other on the gearshift.

I'm about to open the door when he stops me.

"Klara?"

"Yes?" I ask, without turning around.

"Whatever happened on campus today, you don't have to tell me, but I just want you to know that you're not alone, okay?"

And then all of a sudden, I remember the nickname Dario used to refer to Diego. "Thanks, Cangurito. See you later."

I hop out of the car as fast as I can and Diego lowers the passenger window. "Hey! If you ever call me that in class, you're dead, Klara," he shouts after me, swiping his thumb across his neck to emphasize the threat.

I laugh and pretend to shake with fear. "Ooh, I'm scared the little kangaroo is going to attack me!"

"Klara . . ."

"Good night!"

I walk inside, still laughing at Diego's mortified expression when I called him by his childhood nickname. I find Kamila in the kitchen, wearing a black skirt and a dark blue blouse that looks great on her, with her brown hair up in a messy bun. Her white doctor's coat is hanging on the back of her chair and she has a glass of wine in her hand. Andy is bent over the oven, checking something that smells divine. "Mmm . . . what smells so good?" I ask.

Kamila studies my face with those dark blue eyes of hers; she knows me so well.

"Baked chicken, my specialty—we figured we'd wait for you

to have dinner," Andy answers, also seeming to read my face and understand that something has happened.

Although I'm smiling, I know my eyes are puffy and probably a little red from all the crying I've done today.

Kamila sets her wineglass on the table. "Are you okay?"

"Yeah, don't worry."

"I'm not sure if I should worry, but I believe you. I heard you laughing as you walked in, but your eyes . . ."

"I went to visit Mom's grave."

Kamila gasps in surprise. "Really?"

I nod. "I got emotional, but I'm fine now. I'm glad I was finally able to go to the cemetery after so long."

Kamila smiles and walks around the table to hug me. "You're my champion, Klara," she whispers and kisses the side of my head.

Andy crosses the kitchen. "Hey, I feel left out," he says as he wraps his arms around the two of us. "You're both my champions."

We pull apart and Kamila pretends to be annoyed. "Okay, let's eat before Andy gets all sentimental and starts crying into the chicken."

We set the table and start eating. I can't erase the smile off my face and Kamila seems to join me in my good mood. She knows what a huge step visiting my mother's grave is for me. She mouths *I'm proud of you.* And I allow myself to be proud of me, too.

After finishing the food and doing the dishes, I wipe my hands with a cloth to check my phone and see that Kang still has not messaged me. I'm disappointed, but I don't want to send him any texts until I have a chance to talk to Perla, to hear the story from her lips.

I lie in bed catching up on some homework, albeit a little distracted as I try to take in everything that has happened today.

The words engraved on my mother's headstone suddenly pop into my mind: *Every defeat is a step toward victory.*

Maybe today wasn't the best day, but I got to ride home with

Diego and I visited Dario's and my mother's graves; a defeat led to a victory.

"Have you been right all this time, Mom?"

I miss her so much.

Good night, Mom.

27

Tell Me

FRIDAY ON CAMPUS the energy is through the roof and everyone is excitedly talking about the men's soccer team's upcoming game against their biggest opponent to date. Though no one seems to be too worried. They're already making plans for the district finals a few weeks away—who they're going with, what they're wearing—even though the tournament hasn't started and, technically, the soccer team hasn't qualified, either. Apparently, it's more of a social occasion than a sporting event. For my part, I hide under my hood as I walk quietly toward my class. Although Diego and the visit to the cemetery did me a lot of good, my mood is still low. I guess I underestimated how much my encounter with those girls affected me. Another factor is that I haven't heard from Kang since I told him I wouldn't be riding home with him.

I shake my head; I don't want to think about it. My goal now is to talk to Perla. There must be some reason she hasn't shared the details of what happened between her and Kang. Maybe she's not ready to open up to me; we've only known each other a short time and she might not like me prying into a subject that is obviously very sensitive for her. I really like Perla and I want to be her friend.

But we're just getting to know each other, so any awkwardness could end our friendship before it even cements. I don't want to lose the only potential female friend I have, but I'm dying to know what happened.

The more time goes by, the more it becomes clear to me that Yana and her friends did not have the best of intentions. Yana refuses to even look in my direction and the others left me hanging with my hand in the air when I tried to greet them. So why did they act all friendly with me before? I have no idea, but ever since Yana created that TikTok account for me, I've been getting nasty messages from an anonymous profile. Yana wouldn't do something like that, would she?

I sigh, remembering my mother and how she always looked for the light in others. Whoever owns that anonymous account, I truly hope they find the peace they so desperately need.

"People can only appreciate you in the capacity in which they appreciate themselves." My mother's wise words guide me yet again. *"When we hurt someone with our words, we feed their darkness. When we make someone smile with nice words, we expand their light."* Feeling hatred in response to mistreatment leads nowhere—I can't fight darkness with more darkness. Maybe it's a naive worldview, but there are too many negative emotions on this planet. Everyone is a yin and yang, and it's impossible not to be affected by what's going on around us. But I will strive to make a small change, if not in the world, at least in the people around me. I will always try to leave my little light on in the darkness to guide those who need it. I sigh, lost in thought, until suddenly, I hear his voice.

Kang.

He's coming down the hall with three other guys, all wearing soccer team windbreakers, except for Kang, who's wearing a dark blue shirt and jeans. He's laughing.

I'd forgotten how handsome he is. I run my hands through my hair, making sure my wig is in place, and I stand to the side, facing them. Should I say hello? Will Yana and the other girls laugh if they see me talking to him?

Be brave, Klara.

I'm still trying to decide what to do when our eyes meet. I smile. Kang simply nods in greeting. I furrow my brow and my smile fades as I watch him walk past like he doesn't even know me.

Ouch. I feel a tightness in my chest and lean my shoulder against the wall. What was that? He didn't even say hello. I feel like just another fan right now.

I don't understand this change in Kang. Was he really that upset because I didn't ride home with him? Sighing, I walk into the classroom and sit next to Perla behind Diego. I pretend to follow their conversation but I have no idea what they're talking about, so I stare off into space, absorbed in my thoughts.

It hurts.

All through class, as the professor goes on about counseling communication skills, my mind plays the scene on loop: the fleeting glance, the forced, tight-lipped smile. I don't want to believe that those girls were right, because it's too painful, but it now seems like they were telling the truth. Kang got bored or annoyed with me as a project and now he's pushed me aside.

When class ends and everyone leaves, I turn to Perla. "Can I talk to you for a minute?"

"Sure," she says, smiling. She looks to Diego. "See ya."

He studies my expression and seems to hesitate for a second, but finally leaves the classroom. Perla and I are alone, but I don't know where to start.

"What's wrong?" Perla tosses her wavy hair over her shoulders. "You had your head in the clouds the whole class."

I fidget with my hands in my lap. This is harder than I thought. "Perla, the truth is that I don't know how to ask you this. I . . . I don't want to make you uncomfortable, and we get along so well, I'm terrified of ruining our friendship."

"It's about Kang, isn't it?" She doesn't seem angry; that's encouraging.

I nod and she sighs.

"Don't look so terrified." She rubs my arm. "I knew I'd have to tell you sooner or later."

"I'm sorry."

"Don't apologize, of course you'd want to know. You're interested in him, aren't you?"

I nod again.

"Then I think you should hear the whole story. It's not going to ruin our friendship, Klara. I really like you and a past history with some guy isn't going to change that. But let's go—all stories are better over a good latte."

"From the cafeteria?"

She snorts. "There's a Starbucks nearby."

I smile and we make our way across campus. After ordering two nice foamy lattes, we go outside and find a bench on the quad. The day is cloudy, but not too cold. Groups of students sit around, chatting. We silently sip our coffees; I've never been a fan of lattes, but this one is delicious.

Perla looks straight ahead, so I can only see her profile, and lets out a long sigh. I give her the time she needs; I don't want her to feel like I'm pressuring her.

"I grew up in New York until my parents got divorced a couple years ago. In the settlement, my father took the city apartment and my mother got a nice sum of money—enough to buy a huge house here close to family." She pauses for a moment. "But before we moved, they went through the whole divorce process, the fighting. I took refuge in food and put on a lot of weight in a short time. My mother was worried, but food was the only thing that calmed my anxiety. My last year of high school was hell."

"I'm sorry," I say.

"Well, the thing is, by the time we moved here, I was extremely overweight and I was terrified because I had to start college. I was afraid people would shun me or even make fun of me. So I completely shut down. Everyone was in their own world, no one spoke to me, no one knew my name. I had no friends, and my lonely lunches by the garbage cans became routine."

My heart contracts at the thought.

A sad frown forms on Perla's lips. "Those were hard times; I'm not going to lie. I didn't feel like I belonged. I felt invisible and so lonely. But then I started listening to Kang's radio show and I remember thinking he seemed so nice. And he was. I sent messages to the show until one day he wrote back to me through their Instagram account."

I feel a sharp pain in my chest at this revelation.

Me: Is this something you do with all the fans of your show?
Kang: No, only with you.

Was that a lie?

"Shortly after, we began texting every day, and, when we finally met, I was ecstatic. I don't have words to explain how much Kang helped me to regain my self-esteem and confidence; he restored me to the outgoing, cheerful girl I had been when I lived in New York. I realized that I didn't need to be thin to be me, that my appearance has nothing to do with who I am as a person. I did my part, of course, but he gave me the push I needed to find my inner strength. Thanks to him, I started meeting other people and made my first friends."

I listen politely but, inside, my heart is breaking as I realize I was nothing special, that Kang has done the same thing with other girls.

"Anyway, as you know, Kang is very attractive, and he has a magnetic personality. Like a fool, I fell in love with him. I was crazy about him. Our friendship remained the same for a while, until I decided to confess my feelings." A wounded expression crosses Perla's face. "Kang didn't feel the same way. He was very kind, but his rejection hurt like you can't imagine. He told me that he understood the pain of unreciprocated love because he himself was in love with a person he couldn't be with—that his heart belonged to someone else, and that, although this girl didn't feel the same way about him, he still loved her and that's why he wasn't dating anyone and didn't plan to."

I remember Kang's words on the show a while back: *"I have to admit that I haven't been entirely honest with you, folks. The other day I told you that I'd never been in love, but that's not true. My first love was an unrequited love."*

"I told him that we couldn't be friends anymore and asked him not to talk to me because I needed space in order to get over him. He said he understood, and he's respected my request. I finished out my freshman year of college heartbroken, and it took me the entire summer to get over it, but when I started this semester, I no longer felt anything for Kang. I wouldn't dare try to strike a friendship back up with him, though. So here we are."

"I don't know what to say."

"I think I just expected to be treated badly, so when someone was actually nice—when someone showed kindness and understanding—I assumed it was love. As if that's the only thing that could justify him being nice. It's sad, I know."

"You really don't have feelings for him anymore?"

Perla lets out a slight chuckle and rests her hand on my arm, as if sensing she needs to placate my uncontrollable thoughts. "No, I feel grateful for him. I have nothing against Kang. It wasn't his fault that I fell in love with him and I have to accept that he couldn't reciprocate. The only reason I warned you to stay away from him was because you reminded me of myself back then and I worried the same thing might happen to you. I didn't want you to get hurt, but it was wrong of me; you're a different person, and I shouldn't have said anything, since I don't know the nature of your relationship with him. Besides, that was so long ago—who knows if he still feels the same way about that girl? Anyway, that's my story."

"I understand, don't worry." I take Perla's hand and squeeze it gently. "Thank you for telling me; you didn't have to, but you did anyway, so thank you."

She squeezes my hand back. "I needed to explain so we could start our journey as friends off on the right foot."

I smile and stand up. I take a sip of my latte, which gives me a feeling of warmth all over. Perla heads to her next class, and I head to the parking lot to wait for Kamila, unable to stop thinking about what she's told me. My heart hurts and the cracks in it seem to be getting bigger by the minute.

"I sent messages to the show until one day he wrote back to me."

"We began texting every day, and, when we finally met, I was ecstatic."

I don't want to believe it, because it's too painful; Perla experienced exactly the same thing with Kang.

I hear someone clear their throat, bringing me back to reality. Out of the corner of my eye I see a figure at the end of the sidewalk. I turn and I find Kang standing there, his backpack slung over one shoulder, his expression neutral.

My heart twists inside my chest. It hurts to see him, now that I'm certain he doesn't feel the same way I do. It's a completely different dynamic, like I'm just another follower, nothing special to him. We start walking toward each other, getting closer and closer. I clench my fists at my sides. For a second, I'm afraid he'll just walk right past me, like he did this morning. But no, he stops in front of me. His black eyes meet mine and a faint smile forms on his lips.

"Hello, Klara with a K." He sounds so casual, as if it doesn't bother him that we haven't spoken for days. I'm such a fool.

"Oh, so, you're willing to talk to me now that there's no one around?" I ask. Maybe I'm just another Perla to him, but I have to be honest about my feelings: I was hurt earlier when he was so cold to me.

He scratches the back of his neck. "Sorry, I was having a rough morning. I didn't mean to take it out on you."

"No big deal," I say as I turn around and start walking away from him. I don't need to be at campus anymore, nor do I want to be.

Kang walks beside me. "Hey, hey, wait. I'm really sorry, truly. I have something to make it up to you." He hands me three tickets for tonight's game. "It'll do you good to get out and have some fun. You can bring your friends."

Perla's words swirl in my mind. *"He gave me the push I needed to find my inner strength. Thanks to him, I started meeting other people and made my first friends."* Now I understand: He's not inviting me to watch him play. He wants me to go with my friends and have fun. My story and Perla's are becoming more and more alike, and it hurts.

"Thanks," I whisper.

I study the serene expression on his handsome face.

I like you so much, Kang. You were the first person to make me feel again after a long period of emotional emptiness. I'm so sorry I mistook your kindness for love, but it's hard not to when your crush offers you a little attention.

I feel a lump in my throat and I look down at the tickets. "Thank you, I'll invite my friends."

"Great." Kang steps in front of me and walks backward to continue talking while looking at me. "Will you cheer for me when I get out on the field?"

I feign a smile. "Of course."

"Great. I have to go," he says. "See you later, Klara with a K."

"See you later, Kang."

I watch him turn around and walk away until he disappears inside a building. I curse my eyes for filling with tears.

So this is what it feels like? I've read so many stories about love and heartbreak, but for the first time in my life I feel the pain firsthand.

The pain of a broken heart.

28

Calm Me

"GO PANTHERS! GO Panthers! Go Panthers!"

I stand on the bleachers, frowning through the loud chanting all around me. Needless to say, everyone is excited about tonight's game and the possibility of advancing to the finals. The white lights of the soccer field glow in the semidarkness of the dusky orange sky. Sports have never been my thing; I was more of the type to stay after school in the art room reading a book on painting techniques. Then when my mother got sick, I was focused on her, and later on my own health, when it was my turn to be sick. So I've never been drawn to sports and I have to admit I don't understand most of them, not even soccer. But I'm grateful for the existence of Google and its simplified explanations: two teams, one ball, put the ball in the opposing team's goal to score points. Simple. *Thank you, Google.*

To my right, Perla sticks two fingers in her mouth and whistles so loudly that I have to cover my ears. Where did she learn to whistle like that? To my left, Diego is busy chatting with a girl on the other side of him. I envy his confidence and his ability to talk to anyone.

I can't deny how strange it feels to be here. This is the first time I've been in a place with so many people. I don't even know why I came. Maybe I wanted to venture out of my safety zone; crowds are something I've avoided for a long time. And the truth is, here, in the stands, surrounded by so many people, I'm uncomfortable, but Perla and Diego assured me we could leave the moment I felt I could no longer handle it.

The cheerleaders take to the field and whip up the crowd with their pom-poms and black and blue uniforms. They look peppy and pretty, all made up with their hair pulled back. I hear Perla sigh and I look at her. Her eyes are full of sadness and longing as she watches the cheerleaders.

Finally, they leave the field, the crowd quiets down, and my ears get a break. We sit and I turn to Perla. "Are you okay?"

She nods, pursing her lips slightly. "I always wanted to be a cheerleader."

"Oh, then why are you up here and not out there?"

"The world of cheerleading is not ready to accept my kind of beauty." Perla looks at me and shrugs. "Being thin is still a requirement to make the squad."

"Says who?"

"No one comes out and says it, but when I tried out in high school, they gave me excuses like I wasn't flexible, I wasn't motivated enough." She snorts and tucks a lock of hair behind her ear. "At least they didn't just come right out and say I was too fat."

"That's terrible. I'm sorry."

"No biggie. I've learned that my particular brand of beauty is just too much for many people to take, but they'll have to get used to it."

"Your brand of beauty?"

"There is beauty in all of us, Klara. The problem isn't that we come into the world with different faces or bodies. It's not about what we have or don't. The problem is manmade beauty standards;

when someone deviates from those standards, they're made to believe that they're hideous. But that's not true, because we all have our own particular beauty. We're all created different."

"I like the way you see things." I take Perla's hand. "It's very encouraging."

She squeezes my hand. "I think we might be soulmates, Klara."

"Wait, wait, wait, wait . . ." says Diego, and I lean back so that Perla can see him, too. "Soulmates? Moving a little fast, don't you think, Perla? Remember, Klara declared her undying love for me and I rejected her."

Perla rolls her eyes. "If you turned her down, then she's fair game."

"Wow." Diego shakes his head. "Piranha."

"Excuse me?"

Diego puts an arm around me. "Poor Klara is devastated by my rejection and here you come along to prey on her poor heart like a piranha."

I laugh and Perla pushes Diego's arm off my shoulders.

"That doesn't make sense, Diego. Piranha? Where did you get that?"

"Diego," the girl next to him says, tugging on his sleeve.

"This isn't over," Diego whispers before turning to the girl.

The match starts and seeing Kang take the field makes me want to cover my eyes. I'll have to watch him for the entire game, which will only make my broken heart hurt more. Even though it's been a few weeks since I came to the realization he was only trying to help me, the pain still lingers. We haven't talked much since he handed me the tickets for the game three Fridays ago, which I didn't attend; he's been distant, claiming to be busy with soccer practice, preparing for this tournament. As for me, I've tried to keep myself distracted—visiting my mother's grave once again, this time with Kamila and Andy, for the second anniversary of her death; spending time with Diego and Perla; even focusing on schoolwork. Yet, I still miss him.

Seeing him now, he looks so different on the field, so sure of himself, but at the same time so serious, so closed off, so unlike the guy I remember blushing outside the auditorium or smiling at me in the hallway. His black hair is plastered to his face with sweat, highlighting his chiseled jawline, and the black and blue Panthers jersey sticks to his body, showing his defined muscles.

I try not to stare at him, to force my eyes to move to the other players, but, unable to help myself, I always come back to him. This is my first . . . like, love, something? So I assume it's normal to feel sad after finding out that all this time he's just been trying to help me. I can't even be mad; it's not his fault that I fell for him.

I hear a sigh and turn to Diego, who's not looking at the playing field, but at someone else on the sidelines. I follow his gaze, and, to my surprise, I see that he's staring at Yana. The sparkle in his hazel eyes tells me that she's special to him. Or am I imagining things?

"Diego?"

He can't hear me.

"Diego?"

He comes out of his spell and blinks. "Yeah?"

"Are you into her?" I ask, nodding toward Yana.

"She's my ex-girlfriend."

"Really?"

Diego furrows his brow at my expression. "Yes, why are you surprised?"

I shrug. "No reason."

Diego narrows his eyes as if he doesn't believe me.

"Why did you break up?"

He looks away. "I don't want to talk about it."

"Of course, I understand. Let's focus on the game."

Our team scores and the awkwardness of the conversation is dispersed by the crowd's euphoria.

Perla goes to get a drink after I assure her I'll be okay, and Diego resumes his conversation with the girl on the other side of him.

Turns out I lied to Perla. I begin to feel overwhelmed and alone in the middle of the crowded stands. I look down and stare at my hands in my lap, noticing how thin my fingers are, how brittle my nails look. My body has mostly recovered from the chemotherapy, but there are still some parts that have yet to bounce back. I look up and see that it's almost halftime, but something has changed in me. Seeing so many people, all focused on something I'm not a part of, causes my heart to race. I clench my fists and try to discern the shortest way down the bleachers and away from the field. It will take me a long time. I need to get out of here. I can't breathe. I'm going to make a fool of myself in front of the whole school.

"I'm going . . . to the bathroom," I say, short of breath.

I stand up and rush past Diego.

"Klara?"

"I'll be right back."

I hurry past the other people seated in my row and rush down the steps of the bleachers, clutching my chest as if my life depends on it.

I can't breathe.

I try to inhale but the air seems to get stuck in my throat, and I begin to panic. I reach the bottom of the steps and turn the corner to stand against a dark wall hidden behind the bleachers. I can feel my heart in my throat, tears of fright rolling down my cheeks. I can't get any air into my lungs. I'm suffocating.

I'm alone . . . I'm going to die here, alone, no one is going to help me.

With trembling fingers, I pull out my cell phone, but it slips from my hands . . . A tingling feeling spreads over my face and limbs . . . I'm hyperventilating. I'm going to pass out if this keeps up, so I try to remember what Dr. B. has told me: *"When you're having a panic attack, your body goes into fight or flight mode and the rational part of your brain is completely blocked. That's why you can't think clearly and you truly believe that you're dying, even without any real reason to justify this belief. The first thing you have to do is calm your body and your mind to get out of this state of fight or flight and be able to think rationally again."*

Calm my body.

I slide down the wall until I'm sitting on the ground, my legs stretched out in front of me and my hands on my thighs, next to my knees. I close my eyes, raise one hand, and then lower it, letting it fall against my thigh. I then do the same with the other hand, repeating this movement over and over, patting myself in a gentle, quiet rhythm. I focus on this sequence, on the sensation of my fingers as they fall on my thighs, first one hand and then the other, over and over. "I am calm." I repeat the mantra Dr. B. has had me practice. "I am safe, I am"—I swallow—"protected." Whenever my mind wanders back to worrying about my racing heart or my difficulty breathing, I refocus my thoughts on the rhythmic slapping. "I am calm, I am safe, I am protected."

I repeat the words over and over, keeping my hands moving. My breathing begins to regulate, as does my heart rate, but I don't stop. I continue until I can breathe normally. I open my eyes, processing what just happened. A smile spreads across my face and I feel my chest swell with pride. For the first time, I've overcome a panic attack on my own, without anyone's help or assistance. I used the tools Dr. B. gave me and it worked; I was able to get through it. There, sitting in the lonely darkness behind the bleachers, I smile over my accomplishment.

29

Win Me Over

KANG

"SORRY ABOUT THE loss!"

"It was still a great game, dude!"

"We gotta celebrate, man, for even making it this far!"

Words of encouragement continue all around as I pack my uniform away. We lost the match 3–2 and don't get to advance to the National Junior College finals. It stings because our team has won state several times and even went to nationals once, something we owe to Ares Hidalgo, a forward who, in his last year of community college, took the team to epic heights. I often feel the pressure from my team members, because I know that they expected me to follow in the footsteps of that legendary player. I gave it my all; I hope it was enough.

I high-five and thank everyone on my way across the lit-up field. The bleachers are almost empty, with just a few groups of students still gathered around.

"Oppa!" My younger sister comes up to me, giggling.

I smile and ruffle her wavy black hair.

She groans and pushes my hand away. "I told you not to do that, it makes me feel short."

"You are."

"Compared to you, maybe, but I'm actually average height."

"Mina . . ." my mother says. We call my sister Mina, instead of Min-seo, because she likes it better. "Give your brother a break," she says, smiling. "Excellent game, no matter the outcome."

I immediately notice that they are alone—my father has not come with them. And although I expected this, it stings a little.

My mother seems to read my expression. "Your father . . ."

"I know." It's still hard for him.

"It's late. Your sister and I will head home. Drive carefully, okay? And don't stay out too late."

"Okay."

"Oppa, can't I ride with you? Please, please!"

"Mina"—my mother takes her by the arm—"let's go."

My sister pouts dramatically but my mother forces her to turn and follow. I stand there, watching the two of them walk away, a painful reminder that there used to be more of our family. I'm not the oldest brother, that was Jung. But now he's gone.

Would you have come to watch the game, Jung? Would you have dragged our father out to see me play?

I hear the sound of breaking glass and I rush to my older brother's room. I fling the door open. He sits in a corner, shivering, his arms around his legs, hugging them to his body. He looks small and frail, despite being much taller than me.

"Jung," I shout, kneeling down in front of him.

"I can't . . . breathe . . ." he says, reaching out and grabbing my shirt.

It's another panic attack.

Jung had suffered from severe depression and anxiety ever since a car accident in which he nearly lost his life. He spent months in the hospital and required extensive physical therapy to fully regain mobility. When we brought him home, we thought it was all over, that we could put that episode behind us, but we were wrong.

Jung had recovered physically, but mentally he still had a long way to go. I did all the research I could to help him deal with the panic attacks, but I knew that my brother needed professional help and medication. My father's response when I told him broke my heart.

"No son of mine is going to go see some quack," he says, furious. *"A man should be able to deal with his problems on his own; talking about your feelings is for women. As long as you and your brother live under this roof, you're not going to shame me in that way. Tell Jung to stop acting like a fool. He needs to come up for air. It's all in his head—he needs to stop worrying his family."*

"Dad . . ." I beg with tears in my eyes. *"Jung is in very bad shape. Please . . ."*

"Are you crying?" He grabs my chin angrily. *"Kang Jae-sung,"* he says, spitting out my full name, *"you'd better not let your brother's weakness rub off on you. It is your duty to help him, not to become weak like him."*

Weakness . . . Lack of manhood. That's what all psychological disorders were to my father. Men didn't have those kinds of problems; you were weak if you even talked about it.

Jung had only gotten worse: hardly eating, refusing to go out, barely speaking. I couldn't just stand by and watch, no matter what my father said. At only nineteen, I went behind my father's back and sought out a psychologist, paying for the visit out of pocket with my own savings. The therapist referred my brother to a psychiatrist who could prescribe him antidepressants, which he needed to start taking, urgently. We made the first available appointment with the psychiatrist for the following week. I was so worried about my brother that I slept beside him that night, checking on him constantly. I couldn't let anything happen to him. I just had to hold out for one more week, and then the psychiatrist would help us.

Unfortunately, my father got wind of the plan and began interrogating us. He made a huge scene and we ended up missing the appointment.

Two days later, Jung died by suicide. He was twenty years old.

I remember his pale body, his face buried in the sheets, his hand dangling off the side of the bed, several bottles of painkillers lying on the floor . . . I stood frozen in the doorway, my hand on the doorknob, unable to move. I heard my mother's hurried footsteps rushing past me, her wails of pain as she tried to wake Jung . . . and my father's expression of shock and agony as he fell to his knees before his son's bed. I didn't cry, I didn't move, I didn't blink. My brother . . . was gone. He'd been crumbling right before our eyes and we hadn't been able to help him. I didn't do enough. I could've done more; I could've stood up to my father.

Jung . . .

Couldn't you have given me a little more time? Was the pain in your soul truly so great that you had to leave me alone? Jung, I'm so sorry I couldn't help you, that I couldn't save you, even when you gave us so many signs.

I blamed my parents and myself for a long time. I became depressed and, ironically, my father came to my bedroom door one day and said, *"You . . . We are going to a therapist tomorrow. Be ready at eight o'clock."* Then he left.

I wanted to shout at him, curse at him. *"My brother is dead; that's what it took to shake you out of your old-fashioned ways?"*

I saw a therapist and a psychologist for a year, and, when I felt like I'd healed enough, I started college again. I'd dropped out from Duke when I noticed Jung was suffering. I couldn't go back there, not yet—not when it reminded me of all those days I wasn't there for Jung. My first semester at Durham Community College I began dedicating my time to helping others. That's why I started my radio program. That's why I decided I want to major in psychology. For Jung, so that no more lives would slip through the cracks due to lack of knowledge and awareness.

That's also the reason I started playing soccer. It was Jung's passion. I cheered him on at every game while he encouraged me to write songs and sing if that's what I wanted to do. He was the only person who knew I liked to sing, the only one who accepted me fully. And I still couldn't save him.

Whenever I sing at the bar, I picture him in the crowd, alive and smiling at me. Soccer and singing are the things that make me feel my brother the most.

My phone buzzes with a notification, and, as if in mockery, I see it's a reminder about the deadline to sign up for the talent show in Charlotte. When Erick brought it up, I immediately shut the idea down, but I did scan the QR code to the event. Why? I don't know. I haven't signed up yet, and I don't think I will. Right now, singing is a way to feel close to Jung—the bar where I perform has become a safe and comfortable space for me. Exposing myself to others makes me feel like it wouldn't just be for Jung anymore.

I put my phone back into my pocket, and as I scan the bleachers, looking for one person in particular, a pair of hands cover my eyes from behind and I immediately recognize the familiar perfume. I pull the hands away from my face and turn around.

"Hey, champ," she says in her usual mocking tone.

"Hey, Lizzie."

Lizzie has been my best friend ever since we met at camp the summer after third grade. We were inseparable for a long time, deep into my senior year of high school. Then life happened, among other things, and I stopped prioritizing our friendship.

Her blond hair is in a high ponytail and her jean jacket brings out the gray of her eyes. "Kang! That was an incredible goal." She holds up a hand and we high-five.

"You always say that."

"Are you coming to Kyle's party?" Kyle is her boyfriend, another soccer player, who I know well.

"No."

Lizzie scoffs. "You're so boring. You never go to parties! You're twenty-one, you can legally drink, and you're missing all the fun."

"If by fun you mean alcohol, I don't think I'm missing much."

Lizzie rolls her eyes. "You act like an old man—are you secretly like thirty?"

"Don't tell anyone," I say, raising a finger to my lips as if dismayed over having my secret discovered.

Lizzie swats at my hand and starts walking away. "If you change your mind, you know where we'll be."

I watch her move away, waving and smiling to everyone she passes. She was my first love—the first person to set my heart racing, the first girl I wrote love letters to, the girl I dedicated songs to on the radio, hoping she was listening. She stuck by my side when my brother had the accident, when he got out of the hospital, when he took his own life. Lizzie was always there. I was in love with her, but she didn't feel the same way. When I told her how I felt, she gently explained that she was in love with Kyle. There were a few awkward months, but then we resumed our friendship as if nothing had happened.

It was hard for me to see her every day, have her always beside me, without being able to touch her and tell her how I still felt. But I made it through and now I only feel affection for her. Sometimes I wonder if I was really in love with Lizzie or if I just wanted her because I couldn't have her . . . Anyway, being rejected was too painful, and for a long time, it made me believe I didn't want to fall in love ever again.

I walk back in front of the bleachers, scanning the thinning crowd, until, finally, I see *her*.

Klara.

She's sitting in the stands wearing light-washed jeans and that black hoodie I've told her so many times she doesn't need to hide beneath. Her short black hair frames her face. At first glance, she looks so fragile, but she's actually incredibly strong. From the brightness and depth of her eyes, I can tell that she has been through a lot for someone her age, wise beyond her years.

And her smile . . .

Her entire face lights up when she smiles, so dazzling that I have to look away because it sets my heart racing. If she saw herself through my eyes, she wouldn't wear that hoodie anymore; she wouldn't hide. She is so beautiful, on a level that transcends the physical. I love the sparkle in her eyes, the warmth in her smile, her soothing voice.

I stand in front of the bleachers and stare at her—an action that has become out of my control—letting people push past me, some waving or murmuring hello. Klara talks with Perla. I put my hand on my chest to slow the desperate beating of my heart. I know she hasn't seen me, so I allow myself to observe her, not looking away for a second when she smiles. The redheaded guy sits down next to her and I feel a pang of jealousy.

Why is he always with her? The first time I saw them together, he hugged her and she looked so comfortable in his arms that I couldn't help but feel hurt. Klara has been so closed off with me. I've had such a hard time getting the little information I have about her, and seeing her embrace him so readily was painful to watch. I apologized for my immaturity and things were going well until I asked to drive her home from campus at a time I needed her company the most. She agreed at first, but then—and I still don't know why—she changed her mind. To make matters worse, after class, I saw her leaving with the redheaded dude.

I was too upset to talk to her, even though I knew I couldn't say anything about the fact that she chose to ride home with him over me. Klara and I are just friends. What is it about her? I wasn't jealous or controlling with Lizzie, which is why it's so strange that the idea of her liking that other guy makes me go crazy and act immature. So I stopped texting her and I ignored her in the hallway. But then I felt guilty for being so childish, so I gave her tickets to a game, acting all cool and unbothered. She didn't show up, and I wasted more time being upset with her. What I should've done was ask her straight out if she liked that guy. I guess I'm afraid she'll tell me she's in love with him. I still remember Lizzie's pitying expression when she told me she liked Kyle. I can't go through that again, which is why I pushed Klara away even more, pretending I was busy with practice or this and that. To be fair, I become distant with everyone around this time of year. It's a hard month for my family and me, as we add another year without Jung.

"Kang!"

I silently curse whoever just shouted my name because it causes Klara to look at me, and I turn around as fast as I can so that she doesn't notice I was standing there staring at her like the stalker we once joked about me being.

"What a goal!" Yana says, putting her arms around me.

"Hey, thanks," I reply with a friendly smile, trying not to overdo it. I know she has feelings for me—she practically confesses them every time she sends a message to the show. I just wish she'd get the hint I'm not interested and never will be.

"Are you going to the party?" she asks excitedly, gripping my arm. "I don't have anyone to go with. Can I ride with you?"

"I'm not going."

"Why not?" She pouts.

"I'm tired."

"Oh, of course, the game . . ."

"I gotta go," I say, as I begin walking to the parking lot.

Once inside my car, I rest my forehead on the steering wheel, when I'm suddenly startled by a knock on the window, and I glance up. It's the redheaded asshole. As I lower the window, I can't help but shoot daggers at him.

"Yes?"

"Hi, I'm Diego." He holds out his hand and I reluctantly shake it.

"Kang."

"I know," he says, winking. "Klara sent me to ask if you're going to the party, and if we can ride with you."

Klara and Perla walk up and stop behind him, at a prudent distance. Klara catches my eye and then looks away. I swallow.

"Uh, well, I . . ."

Diego leans in through the open window, half his body inside the car, and whispers, "Or should I tell Klara that you spent ten minutes staring at her while she sat on the bleachers? The hand over the heart was a bit dramatic for my taste, but very moving."

He straightens up and circles the car. "Let's go, girls, get in."

Perla and Klara don't move.

I clear my throat. "Yeah, come on, hop in, I'll give you a ride," I say, forcing a smile.

The girls exchange glances, but finally walk toward the car.

Perla automatically gets in the back seat with Diego, leaving Klara no choice but to sit next to me up front.

Don't hide from me.

I turn on music to drown out the silence and steal a glance at Klara, right here beside me, just within reach. My heart races. Somehow I manage to fight the urge to push back her hood.

I focus on navigating out of the parking lot, thinking what an idiot I've been to believe I can control how I feel, that I can keep myself from ever falling in love again.

30

Welcome Me

HAVE PARTIES ALWAYS been this loud?

I cover my ears as we enter the house full of college kids. The place is large and packed with people. My heart is racing and my breath comes fast; I'm not prepared to deal with a social event like this, still a little nervous after the panic attack I had at the soccer field. I tried to get out of it, but Perla insisted she would stay with me at all times. The fact that I'm here with Kang doesn't help matters, either. I've made up my mind to push my feelings for him aside. I don't want to go through what Perla did, mistaking his kindness for something more. After riding next to him in the car, however, I realize how much harder it is to ignore your feelings for someone when they're sitting right beside you.

I follow Perla to an empty corner of the living room and Diego and Kang stop beside us.

"Would you like a drink?" Diego shouts so that we can hear him over the music.

Perla nods. She looks at me, but I shake my head. Mixing alcohol and antidepressants is never a good idea, or so I've been warned multiple times by Dr. B. and my sister—as if I've ever had a drink in my life. Diego then looks to Kang, who also shakes his head.

Diego grabs Perla by the arm and I watch in panic as he pulls her away through the crowd, leaving me alone with Kang. So much for not leaving my side. My heart beats even more wildly, something I didn't think possible. I glance around the room, trying not to look at him, frowning over the volume of the music. I can feel Kang's eyes on me, and I swallow. He leans toward me and his breath tickles my skin, sending a tingling sensation all through my body that settles deep in my stomach. "Do you want to go somewhere less noisy?" That voice I've adored since the first time I heard it now whispers in my ear. It's almost too much to take.

I turn my head toward him, a mistake: Kang is still leaning over me, so his face is now just inches from mine, a hungry look in his eyes. I take a step back and feel my cheeks begin to burn. Kang offers me his hand and I take it, enjoying the sensation of this simple, yet intimate contact. I follow him through the crowd to the kitchen. Someone has brought a thermos of hot chocolate and Kang fills a cup, checks that it isn't spiked, and hands it to me before pouring one for himself. He then guides me upstairs. I'm reminded of so many movies where couples leave a party to find a place where they can have privacy, but I know Kang isn't that kind of guy. Besides, that's for people who *both* want to be more than friends.

We walk down many hallways—this place is like some kind of labyrinth—before we finally stop in front of a pair of double doors and Kang drops my hand to open them. I'm hit by the chilly night air as I step outside. It's a spacious balcony with decorative lights coiled like snakes around the white railing. The view over the backyard is beautiful, with the whole town framed in the distance. Tall trees sway gently in the breeze. Kang walks to the railing, resting his hand on it as he takes in the scenery with his back to me. I bring my cup to my lips and feel the heat coming from it as I inhale the sweet aroma of hot chocolate.

"Sorry about the game," I say, wanting to break the silence.

"It's okay . . . it wasn't meant to be. Besides, there's other things to look forward to."

"Oh, yeah, like what?"

"It's going to snow soon," Kang says, turning to look at me over his shoulder.

"You're crazy, it's not even winter yet."

"I have a feeling."

I smile. "Of course you do."

Our eyes meet and we hold the gaze for a moment. I am acutely aware of the fact that we're alone. I try to calm myself. This is not the first time we've been alone; it's perfectly normal to be alone with a friend.

Kang turns his body toward me and raises his cup in a toast, flashing those dimples I love so much. And then I realize something: Kang is very special to me. His radio show helped me through a very difficult time; he talked me down when I was having a panic attack; he offered me his guidance as soon as he found out we were at the same college; and he's done a lot to help me get back into the world. Why should I question his reasons for it? He's a good person, and he doesn't have to explain himself for wanting to help me.

Having my crush like me back isn't the most important thing in the world. My life has never revolved around guys; I've overcome pain much more intense than heartache. I'm grateful to have met people like Kang, Perla, and Diego, the first friends I've had in a long time. I'm proud to have overcome a panic attack on my own for the first time; to be navigating college somewhat successfully; to have attended my first soccer game; and to be here now, at my first college party, after everything I've been through. These accomplishments buoy my confidence. So, with a big smile, I walk over and raise my cup. "To health, Kang."

We tap our cups together and sip our drinks. The hot chocolate slides down my throat, warming me from the inside.

Having come to terms with what we are, I decide to stand next to Kang to enjoy the view.

"So nice and quiet out here, isn't it?"

"Yeah, I really didn't expect parties to be this loud," I answer.

"You make it sound like it's your first party."

"It is," I admit with a shy smile.

"You haven't missed much," he says.

I turn and lean against the railing.

"If you say so, I believe you," I answer, and before he can respond, I add, "Bat-Kang."

He cocks an eyebrow. "Bat-Kang?"

"Don't think I've forgotten about your nocturnal escapades on Fourteenth Street, Bat-Kang."

He presses his lips together, repressing a smile. "I have to give you points for originality. Anyway, just so you know, the Batman mask looks great on me."

"I don't doubt it," I say before I have time to think. I grimace in embarrassment.

"Oh, really, you don't doubt it?" He looks at me quizzically.

I straighten up and turn away to avoid his gaze. "As if you didn't know . . ." I whisper.

"As if I didn't know what?"

That you're attractive. How hot those dimples are when you smile. How whatever you wear looks great on you.

I fall silent and take another sip of hot chocolate.

"Klara?"

"Beautiful view, isn't it?"

I glance at Kang and see that he's watching me intently, his eyes fixed on me as he answers. "It is." His voice lowers as he adds, "Gorgeous."

Silence. We stare into each other's eyes, and I nervously start playing with the drawstring of my sweatshirt. Kang reaches his free hand toward me and pushes my hood off my head.

"You don't need to hide from me." His hand gently cups my face and I freeze. "I've already told you you're beautiful." He runs his thumb along my cheek. "I promise to cherish every layer you reveal to me, to be in awe of you as much as I am of your beauty. So stop hiding, Klara."

My cheeks are burning, and that strange tingling in my belly is back. These must be the famous butterflies everyone talks about. Right now, with his eyes on mine, his hand on my cheek, my poor lovesick heart wants to start hoping; it all feels so intense and so real. I struggle to focus as my brain and my heart begin to duke it out.

Brain: We're friends, and friends can compliment each other, Klara. Don't get carried away.

Heart: You don't feel this way with a friend, that electricity when your eyes meet.

And as if life had conspired to make this moment even more perfect, snowflakes begin to fall, landing in Kang's black hair, on his clothes. The first snowfall of the year, so early. This moment couldn't be more perfect.

"Kang . . ." I don't know why I say his name. I'm rooted to the spot; I don't want this moment to end.

"Klara."

He opens his mouth to say something else, but closes it, hesitating.

What do you want to say, Kang?

He takes a step toward me, shrinking the space between us, our bodies almost touching, his hand still on my cheek. I lift my head to look him in the eye, our faces just inches apart. A snowflake dances between us and lands on Kang's upper lip. I reach up to brush it off, my index finger grazing his very kissable lips. My mouth falls open. Kang closes his eyes at the contact, and when he opens them, the glint of longing in his gaze makes me want to melt. His hand feels warm on my cheek, and it makes me wonder how it would feel to have it slide down my body while he kisses me. Would he lose his breath and composure if he did? Kang is always so calm and collected; I'm dying to see him lose control. He probably looks so hot when he's excited.

What am I doing?

Kang clears his throat, and I pull away from him before taking another sip of hot chocolate. I pretend to admire the scenery, trying to calm my breathing and my mind.

What was that?

Friends don't have moments like that, do they?

My mind travels back to the afternoon I went to the cemetery with Diego. We were alone and we even hugged, but at no time did I feel what I do now with Kang. It was just a hug between friends.

"It's snowing, let's sit down."

He guides me to a bench on the covered half of the balcony. I sit next to him, keeping a safe distance between us.

"So, umm . . . did you have fun at the game?"

"Yeah, you played so well; I'm sure you already know that, though."

"Why is it that every time you give me a compliment, you assume it's something I already know? Have you ever stopped to think that one compliment from you is much more important than the dozens I've received tonight?"

Why? I want to ask, but I can't. His words have left me momentarily speechless. "I'm sorry," I finally say. "You're right."

Silence falls between us but it's not uncomfortable. We watch the light snow slowly falling and, when we finish our hot chocolates, we throw the disposable cups into a trash can beside the bench.

Kang sighs, stretches his long legs out in front of him, and shoves his hands into his pockets. He's wearing a thick black sweatshirt that does not look warm enough for this cold, and matching black jeans.

He stares out at the snow, his thoughts elsewhere.

What are you thinking, Kang?

"My brother loved snow," he murmurs, so softly that I can barely hear him.

Brother? Kang has never mentioned a brother before; he only talks about his younger sister.

"I never cared about playing in the snow, but he always insisted we go out and make a snowman. He was older than me, but when it snowed, Jung became a child again." Kang has a melancholy smile on his lips.

Jung *was* . . . ? It's the first time I've seen such sadness in Kang's eyes.

"Maybe that's why I like the snow so much now, because it makes me feel close to him," he says. Kang suddenly blinks as if coming back to reality. He looks at me. "Sorry, I got lost there for a minute."

He stands up, pulling his hands out of his pockets, then runs his fingers through his hair. I stand with him and grab the edge of his sweater to turn him toward me.

Before I can think twice, I wrap my arms around his waist and hug him, burying the side of my face in his chest. "I'm sorry, Kang."

He tenses but then puts his arms around me. He smells so good, like soap and cologne.

"I don't know what happened to your brother, but I can hear the hurt in your voice. I'm sorry you went through something so painful."

I hear Kang's heart beating wildly. *Does his heart beat like this for me? It can't be . . .*

Kang hugs me tightly, pressing me even closer against him, and I allow myself to enjoy the warmth of his body, just him and me, standing in the snow; I'll worry about my unrequited love later.

Right now, all I care about is Kang.

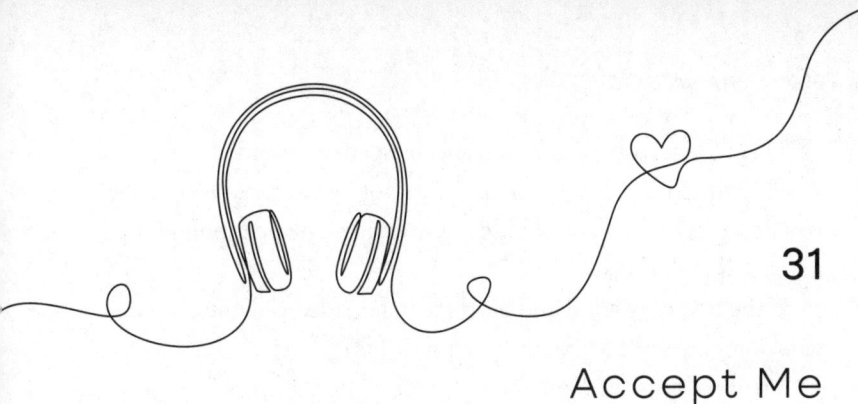

31

Accept Me

THERE ARE MOMENTS in life that can only be described as perfect. It may be something so simple that proves that the beauty of life is in the little things.

Happiness is not a perpetual state; it is a collection of fleeting, perfect moments. Tonight has been a coalescence of many accomplishments: the game with friends in a packed stadium, getting through a panic attack on my own, arriving at a party with friends, and this embrace—my head against Kang's chest, his heart beating in my ear, my arms around his waist, his face nestled against my neck—is the perfect culmination. When I try to pull away, Kang hugs me tighter.

"Just a little longer," he whispers, and his breath tickles the side of my head.

I grin hugely and close my eyes. But, as always, these little moments of happiness are brief. The balcony doors screech open and we pull apart so quickly that I almost stumble forward. Kang scratches the back of his neck and I pretend to cough.

"Kang!" Yana steps onto the balcony. "I thought you said you weren't coming?"

He gives her a friendly smile. "I changed my mind."

She turns her back to me as if I'm not even there. "What are you doing out here? You should come inside. The beer pong tournament is about to start."

Kang takes my hand and pulls me to his side. "I'm enjoying the view out here with Klara. Do you know her?"

"Yeah, of course." Yana fakes a smile. "How are you?"

"Hey," I mumble.

Kang frowns, still watching me. Yana smacks her lips. "So, are you coming, Kang?"

"No."

The disappointment on her face is evident. "It's snowing, you must be freezing." She rubs his arms in an attempt to warm him, but he takes a step back. Yana's hands hang in the air before she lowers them, laughing. "I guess you're not cold . . . Well, Klara . . ." She takes my arm.

I jump. "What?"

"You should come with me," she says, tugging at my elbow. I take a step toward her, unable to refuse. "So you can meet everyone."

I don't know how to respond.

"I'll just steal her from you for a second, Kang," Yana says, smiling and squeezing my hand so hard it hurts.

I turn back to glance at Kang. He looks so sad standing there against the railing, like he doesn't want me to leave. But, like a puppet, I walk back into the house with Yana, who pulls me along as if I were a little girl, her nails digging into the palm of my hand.

"Everything all right?" a familiar voice asks. I look up to see another one of my classmates: Adrian, who it turns out is also on the soccer team.

"None of your business," says Yana with a tone of disgust.

"I wasn't asking you." He looks at me. "Are you all right, Klara?"

Yana steps in between us, annoyed. "It's none of your business, faggot."

My mouth falls open in shock and so does Adrian's, but he recovers quickly. "What did you call me?"

Yana rolls her eyes. "You heard me."

"I don't know what you're talking about."

"Oh, for God's sake, Adrian, get out of my way if you don't want me to tell all your buddies on the soccer team who you really are."

Adrian drops his head and my heart breaks. But Yana isn't finished with him. "I'm glad you know your place; your kind are usually so obnoxious."

She tugs at my arm and Adrian steps aside, dumbfounded. So this is what Yana does. She manipulates people's fears to get her way.

Something inside me snaps, the image of Adrian's wounded expression stuck in my mind. I look down at my hand entwined with Yana's.

Don't let fear of death stop you from living life.

For some reason the words on Dario's tombstone suddenly come to me. Fear has been a constant in my life; it has bested me so many times, but I have gotten up, dusted myself off, and carried on. And thanks to so many moments of vulnerability, so many defeats, so many triumphs over fear, I have a newfound understanding of what my own strength is and how much more it could one day be.

What better moment than the present to put that strength to the test.

I press my lips together and I pull my arm away from her.

Yana turns to me. "What are you doing? Come on, Klara," she says.

The image of my mother's smiling face fills my mind and I feel her gentle caress on my cheek, giving me the courage I need. "I'm not going anywhere with you."

Yana is shocked and speechless, but she eventually recovers. "Oh, don't act all brave now," she hisses. "You know, I did some digging, asked around. It would be so easy for me to go downstairs right now and tell everyone at this party your pathetic story."

Adrian is still behind me, watching us.

"Do it."

Again, she's momentarily speechless. "What?"

"Do it. Go tell everyone my story if you want to. I'm not ashamed," I say, and either because of the adrenaline or how fed up I am in this moment, that's true. "I'm just like everybody else. The only difference is that my wounds are visible, while most people's are hidden. I'm not afraid of you, Yana, and that strips you of any power you may have had over me."

"You are *so* going to regret this."

"I don't think so. I may be thin, I may not have long, lavish hair, I may be fragile and weak, but I've overcome things much worse than anything you could possibly do to me," I say, turning my back on her.

Yana scoffs and storms down the staircase, back toward the party.

I stop beside Adrian and smile. "I've been secretly hoping you and Ben were an item—you look really cute together."

Adrian looks down nervously, avoiding eye contact with me.

I put my hand on his shoulder. "Take your time, but when you're ready to be yourself openly, for the world—or at least Durham—to see, I'm sure you'll have a lot of people cheering you on, including myself. There's nothing to be ashamed of, Adrian. Who you are, who you like, what you've been through, is never anything to be ashamed of."

"Yeah, you're right."

"You got this."

I'm about to walk away when he pulls me into a big hug. "Thank you, Klara."

I squeeze him tightly and, as he returns to the party, I walk back to the balcony—back to the guy who, more than being my crush, has been my friend. I can't repress the huge smile on my face. Now that I've put Yana in her place, my fear of her, her clique, and that anonymous account has completely vanished.

Every defeat is a step toward victory.

You're always right, Mom, even in death.

Confuse Me

IT'S AMAZING HOW much you can learn about a person by exchanging simple questions back and forth. I find out that although Kang loves pop and rock music, his favorite genre is movie soundtracks, especially instrumental scores. His passion for singing was born from making up his own words to the music he loved.

We sit on the bench under the covered part of the balcony. The snow is falling a little faster and the view is perfect. We're facing each other, our knees almost touching; it feels very natural and comfortable.

"Your turn to ask a question."

Kang hesitates for a second. His beautiful black eyes dance around, as if doubting whether to say what's on his mind.

"Kang?"

"Favorite book?"

"That's such a hard question . . . anything by Jane Austen, but if I had to choose, I guess I'd say *Pride and Prejudice*. Yours?"

"Is that why you asked me to quote something from Jane Austen?"

I smile cheekily. "Mmmm, maybe. Do you have something against her work?"

"Nope, it's a good pick. As for mine, I'd have to say *Norwegian Wood* by Haruki Murakami."

"I guess yours is a great pick, too. I see we do have literature in common."

"I told you we did. Favorite kind of food?"

Something tells me that's not what he really wanted to ask. "Italian. You?"

"Korean."

"Of course!" I smile, feeling foolish. "Makes sense." I wait for his next question.

"First boyfriend?"

It's my turn to frown. My mouth falls open; I wasn't expecting that one. "Uh..."

"Who was your first boyfriend?"

"Um... Well..." I can feel myself burning up with each passing second. "I don't have one."

"No, I was asking about your first boyfriend, not if you have one now," he clarifies, undoubtedly noticing that my face has turned bright red.

"It's just that... I've never..."

And then Kang understands. "Really? Wow, that's hard to believe. You're so..." He stops and bites his lips as he looks away.

"And you? First girlfriend?"

"Sixth grade," he says, sounding embarrassed. "Her name was Ria. We held hands and then broke up after one week, but I thought she was the love of my life." He laughs.

I chuckle at the sweet story. And then I don't know if it's because of how comfortable he's made me feel or the fact that we're already on the topic, but, unable to contain myself, I ask, "Do you have a girlfriend?"

"No."

I feel idiotic as I notice a glimmer of hope spreading through my soul.

No, Klara; you were supposed to forget about your feelings for him and enjoy the friendship Kang is offering.

"Why don't you have a girlfriend, Kang—are you in love with someone you can't have?" I joke. "That's impossible to believe, by the way."

"Why?" He cocks his head and stares at me as if dying to hear my response.

"You've got so much going for you, you're so . . ."

"Healthy?"

I smile, embarrassed. "I was hoping you wouldn't remember that."

"I already told you I don't forget anything when it comes to you."

Boom, boom, boom . . . My heart races even faster. Why does he have to say that kind of thing?

We stare into each other's eyes for a second that feels endless. My gaze drops to his mouth and, for the first time in my life, I'm curious about how it would feel to lean in and press my lips against someone else's, especially ones that look so soft and moist. I shake my head and turn to look out at the snow.

Kang takes me by surprise with his next question, almost as if he was reading where my thoughts had gone. "First kiss?"

I swallow and bite the inside of my cheek without looking at him. "I haven't had a boyfriend, so . . ." I leave the answer hanging in the air.

I feel Kang's cold hand on my chin, turning my face back toward him. The moment our eyes meet, my breath hitches.

"I can't believe these beautiful lips have never been kissed." His thumb softly caresses my lips.

I don't know what to say. I can't even move. I appreciate what he just said to me, but I also feel a little annoyed: Friends don't say things like that to each other. Friends don't gently caress each other's faces. I've accepted that Kang only wants to help me and I'm trying to stop looking for romantic undertones in everything he says, but now he's getting my hopes up, saying things that can be misinterpreted. That leads me to wonder if he behaved this way with Perla, because that would explain why she got confused. I put my hand over his and slowly move it away from my face.

He looks hurt.

"Kang..." I begin, knowing I can't go on like this much longer, "I know that ... you like to help people like me. Perla told me about it..."

Kang tenses.

"I want to thank you. You use your radio show to help people." I take his hand in mine. "Thank you so much for everything you do; I feel lucky to have your friendship. And ... I know you probably want to help me with my self-esteem, but you don't have to take it so far."

Kang shakes his head, looking extremely confused. "What are you talking about?"

"You don't have to call me gorgeous, or tell me that my lips are beautiful, or touch my cheek to make feel better about myself. I know you're just trying to help me and, well, I don't want to sound ungrateful, but it's confusing to me ... I'm fine, promise."

Kang frowns and releases his hand from between mine, standing up. I stand up, too. "You think I said those things just because I want to help you?"

"Didn't you?"

He runs a hand through his hair, his back to me.

"Kang, I'm sorry, I didn't mean to upset you. I just want to avoid misunderstandings. Perla told me..."

"Perla? What does she have to do with us?" He turns to me, waiting for an answer.

Us.

"She's my friend and she told me that she mistook your kindness for something more and she fell for you . . ." I say, plucking up my courage. "I don't want the same thing to happen to me."

"Do you think this is how I talk to everyone? You think I go through life messing with girls' heads, misleading them and then rejecting them? Is that what you think of me?"

"Kang . . ."

"Wow . . ." He turns his back to me again, his head in his hands.

I don't understand why he's so angry. More than angry, he seems hurt. He spins around and closes the distance between us in two strides. I step back, pressing my body against the house. Kang puts his hands on the wall on either side of me. I'm hemmed in by his arms.

He wets his lips before speaking, his black eyes sparkling. "No, Klara, I've never said things like this to anyone else." He leans closer, and I feel my breath catch. "I've helped plenty of people, some of them girls; I've talked to them through my radio show. Perla was the only one I'd texted with before, and that was because there were things she couldn't write into the show about, but I've never"—his voice sounds cold and serious—"I've never gotten as close with anyone as I have with you. If I call you gorgeous, it's because you are goddamn gorgeous; if I say that I like your smile, it's because it takes my breath away and makes my heart pound; and if I tell you that you have beautiful lips, it's because, the whole time we've been on this balcony, I've been dying to taste them."

Did I hear that right? My mind is spinning, trying to process what Kang just said.

Kang is so close I can feel the heat of his body against mine. His eyes rest on my lips and the longing in them is evident. He leans slowly toward me, as if he fears I'm going to push him away, but when I don't, he keeps inching forward. I shut my eyes, feeling my heart in my throat.

And then his lips are on mine.

I tense and clench my fists at my sides. His lips are as soft as I imagined they would be. I don't know what to do; I've never kissed anyone before and none of the TV dramas I've watched have prepared me for this. I let him take control. He begins to move his lips against mine and I awkwardly try to keep up. Kang leans his body against me, pressing my back to the wall as he tilts his head, kissing me so gently that a quiet ache stirs beneath my skin. Maybe I'm not kissing him back in the most expert way, but just having his lips on mine is enough to make me feel like I'm on cloud nine. I take his face in my hands and feel his smooth skin, something I've wanted to do ever since I met him.

Kang leans back and my breathing races erratically. I stand with my eyes closed for a few seconds, then open them to see Kang's black eyes glowing out from the darkness. He smiles, dimples in his cheeks.

His voice is deep, full of emotion as he asks, "First kiss?"

I can't help but chuckle nervously. "A guy named Kang."

33

Defend Me

I DON'T WANT to open my eyes.

Kang's lips find mine again, from first kiss to second, so soft and gentle. My heart's on the verge of collapse. I want this magical moment to last forever. Everyone talks about how special a person's first kiss is, but no one discusses what to do when it's over. *Do I smile? Do I thank him? No, of course not.*

When the kiss ends, I pause for a second to open my eyes and look at the guy whose voice has guided my way for so long, whose show was my window to the world when I lived locked inside my room. My first crush, my first friend after everything I went through, and now my first kiss.

My eyes meet his, and my nervousness and fear fade as I lose myself in his hungry gaze. His lips are red and chapped from the kiss.

And then I understand why nobody talks about what happens after a kiss. It's a moment of deep intimacy, of shared complicity. It's a moment in which you see the other person's expression soften, their eyes sparkle with emotion.

Kang gently cradles my cheek. "What have you done to me, Klara?" he asks, grinning. "My heart is about to burst."

Mine too.

I open my mouth to say this when the balcony doors swing open and Kang and I pull apart. From the look on Diego's face, I can tell we weren't quick enough. "I'm sorry, I didn't mean to"—my redheaded friend tries to hide a smile—"interrupt, but we have a situation."

"What happened?"

"Perla got into it with Yana."

I tense up when I hear that name and they both notice. "Where is she?" I ask, following Diego back inside, Kang silently trailing us.

"She's in one of the bedrooms. Ellie is with her, but they wouldn't let me in. I think we should take her home."

I try to remember who Ellie is before realizing she's the quiet girl in class who never takes her eyes off Diego. I think I've seen a certain sadness in her face when she looks at me, as if she imagines I'm interested in him. If she only knew the reality . . .

We enter the house and immediately feel the booming music coming from downstairs. I'd almost completely forgotten about the party.

"Why did she get into a fight with Yana?" I ask, concerned.

Diego shrugs. "She wouldn't tell me."

I don't like the sound of this at all. And it doesn't help that something is up with Diego, who's tense and serious as soon as I mention Yana. I hope he doesn't still have feelings for her. I know Yana is his ex, and while he hasn't shared the story, I have a hunch that she broke his heart.

When I get to the room, Ellie opens the door a crack so that all I can see is the brown scarf she's wearing. She looks at Kang and then Diego. "Perla wants the guys to stay outside."

I glance over my shoulder and smile at them.

"We'll wait here," Kang says, gesturing for me to go in.

Diego nods.

I enter the room to find Perla sitting on the side of a bed, gripping the edge of the mattress. "Perla?"

She looks up and gives me a tense smile. And then I see that her neck is covered in scratches.

"What happened?"

I walk over to get a better look at her neck. The scratches aren't deep, but many of them are swollen and there are a couple faint trails of blood.

"For God's sake, are you all right?"

Perla maintains her calm, trying to convince me that everything's fine. "It's just a few scratches—she got it worse, believe me."

"What happened?" I sit next to her on the bed.

"What happened . . . ?" Perla lets out a long sigh. "Well, I'm sick of it. I've recently come to the realization that the world won't fix itself. Nothing is ever going to change if we don't stand up to people like Yana."

I know what she means; I've had the same thought many times. If we want to see positive change in the world, we have to start with ourselves, with the people around us. More often than not, we don't act, thinking, *What difference can I make in a world with billions of people?* But one change, no matter how small, can mean everything to one person, and that makes it worth it.

I look at Ellie and she averts her eyes.

"What did she do?"

"She was harassing Adrian and Ben," Perla says. "Calling them names. And then"—her eyes flick to Ellie—"she started picking on Ellie for standing in a corner all by herself. What does she think this is? High school? She wasn't gonna get away with it."

I don't dare look at Ellie, because I don't want to make her uncomfortable.

"Anyway, I saw red," Perla goes on. "I couldn't control myself; I've never felt such a strong urge to hurt another human being until tonight, Klara. I've never even had a serious disagreement with anyone, but apparently, I hold a previously unknown capacity for violence."

"Anyone can become violent, Perla. Some of us are able to control ourselves better than others, but, honestly, I'm glad you stood up to that girl. Even if that maybe wasn't the best way to do it."

"I enjoyed every single slap I gave her, Klara. It's scary how much I enjoyed it."

"How are Adrian and Ben?"

"They're fine. They left right after the fight. The truth is that hardly anyone was paying attention to Yana when she was messing with them, but, unfortunately, she had an audience by the time she started in on Ellie."

This time I can't help but look at Ellie. "I'm sorry." I don't know what I'm apologizing for—maybe for the world, for the existence of people like Yana.

"I'm fine," she assures me.

"Ellie . . ."

"It's okay, it was never going to be a perfect night. I was an overachiever, trying too many things at once for my first attempt at socialization."

And that makes me even sadder, because Ellie came out of her shell to go to the game and then come to this party. She was making an effort to improve her social life, to step out of her world of books, and for someone like Yana to sabotage all her efforts just seems so shitty to me.

Perla stands up. "I'm so ready to get out of here, but I don't want everyone to see these scratches."

Ellie removes her scarf, and Perla, understanding her intention, lifts up her hands in protest. "No, no; you don't have to do that."

"Come on," Ellie insists, wrapping the scarf around Perla's neck. Then, still holding the ends of the scarf, she smiles sweetly, and says, "Thank you, Perla. I know I'm socially awkward, shy, too quiet, and reserved. It's something I've been trying so hard to change. I don't want to be the girl who blends into the background, even though it feels like that's all I am. Tonight, though, you made me feel like I matter, like I'm not invisible. Truly, thank you."

One small action can mean everything.

Perla smiles back and places her hands over Ellie's. "You don't need to thank me for anything. It was a pleasure to put Yana in her place. Besides"—she pats Ellie's hand—"we got something good out of it."

"What?" Ellie asks.

"You took your nose out of your books for once and spoke to us."

"That's right," I agree.

Ellie laughs shyly.

Looking at Ellie, noticing how much I see myself in her, I can't help but extend an offer. "Would you care to join our group on campus from now on?"

Ellie puts her hand to her chest dramatically. "I'd love to."

Perla and I imitate her, bringing our hands to our chests.

Then we all burst out laughing.

"By the way." I look at Perla. "What happened to you not leaving me alone?" I smirk at her.

"I'm sorry, Klara! That wasn't my intention. Diego just kinda tugged me along, and Kang was there, so I knew you'd at least be in good hands. Please forgive me." Perla pouts and gives me puppy eyes.

"Stop that. Fine. I forgive you." I laugh.

A knock on the door brings us back to reality.

"Hey, everything all right in there?" comes Diego's concerned voice from the other side of the door.

"Ready to go?" I ask Perla.

She nods and I see Ellie adjusting her hair. I'd forgotten about my suspicion that she likes Diego. And, when we open the door, I realize I'd also forgotten about the tall guy who kissed me a few minutes ago. When I see him, his lips chapped, my cheeks immediately go red.

"Ready to go?" Diego asks, looking at me, Perla, and then at Ellie, whose eyes dart away to avoid his gaze.

Perla smiles in an attempt to ease the tension. "Yeah, let's go."

Suddenly, I have an idea. "Ellie?"

"Yes?"

"Do you need a ride home?"

"Oh, no, I'll take an Uber, don't worry."

"No way, you can ride with us. Kang has to take Diego to pick up his car from the soccer field. I'm sure Diego can drive you home after."

My redheaded friend looks at me quizzically.

"Yeah," Kang says to Ellie. "You can ride with us."

34

Enjoy Me

THE RIDE BACK in Kang's car turns out to be less awkward than I'd anticipated. Diego tells us about all the crazy shenanigans that went on at the party; it's as if he knows that the moment silence falls between us, we might begin to feel awkward. Ellie continuously steals glances at Diego, and Perla laughs nonstop.

As for me, I ride up front, trying to avoid looking at Kang, because every time I do, all I can think about is his face so close to mine and the feel of his soft lips. My heart hasn't been beating at a normal rate the entire car ride, but I've kept my cool.

I glance nervously at Kang and, at that very second, he looks over at me and our eyes meet. His lips curve upward and he winks at me before he looks back at the road in front of him. Something warm and electric settles in my core. I never realized positive emotions could cause so many physical reactions.

We drop Perla off at her house first since it's on the way to the soccer field. Once in the parking lot, Kang stops and Diego gets out of the car, followed by Ellie. My matchmaking plan is working so far. I lower the window. "Get Ellie home safe," I say to Diego with a wink—or, well, an attempt at a wink, because I've never been able to get it right.

He gives me a quizzical look. "What's wrong with your eye?"

I clear my throat. "Good night," I say, then add in a whisper so that only he can hear me, "Cangurito."

"Klara!"

I roll up the window, letting out an evil laugh. As I straighten up in my seat, I feel Kang's heavy gaze on me. "Did you know Diego before?" Kang asks, his voice neutral.

"Yeah, something like that."

"Something like that?" Kang raises an eyebrow.

"It's a long story," I reply, realizing that we're now alone. The last time that happened, we ended up kissing.

I give Kang my address and he drives in silence, the smell of his cologne mingling with the scent of the air freshener tree hanging from the rearview mirror.

I take a deep breath and let out a long sigh.

"So, how was your first party?" Kang asks, stopping the car outside my house.

"Not bad. Hot chocolate, a fight, maybe a new friend, and . . ." I swallow, but say no more.

"And?"

"All in all a good party, with some highs and lows."

Kang turns to me in his seat. "Aren't you forgetting something?" He smiles and his dimples melt me, yet again.

"What?" I ask, nervous. The kiss is something I will never forget, but I can't bring myself to say it.

"I guess I need to remind you of some of the things that happened tonight since you seem to have forgotten." Kang unbuckles his seatbelt and leans toward me, his face approaching mine slowly, allowing me to take in every detail of his handsome features before his lips meet mine.

I'd like to say that I'm somehow magically an expert kisser, but I'm not; although it's easier than before, I awkwardly follow his rhythm. I put my hands on his shoulders and kiss him, my heart beating in my throat and in my ears. It starts slow and gentle, our mouths finding the perfect pace. Then, Kang tilts his head to deepen the kiss and I follow along. My grip on his shoulders tightens as his tongue enters my mouth. This is not gentle anymore, it's passionate, and I can't get enough of it. Heat spreads through my body as our breathing becomes heavy. Kang wraps his arm around my waist to pull me closer and I don't want this to end. Kissing him is awakening so many sensations I didn't know I was capable of experiencing.

The only reason I stop is to catch my breath. We pull apart, and Kang smiles against my lips.

"Do you remember now?" he says, out of breath.

"I think so . . ."

He straightens up in his seat. "What kind of movies do you like?" he asks.

And I don't even know how to talk, how to breathe, how to anything. "Um . . . normal movies."

What kind of answer is that, Klara?

"Normal movies?" Kang laughs and I join him.

"I mean, there's not one particular type of movie that I watch exclusively. If the plot sounds interesting, I don't care what genre it is."

"Well, check the movie listings this week and pick one, okay?"

I look at him, confused.

"I'd like to go to the movies with you, Klara."

"Oh."

"It's a date."

"Oh," I say again.

Kang laughs, and it stirs something inside of me; I wish I could make him laugh all the time.

"How about Wednesday, after the show?"

"Yeah, sure. I'll let my sister know."

"Great."

We're momentarily blinded by a pair of headlights. It's my sister pulling into the driveway. Kamila gets out with two grocery bags; she's the type of person who goes shopping after eleven o'clock at night. Walmart, which closes at two in the morning, is a godsend for her. Kang tenses up at the sight of Kamila rounding her car to go into the house.

"Kang?" I say.

He doesn't answer. His gaze is fixed on my sister, eyes wide with surprise. Does he know her?

"Kang," I say again, and this time he looks at me.

"Do you know my sister?"

"Something like that."

"Something like that?" He's echoing my words from earlier.

"It's a long story."

I decide not to pressure him or demand an answer, because he didn't do that when I gave him a vague response about Diego.

"I better get inside," I say. "Good night, Kang."

"Good night, Klara with a K."

I get out of the car, then stand on the sidewalk waving goodbye as he drives away. I shove my hands into my pockets and head for the front door, unable to keep a smile from curling on the edge of my lips.

What a night!

With each step I take toward the door, my grin grows wider. Kamila comes out of the house to get more bags from the car, but she stops in the doorway, watching me.

"What's with that smile?"

I shrug as I walk toward her, so distracted that I don't see the layer of ice covering part of the path. I slip and fall on my ass in the snow.

"For God's sake, Klara!" Kamila rushes over to help me up, but she slips too, falling and crashing into me. We both burst out laughing.

"Are you okay?" Kamila asks with a giggle.

"I'm perfect," I say, my teeth chattering and my clothes soaked from the snow. I feel happy.

Kamila takes my face in her hands.

"It's been so long since I've seen you laugh like that." Her voice is full of emotion. "You look beautiful."

I put my hands over hers.

"I've been battered by so many storms, but right now I can enjoy the beautiful view."

We laugh, sitting there on the cold ground, because the beauty of life is that the simplest moments are often the most unforgettable. Moments like these remind us, no matter our weaknesses, no matter our burdens, that we'll be able to laugh again one day.

35

Walk with Me

I SPEND MOST of my weekend getting ahead on my reading assignments for both of my classes, using them as a distraction to forget what transpired during the party, both the good and the bad. I sit at my desk as I read for my Personal Health/Wellness class, taking notes by hand. I know it'd be easier to use my laptop, but I prefer to stick to pen and paper. For my American Literature class, I move to the comfort of my bed instead after having spent a few hours sitting. I immerse myself in the words of Kate Chopin in *The Awakening*, realizing how ahead of its time it was.

Before I know it, it's Monday, and fear courses through my body when I arrive on campus. I'm scared to see Yana in class after what happened at the party, fearing not for myself as much as for Ellie, mainly, because I know Perla has grown a thick skin to keep things from affecting her. By no means do I think that Ellie is weak, but, of the three of us, I sense that she's the most vulnerable to whatever Yana may have in store.

Part of me hopes the fight with Perla may have been a wake-up call for Yana, but I have a feeling that she's not the type to let things like that go. As I trudge toward class, I hear laughter and whispers, and, in the distance, I can see Ellie staring at her cell phone, tears in her eyes.

Oh, no. I grab my backpack straps and rush over to her. "Ellie!"

She shoots me a quick glance before picking up her backpack and brushing past me. I rush to catch up with her as she enters the bathroom and locks herself in one of the stalls.

"Ellie..."

"I'm fine, Klara." Her voice sounds pained and I know she's crying.

"What happened?"

"An anonymous account just posted a bunch of stuff about me online, making fun of me for being the same as I was in high school, but I'm fine. I should be used to it by now."

"This is harassment. No one should have to get used to something like that. Come on, we'll go to the dean to report that account, we know who it was."

"It won't make any difference. We have no proof."

"Ellie," I plead, "please open the door."

She swings the stall door open and it breaks my heart to see how red her face is from crying. She's sitting on top of the closed toilet lid, sniffling, her eyes full of tears.

"Hey, maybe you're right," I say, crouching down in front of her and conjuring up my best smile. "But this issue won't just solve itself if we sit back and do nothing. Besides, you're forgetting something very important."

"What?"

"You're not alone." I clasp her hands in mine. "It's one for all and all for one."

Ellie smiles. "Thank you, Klara. But I still don't want to go to the dean's office. Besides, it's not like we can just barge in through her door and demand to speak with her."

She has a point, but I'm not one to give up so easily, at least I'm trying not to be anymore. I march to Mrs. Barnes's office, with Ellie trailing behind me. Outside the dean's office, I explain the situation to her secretary, who, after consulting with the dean, says she has twenty minutes to spare. But it's just as Ellie feared.

"Do you have any proof that it was Yana?" the dean asks.

"No, but we know it was her."

"I don't doubt your words, girls, but in order to file a formal complaint, we'd need proof, especially with a matter as sensitive as online harassment."

"Mrs. Barnes, this is clearly Yana taking revenge. She got into a fight with Ellie and Perla at a party on Friday, after the game, and we're sure—"

"Klara," the dean interrupts, "that happened off-site, not here at the college, so I can't intervene. I can only focus on what happens here. I'll talk to Yana."

"She'll deny it, obviously."

"I'm sorry, but that's all I can do."

Ellie and I exchange disappointed glances. So this is where the system fails us; this is why so many people who experience any form of harassment suffer in silence without saying a word— because nobody will do anything to help them. They tell you to speak up, but, at least here, that's just lip service. When it comes down to things, nothing gets done.

We leave the dean's office and I can see the dejectedness on Ellie's face. I put an arm around her. "Everything is going to be okay," I assure her.

"Ladies!" Perla looks gorgeous today with her hair in two braids on either side of her face. She's wearing a long, flowy baby-blue skirt with a tight white top. Perla's style is so cool and always gives a relaxed vibe. "Are you okay?" she asks Ellie.

She nods.

"I got your message. What did Mrs. Barnes say?"

"That she'll talk to Yana. But I'm sure she'll deny everything."

"Oh, she definitely will, that rat bastard . . ."

I raise an eyebrow. "Wow. Your insults are evolving."

Ellie smiles, and I'm so happy to see it. "We're going to need to work on our insults," she says as we move down the hall.

"Okay," Perla says enthusiastically, "enlighten us."

"Well, we want to keep it classy, not crude. The person won't even understand what we're calling them because they're so wholly uncultured."

"I'm not sure I'm all that cultured," I admit.

"Ditto," says Perla.

"Don't worry, I'll explain every insult to you."

"Perfect."

Ellie sighs and takes our hands. Her serene expression is enough to shift the mood. The simple fact of having someone, of not being alone in hard times, changes everything.

We walk into class together and, luckily, Yana isn't there. Diego has his head down on his desk, and he's wearing sunglasses. I'm sure he's asleep. I sit behind him and begin poking him in the back with a pencil until he wakes up.

"I wasn't asleep," he says, adjusting his glasses.

"You've got a little drool here," Perla teases, pointing to her mouth.

He wipes his face, even though there's nothing there.

"Did you stay up late playing video games again?" I ask, already knowing the answer.

"What video games? Maybe I've been partying and drinking at Congress Social with a bunch of hot girls." He smiles.

I give him an incredulous look.

He sighs. "Yeah, I was at home gaming. It's amazing how time flies when you're playing online. Oh, I played Kang yesterday and I kicked his ass."

"I don't believe you."

Diego gasps exaggeratedly and takes off his sunglasses. "You insult me."

"What games are you into?" Ellie asks, so softly that it's hard for us to hear. She clears her throat. "Maybe you and I can play online sometime."

"No offense, Ellie, but I don't want to have to kick your ass."

She raises an eyebrow. "You assume you'll beat me because I'm a girl?"

Diego scratches the back of his neck. "No, no; I didn't mean that."

"Then, challenge accepted? Or are you too scared?"

Diego smiles slyly. "Challenge accepted."

They stare at each other for a second and Perla and I exchange a mischievous glance. There is a palpable chemistry between them. I can sense it even if Diego hasn't noticed it.

Wow, Klara, you've barely had your first kiss and now you think you're some kind of matchmaker.

My cheeks burn as I remember Kang's face so close, the gleam in his eyes, the feel of his lips on mine . . . A part of me still can't believe it happened. All weekend I was barely able to sleep or pay attention to the things Kamila and Andy talked about. I hope I don't get too nervous if I see Kang today. We've been texting, but we haven't seen each other since the party on Friday. Since we kissed, my first kiss. A huge grin spreads across my face every time I think about that moment. I shake my head and try to pay attention to the lecture, which has just begun.

◆ ◆ ◆

We walk to the cafeteria together after class, rolling our eyes at Diego, who's narrating another one of his crazy stories. Ellie watches him and lets out a sigh. Perla, for her part, shakes her head. This has now become a part of my routine before going home, the cafeteria no longer an unfamiliar setting and the company of my friends making me feel comfortable and safe.

"Have you seen that new action movie that just came out?"

Diego asks. "We should all go together. Going to the movies is more fun as a group."

"I like horror movies," says Perla. "Blood and gore."

"Me too," Ellie agrees. I'm glad she's feeling comfortable enough to open up more, and she seems to have put Yana's revenge behind her. "Not blood and gore, but more suspenseful, psychological horror," she clarifies.

Diego shakes his head. "And here I thought you were such sweet young ladies," he teases them. "Anyway, it doesn't matter what the movie is, we should go, right?"

That reminds me of my date with Kang on Wednesday. Only two days away! I still have to tell Kamila. I remember Kang's strange reaction when he saw my sister. I'm dying to ask him about it, but I don't want to make him uncomfortable. I thought about asking Kamila, but I didn't dare. For some reason, that's way worse.

"That's a great idea. Wanna go this weekend?" Perla says.

I nod; I have no plans. In fact, I think it's the first time in ages that I've had plans twice in one week: with my friends and with . . . Kang.

36

Congratulate Me

"HOW DO YOU feel?"

Dr. B.'s question does not come as a surprise. I'm sitting on the comfortable couch in his office. Honestly, I'm so excited to tell my therapist about all of my recent progress: that I've made friends, that I overcame a panic attack on my own, that I met the guy who brightened my evenings with his voice, that I'm navigating college better than I expected. I want to tell him that he's been right all along, that yes, I will make it through this. It may not be easy, but it is possible, just like the genuine smile that forms on my lips as I answer him. "I'm . . . I'm good." For some reason, my voice breaks because it's been so long since I've been able to utter these words. I feel tears welling up in my eyes.

Dr. B. smiles warmly. "I'm so glad to hear that, Klara." He hands me a box of tissues. "Those tears of relief, of joy, feel good, don't they?"

I nod silently.

"I imagine you have a lot to tell me. What do you say we celebrate with a hot chocolate?"

I nod again and he stands up to prepare it at a machine behind his desk. The smell of hot chocolate fills the office, and a minute later, he hands me my cup and I take a sip before I begin telling him everything.

Dr. B. listens attentively, writing notes here and there. His face occasionally lights up, especially when I tell him about the panic attack I had at the soccer game.

"Bravo, Klara. Have you stopped to acknowledge your accomplishments and congratulate yourself, to say out loud how proud you are of yourself?"

"Not necessarily—at least not out loud."

"It's so easy to say the negative things we think about ourselves out loud, but not as easy to say something positive to ourselves or to congratulate ourselves on an achievement. Do you know why? Because after spending so much time in that place of sadness and fear, you get used to highlighting the negative, to expressing only the bad. Somehow, you forget that positivity has just as much right to be expressed. It's important to smile at yourself in the mirror and congratulate yourself on what you've achieved."

"I don't think I could do that without crying. I'm so sensitive."

"Well, then cry," he says with a shrug. "Tears are another way of expressing our emotions, our deep feelings, which are sometimes difficult to translate into words. Your emotions are valid, your tears are valid, and so is your laughter, your smile. Everything you are as a person is valid and wonderful."

"I still can't believe I'm getting better, that this is possible. The world"—I think of Yana and her friends—"is scary sometimes, but being able to take part in that world is very exciting. It means that"—I think of Kang, my friends, even campus—"I'm not as terrified anymore, that I can leave the house more often, that I can be . . . normal."

"You've always been normal, Klara. But you've had your battles, you've had to fight to regain your mental health."

"It hasn't been easy," I admit, wiping away a rogue tear.

"No one said it was. You're a warrior. I am so proud of you, Klara. Think of the girl who came into my office almost ten months ago, trembling, clutching her sister's hand."

As he says this, I picture myself walking in that afternoon, scared to death of being away from home.

"And now here you are telling me that you can go out alone, that you have friends, that you overcame a panic attack all by yourself . . . You realize how proud you should be of yourself, don't you?"

"Yes."

"I want you to go home after this session and congratulate yourself on everything you've accomplished, okay?"

"Okay."

◆ ◆ ◆

As soon as I get home, I go into my room and close the door. I look around lovingly, remembering when this was my safe place, the space I so rarely left. I remember pacing back and forth. I remember sitting on the floor in the corner, crying, hugging my mother's picture. I remember lying in bed with my headphones on listening to Kang's show, unable to look at myself in the mirror because it made me feel so awful about myself.

I walk now to the mirror and my reflection greets me like always, but it no longer makes me feel bad.

"I . . ." I begin, following Dr. B.'s advice, "I've done a good job." My eyes redden. "I've overcome a lot—I've fallen, I've gotten up, it's hurt, it's burned, but I'm still here." I feel the tears sliding down my cheeks. "I'm strong. I'm proud of myself." I take off my wig and run my fingers through my short hair. "I've conquered so many of my fears, and now it's time to work on my self-esteem. I won't hide anymore; my scars, my suffering, are nothing to be ashamed of." I put my hand on the mirror. "I've made it out into the world. Congratulations, Klara," I say, voice breaking. "Mom, you must be so proud of me." I look at a picture of the two of us and I flex my biceps. "I'm strong," I say loudly. "I'm so strong, Mom."

My mother's smile in the photo fills me with peace and tranquility; I can almost see her there in my reflection, smiling and planting a kiss on the side of my head. *"You're my champion, baby."* I close my eyes, remembering her voice.

"If only I could see you again, Mom. Feel your warmth, smell your scent."

I wrap my arms around myself, trying to remember the last hug my mother gave me, imagining it filling me up with energy, giving me strength. I don't want my memory of her to bring only sadness; I want it to be something that gives me strength, that gives me the courage to go on, because my mother deserves to be more than a sad memory. She was an amazingly wonderful woman who gave me and my sister a great childhood. She deserves to be honored in a positive way.

"I will never forget you, Mom. You will always be here in my heart, with me through every struggle, every victory, every defeat, because you are a part of me, even if you're no longer here."

"Klara?" Kamila knocks on the door.

"Come in."

She enters carrying a box in her hands. Andy is behind her with another, larger box.

"What's that . . . ?" I start to say, brows furrowed.

Kamila hands me the smaller box and I open it. It's an instant camera. Andy puts the bigger box on the bed and I open that next. It's a corkboard in a wooden frame.

"A few days ago, you said you'd like to take pictures of your progress and display them somewhere where you can see them," Kamila says as I admire the camera. "So we wanted to surprise you with this."

I smile and hug her. I couldn't imagine a better sister, someone who remembers everything I say.

"Thank you," I whisper before releasing her to hug Andy.

Excitement runs through me as I look back to the camera. I can't wait to start using it and hang the photos I take with it. This will be my first art project in a long time. My first step back to art. Another step in the right direction. Transformations don't happen overnight, but I know I will keep moving forward and the day will come when I'll hold a paintbrush again.

Kamila sits on my bed and Andy leans against the doorframe. "How's it going?" my sister asks as I sit down on a springy chair in the corner—the newest addition to my room—to open the box with the camera in it.

"Good . . ." I have to tell her that I'm meeting Kang, and I can feel myself turning red. "In fact, I'm going out tonight."

"Oh, yeah?" Kamila sounds surprised and I can't blame her. "Where are you going?"

"To the movies," I murmur.

"Who with?"

Andy seems to notice the red in my cheeks and he clears his throat. "I'm sure she's going with her friends." Andy has the ability to read my mind; he can always tell when I don't want to talk about something. He's much better at picking up on my cues than my sister is, even though she's a psychiatrist.

"Friends?" Kamila asks excitedly, "Can we meet them? You can invite them over if you want, I'll make dinner—"

"Kamila . . ." Andy interrupts.

"Sorry, sorry . . . I'm being too intense . . ." she apologizes. "All in good time. We'll meet them when you want us to."

She and Andy complement each other so well. Kamila is too much, as my mother used to say, too analytical, always overthinking everything, while Andy is practical, straightforward, a laid-back, go-with-the-flow kind of guy. I've never met a couple who balance each other out as well as the two of them. I guess some people are just meant to be together.

"Well, we'll let you do your thing." Kamila stands up. "I can't wait to see your pictures." She smiles. "What time does the movie end?"

"A little after ten o'clock, but we're going for ice cream after, so I'll be home around eleven-thirty-ish."

"If you need anything, don't hesitate to call and I'll come and get you right away, okay?"

I know that "anything" means "panic attack," that she worries I might feel the need to rush home from wherever I am. Basically, my sister is telling me that she'll come running if anything goes wrong, as usual.

"Okay."

Kamila leans over and kisses me on the forehead. "I love you," she says.

I wrinkle my nose in a mocking grimace of disgust. "Sickly sweet, how do you put up with her, Andy?" I joke.

He shrugs. "It's not easy."

"Oh, no, she called me sickly sweet." Kamila pretends to be wounded. "She must be allergic to love."

"I'm not allergic to all love, only yours."

We laugh and they leave as I begin to hang my corkboard and decorate it with colored paper and some of the old Christmas lights from my bed. I can't wait to print and hang my first photos. I stare at my work and turn the camera to me. Taking a deep breath, I smile and take my very first picture. I wait for it to develop, and when it does, I chuckle. I look messy and pale-faced, but I like it. I place the photo on the corkboard and stare at it a bit longer. Gosh, my hair looks so disheveled; I need to shower as soon as possible. Humming, I head to the bathroom.

After showering, I get ready for my date with Kang. I put on black pants and a long-sleeved purple shirt. I towel dry my hair. It's growing quite fast, already covering the back of my neck with a few longer strands down to my ears. I look in the mirror and my lips curl into a smile of acceptance. Loving myself will take time, but it's a start. "What a dazzling smile you have, Klara," I say to myself. Dr. B. recommended I give myself compliments. He says that the hardest thing for many people is to accept their body as it is.

"If only I were taller..."

"If only my eyes were a different shape or a different color..."

"If only my hair was straight. If only it were curly..."

"If only I had bigger boobs or more butt..."

"If only I were pretty, then people would like me..."

"I want to be like her. She's perfect; I'm not..."

Unfortunately, we live in a society in which we are bombarded by images of beautiful people and made to believe that beauty is only one thing, and that if you don't fit those beauty standards, you're flawed. There's not much we can do about that, but my mother always said that every change starts with the self. It's hard to admire your own beauty. Dr. B. illustrated this one session by pointing out how much easier it was for me to see beauty in other girls and let them know it. And I thought back to all the times I'd complimented another girl.

"All the girls I know are beautiful; they all have something unique about them."

Dr. B. smiles and says, "Now I want you to imagine that you see yourself walking down the street. What would you think is pretty about that girl?"

I struggle to come up with something, but eventually I do, and my answer surprises me. "That she has a beautiful smile and very pretty eyes."

Dr. B. seems pleased. "It's easy to see beauty in others, but when it comes to seeing it in ourselves, it sometimes seems impossible. Do you know why, Klara? Because we tend to be our own toughest critics. No one will judge you or criticize you more harshly than you do yourself. No one will be as cruel to you as your own thoughts. It's hard to have good self-esteem if we're always hearing that relentless critic in our head. I want you to pay more attention to the things you think are beautiful about yourself. You told me that you like your smile and your eyes. Okay, so compliment yourself on those things in front of the mirror, every day. It's incredibly therapeutic to look in the mirror and say out loud 'I love my smile.' You may not believe it at first, but over time those positive affirmations will change the way you see yourself."

My phone vibrates and I pick it up.

Kang: I'm outside your house.

My heart starts beating wildly and I take a deep breath.

Me: I'll be right out.

I stand in front of the mirror to position my wig, but Dr. B.'s words spring into my mind. I smile and remove the wig, letting my short curls tumble down over my forehead and ears.

"You have beautiful curls, Klara," I say to myself before I put on my jacket.

I'm afraid of Kang's reaction when he sees me, but I've made up my mind not to let fear rule my life. As I walk to the front door, I picture my mother beside me, Dr. B. winking at me as I pass, and Kamila and Andy clapping. I take a deep breath and pull the door open. The cool night air greets me. Change does not happen overnight, but step-by-step.

37

Rescue Me

BREATHE, KLARA.

The walk to Kang's car takes ages and I am acutely aware of every step, opening and closing my sweaty hands, biting my lip and releasing it, trying on different facial expressions. My heart feels as if it's about to burst out of my chest and I swallow, trying to relax. I'd like to say that my confidence has not waned since I walked out the door, but it has; it's hard to let myself be this vulnerable in front of Kang. His rejection would devastate me, but I know that, if I can be brave enough to show my true self to him, it will be much easier to face the rest of the world this way. Letting out a puff of air, I open the passenger-side door. I get in and sit for a second with my hands clasped in my lap, not daring to look at him.

"Hello, Klara with a K."

I relax my shoulders and turn to face him. Kang is wearing a dark shirt with the sleeves rolled up to his elbows and dark blue jeans to complement his look. He's as handsome as always.

He gives me an approving look as his lips quirk into a tender smile and he reaches out to tuck a curl of hair behind my ear before resting his hand on my cheek.

"I'm glad to see you're not hiding anymore, Klara."

I don't know what to say. I was so afraid. But his voice and his words bolster my confidence. His reaction reinforces my faith in people. Not everyone is going to be critical of someone like me. There are good people, like him, like Perla, like Diego. People who are willing to accept me as I am whenever I'm ready to show them, and I think that the time has now come. Dr. B. is right: It's harder to gain acceptance from ourselves than it is from others.

I smile and place my hand on his. "I've deprived the world of myself for too long," I joke.

"I completely agree with that." Kang runs his thumb over my cheekbone and I lose myself in his eyes. "Welcome back to the world, Klara with a K. There's plenty of bad things about it, but many wonders as well. I'm so glad you're ready to be a part of it."

I'm acutely aware of his hand on my cheek, his face so close. My eyes flash to his lips and I blush. We hear the sound of someone tapping on the window and we both sit back in our seats. It's Kamila.

Before I turn my attention to my sister, I notice Kang cover his face with one hand and turns toward the driver's-side window.

"Hey," my sister says, trying to get a look at the guy next to me. "You left your cell phone." She hands it to me.

"Thank you," I say with an awkward smile.

Kamila is about to say something else when Andy appears behind her. "Kamila, are you coming? Good night, guys, have fun," he says, winking at me, tugging at my sister, who's still trying to see what my date looks like.

I roll up the window and watch them enter the house as Kang starts driving without a word. It's obvious that he didn't want my sister to see him, so I can only assume they know each other, but from where? I have to ask. "Kang," I begin.

"Did you pick a movie?" he interrupts.

"Oops, I forgot."

"Don't worry, I'm sure there are plenty of *normal* movies to watch," he says with a smirk, reminding me of my embarrassing response the other night.

Bravo, Klara.

"You can check the listings on your cell phone," he suggests when I don't respond.

I look out the window, watching the trees go by. I don't know how to ask him about my sister, so I decide to just be direct. I open my mouth to speak, but he seems to read my mind.

"It's a long story." He sighs. "Can I tell you about it after the movie?"

"Okay."

We arrive at the movie theater and get tickets for a thriller, then line up at the concessions stand. When Kang hands me my popcorn and Coke, I grin so widely: it's my favorite snack for listening to his radio show, and now here I am eating it with him, at the movies, on a date.

Kang raises an eyebrow.

"What?"

"I used to always have popcorn and Coke while listening to your show."

He runs a hand through his hair and looks down, but I still catch a glimpse of a crooked smile. Is this guy for real? And am I really out of the house with no wig? It all feels too surreal.

"Used to? So you don't listen to my show anymore?" he asks, tossing popcorn into his mouth as we walk into the theater.

"Why bother, I have the real version now," I joke, shrugging.

"Ouch," he whispers. "So I've lost a listener but gained a girlfriend."

We both stop abruptly. Kang coughs, choking on his popcorn. I pat him on the back. My heart is racing out of control.

"I mean . . ." he says, recovering. "It's a figure of speech . . ."

I don't know if he's flushed because of what he just said or because he almost choked to death on a piece of popcorn.

"It's too soon, I know . . . I'm not pressuring you . . ."

"I know what you meant, Kang," I say, laughing.

He runs his hand over his face. "I'm just such a mess with you."

I scoff. "As if you haven't noticed how much of a mess I am around you."

As we take our seats, I steal a few glances at my date next to me and yelp internally. The movie must be popular because the theater fills up immediately. Sitting next to Kang doesn't make me as nervous as being surrounded by so many people in a new and unfamiliar enclosed space. It took me months to make it all the way to the park with Kamila and Andy. When I started going to campus, it was planned out, with incredible support at my disposal. This, however, is new . . . and new always triggers my anxiety.

Kang seems to notice my discomfort and is staring at me with concern. "Are you okay?"

I nod, my body tense. I take a deep breath as the movie begins. But I know I'm not okay. I'm unable to eat any popcorn, or drink my Coke, unable to enjoy sitting next to my handsome date. Everything takes a back seat when you're having a panic attack, nothing else matters—you feel only fear and the need to flee, to escape. I try to calm myself because I don't want to make a scene, but I'm terrified and it's hard to breathe. Each inhale seems to become caught in my throat, making me feel even more desperate.

"I'm going to the bathroom," I say to Kang, standing up before he has time to respond and pushing past the other people in our row.

Out in the lobby, my breath becomes increasingly rapid.

I need to get out of here. I can't breathe. There's something wrong with my lungs. I'm so scared.

I rush out of the theater and the winter chill hits my face; the fresh air is a shock, offering some relief.

But it's only momentary, because I'm unable to regain control. There's nothing I can do to make myself breathe normally. I'm not okay.

You have to calm down, Klara, breathe. But I can't.

But then I conjure Dr. B.'s encouraging words in my mind. *"You are in control. Even when you feel you're at your worst, remember that you are in control. And remember that it will pass, Klara, hold on to that; a panic attack is always going to pass."*

It's going to pass.

I move away from the entrance, walking with one hand along the wall until I turn and step into a dark and desolate alleyway. Hyperventilating, I press my back against the wall and slide down to the ground.

Come on, Klara, you've done it before, you can do it again.

I stretch my legs out in front of me, close my eyes, place my hands on my thighs, and begin to raise and lower them in that rhythm I know so well.

I am calm, I am safe, I am protected, I repeat over and over.

I exhale, tears streaming into my mouth.

I am calm, I am safe, I am protected . . .

My hands continue to move in rhythm.

I know what this is. This is a panic attack, and I know it's going to pass. I'm in control because I know exactly what it is. A panic attack.

I repeat those words over and over, ignoring my cell phone vibrating in my pocket. I'm sure it's Kang. He must be worried, but before I answer him, I need to get through this.

After a few minutes, I'm breathing normally again. I look at the parked cars in the distance and I feel the cold of the nighttime breeze.

I did it. I was able to get through a panic attack again, on my own.

I remember Dr. B.'s suggestion that I congratulate myself out loud. "Well done, Klara," I whisper, hugging myself and rubbing my arms. "You did a good job."

I stand up and walk out of the alley back into the light, both literally and metaphorically.

"Klara!"

Kang, standing outside the entrance, runs toward me, visibly concerned. And he grows even more worried when he sees my face.

"Hey, are you okay?"

I tell him the truth. "I had a panic attack."

I search his face for any hint of disapproval, but he just sighs and pulls me into a hug. I stand there for a second, not reacting, until I finally wrap my arms around his waist. He smells so good and his warmth is so comforting.

"You scared me," he admits as he rubs the back of my neck.

"I'm sorry."

"No, don't apologize." He leans back and takes my face in both hands. He looks at me with those black eyes that exude honesty. "I want you to understand that this isn't something you have to hide from me. I know we're just getting to know each other, but you can trust me. You don't have to face everything alone. Let me help you. I *want* to help you."

I put my hands on his. "I know, but there are some battles I have to fight on my own, Kang." I offer him a sad smile. "There are times when I have to be my own knight in shining armor."

He runs a thumb over my cheekbone as his eyes fall to my lips.

"I know the timing isn't the best, but I'm dying to kiss you."

He looks surprised when I nod, blushing, and then he presses his lips to mine. For a second, I forget what just happened, and the world around me falls away. All I feel are Kang's soft lips against mine. He holds my face gently and I grip his arms when it feels like my legs are about to give out beneath me.

It's amazing how much things can change from one moment to the next: I just had a bad panic attack, but was able to get through it on my own; I couldn't handle a regular movie date with the guy I like, but now I'm kissing him. I guess that's what life is: a collection of good and bad moments. Right now, I want to focus on this good moment; dwelling on the bad won't change it.

Kang pulls back, his face still hovering close to mine. "Damn,

Klara, you have no idea what you do to me," he says, nestling his nose against mine, his chest moving rapidly. He gives me another short kiss.

"I can say the same about you." I smirk.

Kang straightens up and drops his hands from my face. "Should we go get some ice cream?"

"Yes." I take his hand and he looks down, blushing.

"We have a lot to talk about, Klara with a K."

We hold hands as we walk to his car.

"Over ice cream, I'll tell you about someone very special to me: my brother, Jung."

Confide in Me

KANG

TWO LARGE CUPS of ice cream on the table between us. I play with the spoon as I prepare to tell Klara everything I remember from that day—every detail, every emotion.

I squint in the bright light of the hospital hallway. My eyes are irritated from crying so hard at my brother's funeral. I walk past nurses and doctors who look at me without saying a word. They're probably used to seeing people crying in these halls.

In my hand, I clutch a small slip of paper I received only days ago with the name of the psychiatrist who was scheduled to see my brother. I walk quickly, checking the office doors for the name. I'm a mess, I don't even know what I'm doing.

I turn a corner into an empty hallway where I finally find the door with the name I'm looking for. I knock desperately.

A nurse opens the door and looks at me quizzically. I can see her desk and another door behind her. I imagine it leads to the doctor's office.

"Can I help you? Are you okay?"

"Where is Dr. Rodríguez?"

The woman frowns and looks me up and down. I'm still wearing my black suit from the funeral. I'm disheveled and I don't even want to imagine what my face looks like.

"Dr. Rodríguez is making her rounds. She should be back any minute. Do you have an appointment with her?"

I shake my head.

"Are you all right? What's your name?"

"Kang," I whisper.

"Well, Kang, do you want to come in and wait? The doctor will be back soon."

"No, I don't . . ." I crush the slip of paper in my hand. I notice movement to my right and turn to see a young doctor with dark hair in a messy bun walking down the hall toward me. She's wearing a white coat and has one hand in her pocket while the other holds a plastic cup of coffee.

"Dr. Rodríguez, this young man—"

"You!" I say from between gritted teeth, running toward her with my fists clenched. "You!"

She doesn't say anything, just watches me.

"Why couldn't you see my brother the day we came to the psychologist? Why?! He was already here, you would've only had to see him for one second, one fucking second!" I don't usually talk like this, but I'm out of control. "That would've been enough! Why? He was so bad off, he needed you to see him, but instead you were off that day, probably on a fancy vacation instead of doing your job." Tears of rage flood my eyes, but I don't let them fall. "My brother is dead because of you!"

Dr. Rodríguez's expression softens and her eyes fill with sadness.

I take another step toward her, pointing at her. "My brother is dead! Because of you!"

"Kang . . ." the nurse behind me starts to say, but the doctor raises a hand.

Why doesn't she say anything?

"You could've saved him! You could've . . ." I choke on the sobs stuck in my throat. "I just left his funeral. I had to say goodbye to him . . . He was only twenty, he . . ." I pause, struggling to breathe. "I couldn't save him. I . . . I did what I could, but . . . If only you had seen him that day, if only . . ." I take a step back, wiping my tears. "If only . . ." I rub my chest, pain coursing through my body just as it did the day I found Jung dead in his room. "You could've saved him, and I didn't do enough, and now I can't do anything, because he's dead . . ." I say through the tears. My knees give out and I crumble to the ground. "He . . . there's nothing I can do now; it's too late."

The doctor hands her coffee to the nurse and sits down in front of me. There is evident sadness in her expression, but at the same time she transmits so much peace. "You can cry, scream, insult me," she says. "It's okay, Kang. It's okay to express what you're feeling. And if anger is the predominant emotion in your heart right now, I want you to know that it's completely normal. All that pain, rage, helplessness, and guilt are completely normal, Kang."

"How can you be so calm when my brother is dead because of you? You wouldn't see him that day and he'd be alive if you'd done your job." My words are fueled by anger. "Why didn't you just do your job that day?! Why?!"

"I wasn't at the hospital, Kang. I wasn't on call. If I had been here, I'm sure I would've fit him in . . ."

"Excuses! They called you and you decided not to come, didn't you?"

"Not this time, Kang."

"Bullshit!"

She sighs, her eyes reddening slightly. "My mother died that week."

At her words, it's as if a bucket of cold water has doused my anger, cooling it down immediately.

The doctor takes a deep breath to keep herself from crying. "But *that's not important right now. Would you like to come into my office for a while?"* she asks.

I feel like shit. "I'm sorry . . . I . . . I don't know what I'm doing . . . I'm so sorry . . . I don't know what I was thinking coming here. I just . . ."

She puts a hand on my shoulder. "It's okay, Kang." She rubs my back gently. "I'm very sorry about your brother's death, and if it's okay with you, I'd like to help you deal with all this."

I shake my head, silently crying. "That's not why I came."

"Maybe not, but since you're here, I think it would do you good to talk to someone."

"I don't even have an appointment."

"Don't worry about that—if I tell you I have time to talk, it's because I do." She stands up and offers me a hand.

I hesitate, but then Jung's sad face flashes in my mind and I think about how different everything would've been if he'd gotten help when he needed it. So I take the doctor's hand and follow her into her office.

Dr. Rodríguez was my psychiatrist for the year it took me to process my grief. And she became very special to me. I'm eternally grateful to her, but I didn't want to see her in front of Klara; at least not until Klara heard the story from my mouth.

I wish I didn't have to tell Klara such a tragic tale on our first date, but sooner or later she'll want to introduce me to her sister, so it's better that she knows.

I take a deep breath. "My older brother Jung died by suicide."

Klara opens her mouth and reaches across the table to take my hand. "I'm so sorry, Kang."

"My father didn't believe in depression, in anything to do with mental health. He said it was all a matter of willpower." It feels good to talk about this without wanting to cry. "He wouldn't let my brother see a therapist, even though he was suffering from a deep depression after a car accident. I thought I could save him."

I smile sadly to myself. "I guess we always want to be heroes for the people we love."

Klara squeezes my hand gently.

"One day, Jung couldn't take it anymore and he took his own life." I need another deep breath to continue. "It tore me apart. I . . . I can't explain in words the pain I felt, that I still feel. I loved my brother with all my heart—we were very close. It was an extremely difficult time for me."

"I can't even imagine, Kang, I'm so sorry." Klara's voice transmits calm.

"Look at me, telling you all this on our first date . . . I'd totally understand if you didn't want to see me ever again," I joke, trying to alleviate the tension caused by my confession. The truth is that my heart wouldn't be able to take it if she didn't want to see me again. I study her, searching her small face for any sign of rejection, but I find only a reassuring smile.

She shakes her head. "Thank you for being willing to tell me what happened to your brother," she says.

I stare at her. I want to hug her, kiss her, but I hold back because I don't want to be too intense. I don't want to do anything that could ruin what we've started to build. I guess I like her a lot more than I thought. I sigh before continuing. "Anyway, before Jung . . . died, I took him to a psychologist who referred him to a psychiatrist . . ."

"To my sister . . ." she guesses correctly.

I nod. "Yes, but we never made it to the appointment because my father wouldn't let us, and then it was too late. I . . ." I remember my anger as I marched down the hospital hallway prepared to confront that doctor. "I was so angry the day of Jung's funeral that I went to the hospital to tell Dr. Rodríguez off for not seeing Jung. But she told me she wasn't at the hospital that day because"—Klara waits patiently—"because your mother had died that week."

She tenses up and pulls her hand away from mine, then looks away. It's a sensitive subject and she didn't expect me to know.

"I became your sister's patient that day," I continue. I don't want to bring up her mother; she's had a hard enough night already. "I'm so grateful to Dr. Rodríguez. Your sister is an excellent psychiatrist. She helped me so much."

"Is that why you were hiding from her, so I wouldn't see that she knew you?"

"I wanted to tell you myself."

"I understand." She reaches across the table, intertwining her hands with mine. "Thank you for telling me, Kang . . . I know all too well how difficult it is to talk about the death of a loved one."

Again, I stare at her. She seems unreal to me: the understanding expression, the sweet smile on her lips, the sparkle in her eyes, the tousled curls around her face . . . Everything about her is so genuine, so beautiful. Klara transmits such a sense of peace . . . I can't help but be in awe of her.

"I like you a lot, Klara," I let out.

Her eyes widen in surprise and her cheeks immediately blush. I imagine I must be just as red.

"I . . ." She pauses, and I give her time, although I can't help but feel nervous. "I like you too, Kang."

We sit in the bright, colorful ice cream shop, smiling at each other and chatting comfortably. I don't want the date to end. I never thought I could feel this way about a girl so quickly. I was able to talk to her about my brother without crying and I even got up the courage to tell her how much I like her. There's something special about Klara that makes me want to open up to her, because she listens without judging, accepting me as I am. I've never known anyone else like her.

Klara with a K is one of the most incredible people I've ever met. I will do my best to stay a part of her life for a long time.

39

Catch Me

ALL IN GOOD *time*, I remind myself. Kang told me about his brother and my heart breaks as I imagine what he must have felt when he found Jung dead. The helplessness, the guilt. I don't want to get into the sad story of how my mother died, not tonight. It's his turn to open his heart to me. There will be time for me to share my story with him on future dates. There's a special connection created with someone who has gone through similar pain: the feeling that we're no longer so alone, so misunderstood.

"You got very quiet all of a sudden," Kang says.

"I'm just thinking crazy things."

"Crazy? Like what, try me."

"No, another time." I smile nervously; even though I feel comfortable with him, his presence still makes my heart flutter. I have to look away from him when I gaze into the depth of his eyes. "When are you going to invite me to see you sing at the bar on Fourteenth Street?"

Kang raises an eyebrow. "Klara, it's our first date and you already want to commit a crime together?" he jokes.

"Oh, come on, singing in a bar is not a crime."

"It is if you're underage, which you are."

"Can't you persuade the owner to let me in? Just turn on your charm."

"I think you're overestimating my charm." He rests his elbows on the table and leans toward me. "Am I charming?"

Without meaning to, my eyes drop to his lips and I instantly remember the feeling of his kiss. I scrape the bottom of the ice cream cup to buy myself time, though there hasn't been any left for a while now, then place my hands in my lap. "As if you didn't know . . ."

He leans back and I'm grateful for the distance between us. "Maybe I don't know, Klara."

"I'm not going to tell you how charming you are, Kang."

"Ouch, why so hostile?" He runs his hand through his hair, tousling it, which makes him look even hotter.

"I'll tell you how charming you are when you take me to see you play at that bar."

"Oh, are we negotiating now?"

"I learned it from you," I say, shrugging.

I remember all the times Kang got information out of me. It seems like a long time ago, back when I was still stuck in my room, not going out, and the thought of seeing him someday hadn't even crossed my mind. Yet here we are, face-to-face, having our first date.

"Fine, if you don't want to take me to see you play, then at least tell me the story behind the mask."

Kang looks down at his empty cup, moving his spoon around, as if contemplating what to say. I'm about to tell him we can save it for another time since he's already opened up so much to me, but to my surprise, he takes a deep breath, then begins. "I only ever played for my brother." He pauses. "He was the one who believed in me, who swore I belonged on a stage even when I laughed it off. But after he died . . . playing didn't feel right anymore. Music was ours—something that existed in late-night jam sessions, just the two of us. I wasn't ready to share it with the world, not without him. The mask . . . it keeps it that way. It lets me play without feeling like I'm giving away something that was only his to hear. Up there, no one knows me. No one sees me. And for now, that's the only way I can do it. It's stupid, I know . . ."

I place my hand on his and rub it gently with my thumb. "It's not stupid, Kang."

He offers a barely-there smile, then says, "As much as I've enjoyed sharing ice cream and a painful part of my past with you, and as much as I wish this day would never end, I don't want Dr. Rodríguez to get mad at me for having you miss your curfew."

I sigh, but give in. "You're right. We should head out."

All the way home, I pester him about inviting me to see him play. I really want to hear him sing. I can't even imagine how his voice might make me feel.

Suddenly his phone rings and he hands it to me. "Can you get that? Tell him I'm driving."

It's a video call from Erick. Suddenly I remember that I'm not wearing a wig. I don't feel brave enough to face someone like Erick. I stare at the phone in my hands for a few eternal seconds as thousands of thoughts flash through my mind. Kang calls out to me, but he sounds distant.

Erick is going to laugh at you.

No, he won't.

Maybe not, but he'll pity you, like everyone does when they see you without a wig. Remember the sad looks at the hospital when you got your treatment?

I close my eyes and picture my mother's smile, how beautiful she looked even without hair. *"It's just hair, baby, it'll grow back,"* she said, winking. *"Let's look on the bright side: I won't have to wear a hairnet when I'm baking my cakes anymore."*

I inhale deeply, puffing out my chest and feeling the air fill my lungs, and then release it all before accepting the video call.

Erick appears on the screen with messy hair, sitting on a sofa.

"Hey," he says, looking confused when he sees me.

"Hey."

"You're not Kang."

"Nope."

"I'm driving!" Kang shouts and I turn the phone so Erick can see him. "What do you want?"

"That's how you say hello?" Erick snorts. "Klara"—I turn the phone back to me—"can you believe how he treats his best friend?"

He doesn't even seem to notice that I am not wearing my wig, and here I was on the verge of a nervous breakdown about it.

"Sometimes, our anxious mind causes us to worry about other people's reactions or perceptions and we give life to an entire cycle of anxiety even though these thoughts have never even crossed their minds. We create anxiety based on assumptions." Dr. B.'s words return to me. How right he is.

"Don't be dramatic, Erick. What do you want?" Kang asks.

"I was going to ask for the notes for Professor Johnson's upcoming final, but actually, better question is, does she know?" Erick asks, and Kang frowns.

"Know what?" I look at Erick for an answer.

"Kang finally signed up for the talent show in Charlotte—you going with us to cheer him on or what?"

"Ah . . . I . . ."

"Erick, leave her alone. I don't even know if I'm actually going," Kang explains, shaking his head.

"Come on, man!" Erick whines, but I'm suddenly distracted by Kang as he motions for me to give him the phone. I hand it to him.

"Bye, Erick."

"Wait—"

And Kang hangs up. "Sorry, Erick can be a pain in the ass."

I lick my lips. "So . . . are you . . . going to the talent show?"

"I don't know yet."

"You should go," I say with a reassuring smile.

"Would you go with me?"

My smile fades.

Charlotte is three hours away by car and one hour by plane. Neither option sounds like something I'm capable of handling at the moment, especially after my panic attack tonight. I've grown comfortable around campus, but a road trip so far away is another level. It's in this moment that I realize I still have more work to do.

Kang glances at me. "Is that a no?"

"I don't think I'm ready yet."

"That's okay. Like I said, I don't think I'm going."

"Is it because of what you said earlier?"

Kang runs a hand over his face while keeping his other hand on the steering wheel. "Yes . . . No . . . I . . . I don't know. I may not be ready for it."

"I get it." I nod.

We ride in silence the rest of the way, both of us deep in personal thoughts, until Kang pulls up outside my house. He rests his forearm on the steering wheel and turns to me.

"I had a great time," I say. "Tonight was . . . very special to me."

"I'm so glad. That means . . . second date?"

"Of course," I say, too quickly, and then grimace with embarrassment.

Kang smiles and his adorable dimples appear. He takes off his seatbelt and leans toward me. His face isn't even close and I've already closed my eyes, squeezing them tightly shut. His lips brush mine and I can feel my heart beating in my throat. Kang kisses me softly, giving me time to catch up with him. I put a hand on one of his shoulders and kiss him slowly. After a few seconds, he speeds up the movement of his lips against mine, tilting his head to deepen the kiss as he puts a hand on my waist and pulls me closer to him.

I squeeze his shoulders and feel the kiss growing in intensity. Kang's breathing becomes heavy and so does mine, whether because of nerves or the sensations this kiss awakens. His hands around my waist grip me longingly and it's as if the heat from that contact penetrates my clothes and makes my skin tingle. Kang's kisses become more passionate, and when I feel his tongue, I lose all sense of where we are. I want . . . I need to feel more of him, *all of him*.

A moan escapes my lips and becomes trapped in his mouth. I can't stop, even though I know I have to; this is addictive. I pull away to pant. Kang rests his head against mine and kisses my nose before straightening up in his seat. We're both out of breath, flushed, with swollen lips. He bites his lower lip and gives me a crooked smile.

"Good night, Klara," he whispers, and I can't help but smile, too.

"Good night, Kang."

I go inside, walking on air.

◆ ◆ ◆

I've spent the entire weekend buried in textbooks, my hand cramping from nonstop note-taking, until I finally force myself to take a break. With a sigh of relief, I grab my popcorn and Coke, settling in just as Kang's special Sunday broadcast begins, something he gives his listeners to make up for shows he misses due to holidays. It's a completely different experience now that I know him and we've shared so much; now, my interest in him has become tangible, real. I replay our last kiss over and over in my mind, my cheeks instantly flushing.

As soon as he finishes his show, Kang calls me.

"We have to go see them play live one day," says Kang, talking about one of the local bands he promotes on *Follow My Voice*.

I take the last sip of my Coke. "I love that idea."

Kang sighs. "I already have our next date planned. We're going to Carowinds. How about Saturday?"

The smile fades from my face. Carowinds is a popular

amusement park a few hours away. Kang talks excitedly about all the rides he wants to go on. The joy in his voice is so evident that I don't dare interrupt. "What do you think?" he asks.

"It's..." I don't know how to vocalize my fear of an amusement park. "I don't know... I'll think about it."

"Oh." His voice betrays his disappointment and I feel bad for not being able to match his enthusiasm. "You're right, I'm sorry, I made plans without running them by you."

"No, it's fine, it's just..."

"We can do something else, it's no big deal."

"It's okay. You just took me by surprise, that's all."

"We don't have to do anything you're not ready for, Klara. You know that, right?" He sounds reassuring, and I hate that I have taken his excitement away.

"I know." I sigh. "Let's talk about this tomorrow. I've had my head deep in textbooks all day. I'm a little tired."

"All right. Good night, Klara."

"Good night, Kang."

We hang up, but I continue to replay the conversation. I stare out the window of my dark room, sadness running through me, for quite a while. Kang has so many things he's passionate about, so many things he'd like to do. Will I limit him? That's the last thing I want. I'd like to be able to share in his passions and interests. I couldn't handle the idea of going to Charlotte to support him for the talent show, and now I can't handle the idea of the amusement park. Yes, it's just a theme park for now, but is this what's in store for us? Is this what we will look like moving forward? I didn't consider how all my fears could limit our experiences together. I guess the small progress I've made clouded my judgment. Either way, he doesn't deserve that. Maybe I rushed into a relationship without looking at the bigger picture.

I'm crazy about Kang and I care about him too much to want to be an obstacle in his way. Maybe I'm overthinking it, but my anxiety is through the roof as I go over a million possible scenarios.

Unable to fall asleep, I conjure Dr. B.'s words to calm my mind and stop this cycle of negative thoughts. Even if I manage to get to sleep tonight, I know that a part of me will still harbor these doubts.

◆ ◆ ◆

Days turn into weeks, and before I know it, Thanksgiving break comes and goes in the blink of an eye. After my movie date with Kang, I try to go out without a wig on every date—movies, coffee, dinner, a regular park (not an amusement park), my favorite bookstore—and it eventually leads to walking around without one at home. As the days go by, I grow more confident in letting it go, especially with Kamila and Andy encouraging me over Thanksgiving dinner to try it out on campus.

But now, standing just outside the main entrance, hiding behind a small tree and biting my nails, I immediately feel like I've made a mistake—I'm even considering calling Kamila to come back and get me. What if Yana starts harassing me? Even though she's left Ellie and me alone so far, maybe she's been waiting for the perfect moment to strike again.

"Hoodie?" I hear Diego's voice from the other side of the tree and I lean over to see him right in front of me.

"Ah!" I jump in surprise and take a step back.

"What are you doing?" he asks, staring at my hair. "Beautiful curls, Hoodie."

"Thank you."

He raises an eyebrow. "Is that why you're hiding back here?"

"I think I might go home. I'm not feeling very good today."

Diego narrows his eyes. "Oh, no, Hoodie." He waves his index finger in my face. "You're not going anywhere. Hiding behind a tree, what a cliché."

"Says the guy who hides his feelings behind jokes." I cross my arms. "You have your own clichés too, Diego."

He huffs exaggeratedly. "I have no idea what you're talking about."

"Mhm, sure."

"You're delirious. This tree"—he checks the branches—"must contain some hallucinogenic substance."

I punch him on the shoulder as he continues to examine the leaves. "Go to class."

"Without you? Never!" He takes me by the arm. "Come on, Tree Girl, class is about to start."

I wrench myself away from him. "I'm not going, Diego."

"I thought you might say that." He pulls out his phone. "I need backup," he says into it. "Tree next to eastside entrance."

"What are you doing?"

He hangs up and smiles victoriously. A few seconds later, Ellie and Perla appear.

"Diego!" I say, my hands on my hips as I give him a murderous look.

My two friends join us behind the tree, smiling when they see me.

"You look beautiful!" Perla hugs me.

"I'm proud of you," Ellie chimes in.

This moment, surrounded by the warmth of friendship in the winter cold, I may be as happy as I've ever been. Two persistent negative thoughts that tormented me for a long time have been vanquished.

No one will ever want to be friends with you, Klara.

Well, look at me now, surrounded by them.

People will only ever pity you.

No, I can also inspire others to feel proud, as Ellie just told me.

In my mind, I give those two negative thoughts the finger, my smile widening.

40

Hold My Hand

THERE ARE BATTLES we can face alone—that we must face alone, in fact. But there are others in which help and support are essential. When you need someone to hold your hand, for example, as you walk into college without your wig, exposing your short hair to the world for the first time.

I slow down and squeeze my friends' hands. I glance over to see Diego on one side smiling encouragingly and Perla on the other, eyebrows raised in an expression that says "*You got this, babe.*" They each return a firm squeeze and I continue on.

It seems to take forever, until finally, we reach our classroom. Everyone has already taken their seats and their gazes linger on me for a few seconds, but then it's all business as usual, and I am grateful for that. I turn around to hug my friends. "Thank you."

Diego playfully taps my head with his index finger.

"Thank you?" He shakes his head. "Um, I only accept payment in ice cream."

"I'll settle for a coffee," Perla says, winking. "It's a date."

I smile. "Deal."

I can't believe I've been going to college for close to three months now. Every day college becomes more bearable. I have to admit that there are days when the fear comes knocking on my door and shakes up my day, but I've been able to handle it. The urge to flee desperately back home comes less and less often. With my mantra and breathing exercises, I'm able to control the urge to burst into tears or run away. Of course, there are days when I feel like I can't take it anymore, and then I allow myself to go home early or ask to speak to Ms. Romes. I've picked my battles, and I think that has helped me stay the course.

After class everyone stands and begins chatting. Finals are around the corner, and we're gearing up for winter break. With class out, there will be more parties; everyone is excited to sleep in, to forget about college for a while. I, however, don't want to leave. I've just arrived. I'm still getting used to everything and I'm terrified that, after being stuck at home, I might have trouble getting back out again. I guess some fears will stick with me no matter how much time passes.

But it's not only that; Christmas is a challenging holiday for me. It was always the time of year that my mother spent hours in the kitchen preparing delicious meals, and I have so many memories of exchanging gifts, singing and laughing together. It's the time of year when you're supposed to be happy, but it just makes me melancholy and sad.

"Klara?" Ellie waves her hand in front of my face. "You haven't heard a word I've said, have you?"

"Huh?"

"Do you have plans after class?"

"Of course she has plans!" Perla says before I can answer. "She's having a coffee with me."

"I guess a deal's a deal . . ." I say with a shrug.

"Excellent," Ellie says and sits down next to me while Perla walks over to join Diego, who's speaking with Adrian and Ben.

"Klara, I have to tell you something."

"Tell me everything."

Ellie carefully adjusts her glasses and bites her lip, glancing around. "Diego asked me out," she whispers.

"What?!" I shout, causing several people to look in our direction. I laugh nervously and Ellie turns red. "Sorry, sorry," I say. "That was unexpected." Everyone goes back to their conversations as I repress a squeal, feeling as excited as when the stars of the Korean dramas I watch finally realize their feelings for each other and kiss. "I'm so happy for you," I tell her from the bottom of my heart. I know it means a lot to her to have been able to talk to Diego after all the time she spent watching him from afar, never getting up the nerve to approach him.

"I still can't believe it," she says. "We were playing online, I was kicking his butt, and we were joking around like always when all of a sudden, he asked me if I'd like to go out with him. I thought my headphones might be playing tricks on me at first and I had to make him say it again. Of course, I said yes! So tomorrow we're going to the movies!"

"How romantic!" I clasp my hands together and press them against my mouth. "I want to hear everything after. Well, maybe not everything, but as much as you're comfortable sharing."

"Everything, of course. I know you made this happen."

Perla high-fives us before dragging us both for coffee and girl chat.

◆ ◆ ◆

After lunch, as we make our way toward the exit, we hear a great commotion of voices and soon see a group of guys moving toward us, led by Kang. They all pass us, except Kang, who stops in front of me.

"Hey."

I bite my lip. "Hey."

Diego, Ellie, and Perla exchange glances.

"We'll see you at Starbucks," Perla says.

I nod, keeping my eyes on the guy who whips up a whirlwind of emotions in me.

Kang smiles and runs his fingers through my curls. "You're so beautiful—I'm a lucky guy."

I blush. I can feel people's eyes on us as they pass and it makes me uncomfortable, so I try to stay focused on Kang. "How was your day?"

He shrugs. "Just another day. I'm not excited about winter break, for, like, the first time ever."

Me neither.

"Oh, yeah, why's that?"

"Because I won't get to see you every other day."

Kang reaches out and takes my hand. I squeeze his nervously as we look into each other's eyes. I hear people whispering behind us, but I try not to let it affect me.

"Klara Rodríguez, I'm so glad I bumped into you." Ms. Romes's secretary approaches me. "Ms. Romes was looking for you—you're needed in the counselor's office."

I feel a tightness in my chest and I drop Kang's hand, taking a step back.

"Klara?" he asks with a frown.

An unpleasant feeling travels from my throat to the pit of my stomach as I walk away without a word to Kang. Everything around me becomes blurry and confused. I hear Kang behind me. It's a struggle to walk, like I'm dragging heavy stones tied to my heels. As I move down the corridor, I notice my breathing is shallow and I clench my hands into fists at my sides. A memory echoes in my mind. *"Klara Rodríguez, to the office urgently."*

The last time a counselor summoned me to their office was in high school, when my mother had to be taken to the emergency room after one of her chemo treatments. The side effects had made her so ill that we'd almost lost her that afternoon. I still remember the look on the principal's face when she told me to sit down and try to get ahold of myself while we waited for Kamila to pick me up and take me to the hospital to see Mom.

The hallway now seems too narrow and voices sound far away, as if sounds can't reach me over my racing heartbeat, which I can feel in my ears, in my chest, in my limbs.

"Klara, sit down. It's about your mother."

Near the end of the hallway, I stop and lean against the wall, holding my chest.

I can't breathe.

Yes, you can.

Come on, Klara.

"Are you all right?" someone asks, but all I see is a blurry figure. At some point, my eyes have filled with tears. "Klara, can you hear me?"

No.

Hands take my shoulders, but I brusquely push them off. "Leave me alone!" I shout, and my gaze clears to reveal Kang with a hurt expression. I shake my head; I don't know what to say. "Leave me alone..."

I don't want him to see me like this; I don't want anyone to see me like this. My heart is beating out of my chest and I can feel the fear coursing through my veins straight to my mind, convincing me that I'm going to die in the next few minutes. And then comes the numbing sensation, because I'm breathing so fast that my lungs don't have time to get the oxygen they need... I'm hyperventilating.

As I make my way down the hall, Ms. Romes comes rushing toward me. I guess someone told her what was happening. "Klara!" She puts a hand on my shoulder. "Hey, hey, you're all right, you're all right, come on." She guides me into her office—a corner of calm, as she calls it.

"I need to go to the hospital. I feel... bad..." I say in a hoarse voice. "I can't breathe ... The ..." I look for my phone. "The nearest hospital is ten minutes away. Please, I need a doctor."

"You're going to be okay, you're going to be fine ... Let's breathe together."

"I can't."

"Yes, you can, you've done it before."

"No, the hospital ..."

"Come on, Klara, we can get through this." Ms. Romes puts an arm around me. "Come on, you're safe, let's breathe together," she whispers, using her slow breaths as an example. "Come on. One ... That's it, slowly ... You're hyperventilating, that's why you feel like this. But you're fine. Remember your mantra, come on."

"I am calm"—inhale—"I am safe"—exhale—"I am protected."

"Again."

"I can't."

"You're doing great, Klara, come on."

"I am calm. I am safe. I am protected ..." I repeat, slowly inhaling and then letting the air out. I take another slow breath, still aware of the tingling in my limbs. I'm trembling, my muscles tense, my heart pounding.

"That's it, that's it, Klara, come on, keep breathing just like that," says Ms. Romes, rubbing my arms gently. "Breathe ... One ... two ... Let it out, come on."

The tingling sensation stops and, little by little, I am able to calm down while continuing to breathe deeply. And then comes the crying. I begin to sob uncontrollably right there in Ms. Romes's office.

"That's it, it's all over now, Klara. You did so well."

She pats my head and I cling to her arm, unable to stop crying. "I was so scared."

"I know, I know, but you handled it well."

"No, no ... I lost control this time ... it's gonna keep happening, I can't live like this ..."

Ms. Romes leans back and places a hand on each of my shoulders, her face level with mine. "Look at me," she says firmly. "You're a champ; I'm so proud of you."

"*You're my champion, baby.*" My mother's voice echoes in my mind.

Ms. Romes silently allows me to sob for a moment and then offers me a box of tissues and some water.

"I'm sorry, I don't know what happened."

"Don't apologize, Klara. I'm glad I could help you through it. I'll always be here if you need me."

"I wouldn't have been able to get through this panic attack on my own. It was very . . . intense. I thought I could control everything on my own, but this is the second time in a month. I keep thinking I'm having victories. I'm so deluded!"

"Don't say that. Remember that panic attacks are not something you can control, but you can learn to manage them with the tools that work for you. And you're doing exactly that. You're doing great."

"*Great* is not the adjective I would use."

"Then how about *wonderfully*?" Her smile is so genuine that I can't help but smile back. "Do you know what the trigger was? The people in the hallway? The noise? Or maybe there wasn't even a trigger, that can happen."

"I think it was the secretary, when she let me know you'd been looking for me."

"Why?"

"The last time I was called to an office, in high school, my mother had been hospitalized." I'm surprised I'm able to say this out loud without my voice cracking.

"Oh, I'm so sorry. We'll find a different way to contact you, okay? We don't need reminders of sad moments."

"Thank you." I stand up but then remember that I still don't know why she called me here. "What did you need?"

Ms. Romes shakes her head. "It's nothing. I just wanted to talk to you about scheduling."

"Oh."

"I was wondering why you haven't enrolled in any art classes for next semester, Klara?"

"I don't know."

"I'm not trying to pressure you, but you won an award a few years back for your paintings, right? You must be very talented."

"I don't know how to explain it . . . Painting was so much a part of me, so connected to my emotions and identity. And now . . . I have no idea who I am. I'm terrified to stand in front of a canvas and see what I might paint, given my current state of mind. My paintings have always been so colorful, so vivid, so uplifting. I can't imagine what they'd look like now. I think that, for the time being, I'd rather not."

"I get it. You don't feel you'll be able to enjoy it, to truly feel it. But don't you miss painting?"

"Every second of my life."

"Let's go."

"Uh, what?"

"Let's go paint."

"Ms. Romes, I can't, not now. I've had enough for today."

"Okay, I understand. Take as much time as you need."

She smiles one last time and leaves her office. Now alone, I picture Kang's pained face. I'm not ready to see him and I might run into him in the hallway, but I go out anyway, heading first to the bathroom to wash my face. I feel unbelievably low from this panic attack, my spirits at rock bottom. It's almost as if I take one step forward, getting my hopes up, only to take two steps back.

I go into one of the stalls and lower the lid so I can sit. I want to do some more breathing exercises, but I can't stop seeing Kang's hurt expression when I pushed him away from me.

I feel exhausted and devastated, because I know what I have to do. I recall the conversation I had with Kang about the amusement park, how excited he was and how I couldn't share in that feeling because of my fears. And now I've just pushed him away, literally. My mind is a whirlwind of negative thoughts, made worse by what happened today.

What am I doing? I don't want to hurt Kang, but I'm beginning to see that, with me beside him, he'll only be subjected to more scenes like the one today. I have nothing to offer him and will only hold him back.

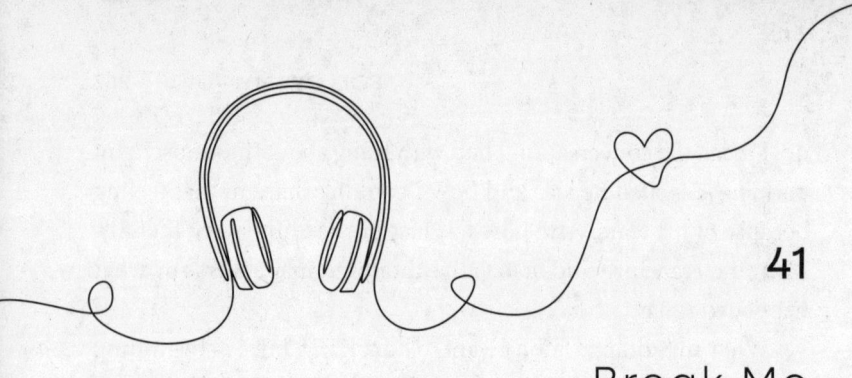

41

Break Me

KANG

"ARE YOU IN, Kang?" Erick asks. "Are you down to hang after class?"

"I don't know."

It's Friday, the last day of class before finals, but I'm not even excited about winter break. My mind keeps wandering back to what happened with Klara. I check my phone. The last text message I sent is still unanswered. I know she's okay because I asked Perla about her; but I need to hear it from her lips, to make sure everything is okay, that we're good.

When class ends, I rush over to Klara's classroom. I arrive at the exact moment she walks out, flanked by Perla and Ellie. She smiles at something Perla says, and I'm relieved to see her looking so calm. But when she sees me, her smile fades and she looks away.

"Hey," I say, waving.

Ellie and Perla each respond with friendly smiles.

Klara says nothing.

"Can I talk to you for a second?" I ask.

Klara nods, still without meeting my eyes, and turns around for me to follow her, leaving Ellie and Perla behind. I'm not surprised when we end up in front of the auditorium. The memory of the first time we met immediately puts me in a good mood.

"Did you bring me back here to tell me that I'm *healthy*?" I joke.

A slight smile tugs at her lips, but that's all I get in response. She seems tense, with her hands clenched into fists at her sides and her eyes fixed on the wall. Something's wrong. *Why won't you look at me?* My good mood devolves into anxiety and fear. Maybe I've done something wrong and ruined what we had between us.

"Kang, I think I . . . I jumped the gun on this. I'm sorry." Her voice is a whisper.

"You jumped the gun on what?"

"You and me."

This catches me completely off guard. I search her face, unsure of what I'm looking for in her expression, I guess some kind of hint that will help me understand what's going on, but I find nothing. "What are you talking about, Klara? Is this because of what happened in the hall the other day? Did I do something wrong?"

"No." She shakes her head and finally looks at me, eyes filled with sadness. "I've made a decision and I hope you'll respect it."

I'd do anything she asked me to because I care about her, perhaps even love her, but this . . . it hurts. I don't know what to say; I've put my whole heart into us, into her.

"I have the right to ask, Klara. Why?"

"I've made up my mind."

"But why? You're breaking up with me . . . and you won't even tell me why?"

"I'm sorry. I need time, Kang."

"Time?" I ask with a frown. "I can give you time, Klara, all the time you need."

She falls silent, but her eyes are red when she looks back at me.

"I hope you have a good winter break, Kang." She gives me a forced smile, and then turns around and walks away.

I want to stop her, to shout at the top of my lungs that she's hurting me and I don't understand why. But I restrain myself. She doesn't need a guy who won't respect her decision on top of everything else she's been through.

I stand there in the hallway that holds such beautiful memories of Klara, now the scene of a difficult conversation that has left me heartbroken.

◆ ◆ ◆

After getting home, I find myself playing my guitar, humming a melody that matches the way I'm feeling tonight. Klara's tormented expression keeps replaying in my head. The notes are sad and I can't stop recalling every word she said in hopes of finding an explanation. I know the mature thing to do was to let her go, but I'm beginning to wonder if I should have insisted she give me a reason.

She's had enough, I remind myself. The last thing she needs is someone pressuring her to say things she may not be ready to say.

This still sucks.

I really thought we were doing well.

Someone clears their throat, and I look up to see my father in the doorway of my room. I stop playing.

"You can keep going," he says with a polite smile.

"I was just humming nonsense," I explain. My father found out I play the guitar after Jung's death. I stopped hiding it from him because at that point, I was so angry at him that I didn't really care about what he thought of me.

My respect for him died along with my brother. He seems to know that because he has never made a comment about my playing.

"Who taught you how to play?" His question catches me off guard. He's never shown any interest.

"Jung took me to a few private classes," I reply, wary and confused. Why is he curious?

"Mmm, of course." There is no sarcasm or malice in his tone, just acceptance that my brother was the kind of person to encourage you to fight for your dreams. He folds his arms across his chest. "Your mother told me you play in a bar."

I swallow and hesitate. "Yes." Is he going to lecture me about it?

"I'd like to go."

"What?"

"I'd like to go and see you play."

My heart races. Even though I've lost respect for the man and a part of me is still working on the anger I felt toward him after what happened, he's still my dad.

"You don't have to do that," I retort.

"I know, but I want to," he replies. "Just a heads-up, if you are not good at it, I will let you know. I am an honest man."

I chuckle. "Right."

He turns around and, out of nowhere, I find the courage to invite him to see me play sooner than I expected it. "Actually," I start, and he turns to me, listening, "there is a talent show in Charlotte next month. You and Mom can come if you want."

"Talent show?" He raises an eyebrow. "Sounds interesting. Okay."

"Okay," I say with a smile.

42

Release Me

OVER THE PAST week, I've relied on my friends for a distraction, meeting up for study sessions to prepare for finals. I haven't talked to anyone about Kang, because I don't think they would understand, and because I don't even know how to explain it. I like Kang a lot, but I don't want to hurt him after everything he's done for me. I'm still processing so much that I don't know if I can deal with anything else right now; I need time.

I want to spend winter break taking in all the changes I've experienced. I want to focus on my victories and be comfortable knowing setbacks will come. I want to strengthen my relationships with my new friends. And even though Kang is part of the group of good people who have come into my life and helped me make positive changes, worrying about the negative effect I may have on him is too much for me to handle right now. Maybe it's selfish of me, but . . .

After taking my Personal Health/Wellness final, without realizing it, I've made my way to a completely different building, through a hallway where the art classes are held. Standing in front of an open door, I'm hit with the smell of fresh paint. I see blank canvases, unfinished works, and completed paintings. I've spent a lot of time in classrooms like this one. I can almost see myself sitting there, headphones on, listening to music, my head bobbing to the beat as I paint. I can also picture my mother coming in, smiling, to remind me that I've lost track of time again and she's come to pick me up.

"It must be hard, I imagine." I'm startled by Ellie's voice suddenly beside me. "I mean, it must be hard to lose something that used to be so important to you."

The memory of my mother's smile as we walked out of the art classroom, joking and laughing, is still so clear in my mind. "It is hard."

"I know it doesn't compare to everything you've been through, but I imagine I would feel something similar if I couldn't read. Books are my way of escaping reality, losing myself in other worlds."

I sigh. "It's not just that I'm not able to paint anymore. It's that I associate painting with sadness," I say. "One day I just became afraid to paint, to see that sadness in my paintings."

"Our brains work in strange ways, don't they?"

"I think our brains have many ways of dealing with trauma so that we can survive."

Ellie takes my hand. "Come on, my finals are over for today."

I follow her silently. That's not the only thing that's over.

◆ ◆ ◆

I'm back between my four walls.

I now find my room stifling, boring. It used to be my safe haven; I've spent so much time here. That all seems like a distant memory even though it's only been a few months. Things can change so much in just a short time. When we're in a slump, in the dark moments, we believe that we'll feel that way forever, that we'll never get better. But that's not true. We just have to push back against that belief that sadness lasts forever or that crippling anxiety will be our daily bread. We have to accept there will be good days and bad days, and hope there will eventually be more good ones. It's something I'm still working on believing.

"Are you ready?" Kamila pokes her head through the half-open door. "They're here."

I smile and then sigh as I approach the mirror. I still struggle with my reflection, with what I see, but I'm learning to love myself a little more every day. I'm ready for the Christmas party my sister has arranged in order to meet my friends.

"You look great," Kamila assures me.

"You don't have to compliment me all the time."

"Yes, I do. Before, Mom . . ." Kamila's voice trails off. "Mom always gave you compliments, so now it's my job."

"Well, you're doing a terrible job."

She laughs. "Believe it or not, I love your cruelty."

Kamila wears a casual black dress with an apron over it, stained with flour and other mysterious substances. I am immediately reminded of my mother, who used to spend all day in the kitchen around this time of year. It's the first time Kamila has baked anything since Mom died, and that brings a tightness to my chest.

"What did you make?" I ask, trying to sound calm even though it makes me very emotional.

She dusts some flour off her apron. "Strawberry shortcake."

Mom's favorite.

We both fall silent for a moment, not feeling the need to say anything. This is a huge step for Kamila, who has also had a very difficult time, and I'm happy that she's making progress.

"You've been such an inspiration to me, Klara," she says warmly. "Seeing you take classes this semester and make friends has motivated me to take a few steps myself. So"—she holds up her hands—"we'll have strawberry shortcake for dessert."

I walk over and hug my sister tightly. "You're doing great, Kamila," I whisper against her hair.

"The cake might be horrible, Klara, don't congratulate me yet," she jokes.

I laugh as I pull away from her. "Thank you."

"For what?"

"For helping me, for always being there, even while you were fighting your own battles. You're the best sister in the world."

Kamila's eyes redden and she throws her head back, huffing. "No, no tears! Come on!" She loops her arm through mine and we go out into the living room where Diego is standing beside Ellie. "Hoodieeee!" Diego says, wrapping me in a huge, warm embrace. I give Ellie a hug and the doorbell rings. Andy opens the door for Perla, who squeals when she sees us.

"Hey!" she says, corralling us into a group hug. "It's been five days and I literally feel like it's been years since I've seen you guys, I missed you so much!"

We sit down. Perla introduces herself to Andy and Kamila and jokes with Ellie and Diego. My sister seems charmed as we begin serving ourselves. I sit next to Andy, who is wearing a big smile. He nudges me with his elbow. "Where's the famous radio host?" he says.

"I don't want to talk about it," I whisper. "Diego, pass me the salt," I say, and Andy seems to get the message.

Perla is telling a funny story about New York and some pigeons when my cell phone vibrates with an incoming message. I open it and a feeling of warmth and sadness fills my heart. It's from Kang: *Merry Christmas, K.*

I send a Merry Christmas message and then put the phone away. Ellie and I exchange knowing glances. For some reason, she's the only person I've told about what happened between Kang and me. It's strange how we can develop an instant sense of trust with certain people, unexpectedly.

The truth is that I miss Kang a lot, in spite of everything. He and I used to talk or text every day, even before we started dating.

"It was awesome, wasn't it, Klara?" Diego's voice brings me back to the present moment, around the table.

"What was awesome?" I ask.

Perla shakes her head. "Klara has her head in the clouds, as always."

"I was saying that Kang's last show before the holidays was great, wasn't it?"

Oh . . .

Diego waits for me to respond and it takes him about four seconds to realize that I didn't listen to the show. "Did you miss it?"

Now everyone's attention is on me, and I don't know what to say.

"Wasn't that the day we watched *Queen of Tears*?" Ellie says. I've told her about that Korean drama several times. "We were so wrapped up in it that the time got away from us," she lies effortlessly.

Diego is still looking at me, eyes narrowed.

"Yeah, I guess it slipped my mind," I say, trying to sound convincing.

Perla looks at Ellie and then at me, but says nothing.

I know I have to tell them that I broke up with Kang, but this isn't the right time.

"Here comes dessert!" Kamila saves me by showing up with the strawberry shortcake.

It looks beautiful, and, tasting it, it's clear that my sister has inherited my mother's baking skills. It's delicious.

We toast and eat the cake that means so much to my sister, smiling and wishing each other a Merry Christmas, my heart overflowing with love.

43

Paint Me

AFTER MANY CONVERSATIONS with my friends, Kamila, and Andy, I decided to keep a similar schedule as the previous semester—one in-person class (ART-111 Art Appreciation) and one online (ENG-232 American Literature II). But going back to college for another semester after winter break is as hard as I thought it would be. Although I've been bored within the confines of my room, it was easy for me to fall back into a pattern, allowing myself to feel safe and protected by those four walls.

Back on campus, I constantly scan the halls for Kang. I haven't heard from him since that Merry Christmas message and, while I appreciate his respect for the time I asked him to give me, part of me—the immature, hardcore romantic—wishes he would seek me out, fight for me a little like in the TV shows and Korean dramas I love so much.

I have an appointment with Ms. Romes as soon as classes are back in session. She greets me with a handshake and leads me out of her office into another hallway. We walk up a stairway and down another long corridor and I know where she's taking me. We're in the Arts wing.

Ms. Romes stops in front of a studio art classroom and checks the time on her phone. "The class starts in a few minutes, so Mann must be on her way if you'd like to meet her."

"What are we doing here?"

She points to a sign by the door and smiles. "ART-240 Painting I."

"No," I instinctively say.

"Let's just go inside, okay?" Ms. Romes suggests. "Just to take a look around."

"But . . ." I pause for a second, thinking about it.

"I'll be right here if you need me."

"I need more time; I have to take it little by little."

She nods. "Okay."

So, the first day, I just stand in the doorway looking at the empty classroom for a few minutes before the instructor or students arrive. On Wednesday, I watch part of the class from the hallway. On Friday, I feel bold enough to sit in on an entire class beside the open doorway as the students work their magic. The next Monday, I walk by the studio art room but no class is in session. I open the door and stand there, motionless. Then I take a deep breath and enter. The first thing that hits me once again is the smell, the scent of fresh paint that I know so well.

I close my eyes and inhale. *"You're an amazing artist, baby!"* The smell brings my mother's voice straight back to me, like a stab to the heart.

I open my eyes and see all the canvases, the students' works in progress, some still gleaming with fresh paint. The only light comes from the large windows on one of the walls, which frame the snow outside and a leafless tree, making it seem as if the art studio has been abandoned by the cold world. It's almost dreamlike.

I walk among the paintings, some very simple and others very detailed. I run my finger across a blank canvas, admiring the texture. And I remember my art teacher from high school.

"Another portrait of your mother, Klara?"

From the moment I found out about my mother's cancer, I became obsessed with immortalizing her face. I painted portraits of her nonstop, trying to get it right. My teacher didn't know what was going on at home; I was becoming more and more closed off.

"Portraits were last month's theme, Klara. You're very talented, but I can't put another portrait in the student exhibit."

I say nothing.

She sighs. "Why don't you take a break? You can rejoin the art club next month after the exhibit."

I stare at my mother's portrait. I'd been trying to capture the beauty of her hair, which she'd already begun to lose. I force myself to smile at the teacher. "Okay, I'll come back for the painting when it dries."

That was the last picture I painted. On some level I think I like the fact that it was of my mother's face.

"Klara Rodríguez," an unfamiliar voice calls from the door. I turn to see Mann. She's tall and thin with white hair in a messy bun. "Talented painter from Cooper High School, winner of several district art contests going back as far as elementary school. I've seen you watching the classes. I'm glad you finally came in, welcome."

"Thank you."

Mann studies me for a few seconds and then begins walking toward me. "Shall I prepare a canvas for you?"

"No." I shake my head energetically.

"Why not?"

"I didn't come to paint."

"Really? The look in your eyes seemed to suggest the opposite."

I don't respond.

"When was the last time you painted?"

"A long time ago."

"Why?"

"I don't know."

"What are you afraid of, Klara?"

My eyes linger over an almost finished painting of a sunset. "Of myself." The words leave my mouth of their own accord.

"Are you afraid of what you might see of yourself reflected on the canvas?"

"I guess."

"So?" she says, as she begins to set up a canvas and paints.

"So?"

"So, aren't we artists all a jumble of emotions, of fears? Isn't our very sensitivity what enables us to be inspired?" Mann says with a smile. "Art is always an expression of the artist's inner life. We don't remember a painting for its beauty, but for how it made us feel when we looked at it." She guides me over to the blank canvas. "You don't have to paint anything elaborate. I just want you to permit yourself to touch and feel the paint, to shout out your fears, if necessary, to release all your emotions."

My hand trembles as I sink my fingers into the black paint. It's been so long. I lift my hand and watch the paint drip down my fingers and into the center of my palm. With tears in my eyes, I press my hand against the canvas.

"Oh, you've painted another portrait of me, baby. It's wonderful, and look how beautiful my hair looks. Hopefully it will grow back looking like that again soon."

I pull my hand away from the canvas. "I can't."

Mann takes my wrist and places my hand back on the canvas, moving it smoothly to create sinuous black lines. "Yes, you can." She takes my other hand and dips it into the red paint, then moves it across the canvas to make red lines beside the black ones.

I feel tears begin to roll down my cheeks and drip from my chin. I sigh and feel a sob caught in my throat.

"Cry, scream, do what you have to do. Your art is your exit, the doorway out of all that."

"I'm broken . . . Everything I create will be broken."

Mann releases my hands. "Art is to console those who are broken by life," she whispers.

"Vincent van Gogh said that."

I press both palms against the canvas and the paint squishes through my fingers as I lick salty tears from my lips. "Cancer sucks," I say in a whisper. "I hate it—I hate that it took my mother from me." I slap the canvas hard and scoop up more paint. I continue tracing lines and tapping out shapes with my fingers. "I hate that it ravaged my body and ruined my mind. I miss my mom so much. And I'm so tired of living in fear. I'm . . ." My voice breaks.

Mann puts an arm around me and I turn to her, crying against her shoulder. "Pssst, Klara, you're an artist. Welcome back." She turns me around to face the canvas.

I look at the marks I've made and they somehow make sense to me. I can see anger and sadness, but I also see what I could create from them.

"Take as much time as you need," Mann tells me as she heads for the door.

After taking a few minutes to compose myself, I start pouring some colors onto a palette, then take the brush and use black to create a figure in the middle of the chaos, outlining it in white to make it stand out. It's clearly a girl. I add a darker shade of red and touches of gray to create a chaotic, fiery background. At the girl's feet I add more grays, like ashes fallen from the flames of the sky.

I remember one night I sat shut away in my room listening to Kang's show and I began to trace the full moon with my finger on the windowpane. I now use white to paint the moon in the red sky. As I paint, the smiling faces of my mother, Kamila, Andy, Dario float through my mind, along with all the new people who have entered my life: Diego, Perla, Ellie, and . . . Kang. Through the chaos, fire, ashes, and darkness these people have been my full moon, there to light my way.

I lose track of time and it's not until someone opens the door that I realize how long it's been. I stop painting as Mann enters. "How are we doing?"

I shrug. "It's nothing special."

"Let's see," she says, stopping before the canvas, resting her chin on one hand. "Wow. It's beautiful, so much . . . pain . . ." Her voice trails off.

"Thank you," I say, even though I think she's just being polite.

"Thank you for returning to painting. I can tell that you're going to make an important contribution to art, Klara."

I fall silent.

"By the way, your friends are outside looking for you," she says.

"What?" Ellie texted a while back and I told her I was in the art studio, but I didn't expect her to come. I wipe my hands but the paint has stained my fingertips. I don't mind; it feels good to get my hands dirty again. When I get downstairs, I'm surprised by the sound of cheers and clapping from my friends standing at the end of the hallway.

"Klara! Klara! Klara!" Perla, Ellie, and Diego chant in unison.

I take a deep breath to keep the tears from coming; I've already cried enough today.

"It's okay to celebrate small victories in a big way, Klara."

I smile and start walking toward them, shaking my head.

"You guys are totally crazy," I say as I hug each of them.

"Oh, shush! You're finally painting again! I'm so happy for you."

"It's no big deal," I say quietly.

"Don't sell yourself short. Of course it is. When Kang asked my mom to help you get back into art, I honestly didn't think it would work," Perla says.

"What?"

"It was supposed to be a surprise," Diego says. "Kang was the one who gave Ms. Romes the idea to walk you to the art room. He told us about it, too, so we could encourage you, but he asked us not to say anything. I guess we're not very good at keeping secrets."

I freeze. Kang did all this for me, even though we're not together, even though I asked him to give me time to think. My mind travels back to the first time I listened to his show, to our first text messages, the hallway outside the auditorium where we first spoke, the party, the hot chocolate, our first kiss, our date to the movies (and the many dates after), our conversation at the ice cream shop, his deep black eyes, his warm smile, those dimples . . .

And I'm overwhelmed by all my feelings for him, which I've been trying to ignore for the past month and a half. I want to see him, to hug him, to tell him that he's too good for this world and that staying away from him has been so painful, that I only did it because I thought it was the best thing for him, but . . . is it?

I call him, but his phone goes straight to voicemail. Ah, that's not good. I rush through the building, with my friends chasing behind me.

"Klara?" Diego calls out from behind. "What are we doing?"

"I need to find him," I say, out of breath.

"He's not on campus!" Perla says, stopping me.

"What? How do you know?" I ask.

"He's in Charlotte." She says it as if it's the most obvious thing in the world.

"Oh . . . the talent show. What time does it start?"

"Kang said at seven."

I look at the time. The talent show starts in three hours. If we leave now, will we make it? Can I make it? I want to talk to him; I want to be there for him. He wasn't sure about being able to perform and he took the risk; he's facing his fears. Maybe it's time I face mine. This can be the beginning of me going out in the world beyond this small town, conquering a road trip.

I look at my friends.

I'm not alone.

"Are we doing this or what?" Ellie asks, excited.

"Doing what?" Diego furrows his eyebrows.

"Rushing to Charlotte to make a romantic gesture," Ellie explains. "How are you not catching the vibe, Diego?"

"Oh." Perla beams at me, catching on herself. "Didn't take you for a romantic, Klara with a K."

I take a deep breath. I can do this. I can . . .

"Hey." Perla holds my hand. "We'll be with you the whole time, and if at some point you want to come back, we can, all right?"

I nod.

"Let's go." Ellie cheers as we head out to the parking lot.

I take another deep breath as I climb into the passenger seat and Diego drives off.

Love Me

ROMANCE MOVIES HAVE lied to us.

How come the main character always makes it to the airport on time? There is nothing romantic about driving in the cold of January and facing Charlotte's traffic as soon as we come close to the city. Finding parking is also a nightmare. I really don't think we are going to make it. The sun is gone, and the talent show has already started. I'm crossing my fingers for Kang not to have played yet.

We reach the grass, and the PNC Music Pavilion is right in front of us: The amphitheater looks good, with purple lights and gold streamers hanging from the ceiling. There is a band presenting their set and everyone is cheering for them. There are lots of people here, and I push that realization out of my head because unfamiliar crowded places are still not a favorite for me.

We are working on it, I remind myself.

There is a board on the left side of the stage, and I look at the list of people presenting. When I find Kang's name, I'm relieved that he still hasn't played yet. There is another band after this one, and then it's his turn.

We made it.

We move through the crowd until I'm standing against the wall in the front. I want him to see me. I want him to know I'm showing up for him despite my fears. Perla hugs me from behind and Ellie holds my hand.

It's his turn. Kang walks on stage, guitar in hand, and stops in front of the microphone. His hair is messy around his face, and he looks a little pale. He's nervous. No mask. I'm proud of him.

"Hello, I'm Kang, and I'll be playing an original song I wrote for my brother." His voice is not steady. He's super nervous.

"Yes! Go Kang!" I scream as loud as I can.

His eyes fall on me immediately, and even though he seems shocked, his expression relaxes, his shoulders loosen. I nod and mouth *"You can do this."* He smiles and focuses back on his guitar. A soft melody brings the whole place into silence, and he begins:

Leaves are falling, orange tints the sky,
The chilly breeze is here, and I'm holding my guitar.

Everything is the same, except you're not here this time,
And every season that passes without you feels like a crime.

So many snow angels left for you to build,
So many dreams waiting to be fulfilled.

Life isn't fair, and death isn't much better.
Jung, I've written you songs and a million letters.

In hopes they will heal me,
In hopes they will mend me.

Losing someone you love is a pain that never leaves,
Never quavers, stays in constant grief.

But tonight, I'm healing and honoring you,
I'll look for you in the snow angels, in the falling leaves, in the melody from the strum of my guitar.

No matter how much time passes, I hope you can follow my voice
Because I'll always sing for you with love and joy.

My sight is blurry and I'm pretty sure everyone around me is sniffling. The lyrics, the soft guitar, the genuine grief in his voice. This is a side of Kang I've only seen once before. This is the raw, unfiltered Kang that carries the heavy grief of losing his brother. It's heartbreaking, but beautiful. Maybe art is just an outlet for all of us, a way to expose to the world our deepest pain and, in a way, release it.

Diego starts the clapping, and everyone follows with cheering. Kang gets off the stage and runs toward me.

"Kang—"

He pulls me into a hug. "Thank you for coming," he whispers and kisses the side of my head. "Thank you."

We break apart and I look into his eyes.

I have so many things to say to him that I don't know where to begin.

"I want you to listen to me, okay?" My voice trembles with nerves, and I take a deep breath. "I'm sorry . . . I'm sorry that I pushed you away without giving you the explanation you deserved. I thought I was doing the right thing. I didn't want to ruin your life." I pause to take another deep breath.

"Klara . . ."

"I'm a mess, okay? It's literally a constant struggle every day, and I'll have lots of good days but plenty of bad days, too. And you'll see me laugh and cry, and maybe there will be more panic attacks, maybe I'll want to shut myself away in my room again. I don't know what's in store, but I do know that you can't save me because love doesn't cure depression and anxiety. Love can give you strength, it can provide a reason to keep going, and that's a lot, for sure.

"I know I'm more than my problems, Kang. I'm kind, I'm a good friend, I can paint, I have a dark sense of humor and an unhealthy obsession with TV dramas, and so many other things that make me who I am. I am so much more than my depression and anxiety, but my depression and anxiety are part of me, too. So if you want to be with me, you need to know what you're getting, the whole package." My chest rises and falls. I feel like I've laid my heart bare.

Kang studies me silently, processing everything I just said. "Klara . . ." He takes the last step toward me and his hand cradles my cheek. I can feel the warmth emanating from his eyes. "I fell in love with the whole package a long time ago."

My heart is about to burst. I bite my lip. "I worry that dating me might not be good for you." I have to say it.

He sighs. "Every day is a struggle for me, too. I'm still getting over the loss of my brother; I still have days where I'm consumed by guilt and I feel like I've regressed in my forward momentum. I know you're right, we can't save each other, but we can be there for each other, along for the ride, right?"

"Yes."

Kang leans toward me and I hold my breath until his mouth meets mine. It's a kiss full of so many emotions, so much sincerity, that I clench my hands at my sides, bracing myself, soaking it all in. Our lips touch and it's sweet and delicate.

Gosh, I hate admitting that the romance movies were right after all. This is so romantic. We are kissing in the middle of a crowd filled with strangers, my best friends a few steps away from us.

We pull apart and Kang gives me a kiss on the forehead before putting his arms around me. "I missed you, Klara with a K."

"I missed you too, Bat-Kang."

He laughs quietly.

Someone behind us clears their throat. We turn to see Diego, Ellie, and Perla. *Oh, God, did they hear everything?* Judging by the tears in Perla's eyes, I'd say yes.

"Ready to drive back and celebrate?" Diego offers me a high five, grinning.

I grin back. "Ready!"

"Are we not going to wait for them to announce the winners?" Perla asks.

Kang grabs my hand, and says, "I won."

◆ ◆ ◆

By the time we get back to Durham it's past midnight and everything is closed, so we have no other choice but to celebrate at my house. Kamila and Andy don't seem to mind. Kang's parents drop him off at my house and go home because they have work in the morning.

I introduce my boyfriend to Andy. "Nice to meet you, Kang." Andy holds out a hand and Kang shakes it.

Kamila smiles.

"Dr. Rodríguez," Kang says.

"That's Kamila to you," she says, and hugs him.

We cook some pizza and eat around the kitchen counter, as Kamila confesses she purposefully left Kang's radio show on for me to listen to that first time. She thought Kang could be a voice of reason for me, that I could find motivation and inspiration in his words. And she was right.

I'm amazed at how much my life has changed in the past few months, and how each of these people has done their part to help me. If someone had told me a couple months ago that I'd be here, I wouldn't have believed it. Me, friends? Me, in college? Me, dating my crush? No way. The hardest part of depression was the feeling that my sadness and fear would be all I'd ever have in life, that it would never get better, that every day would be the same: empty, meaningless, dominated by permanent fear. It's so easy to underestimate our strength, our ability to make progress, to take one step after another no matter how small. No matter how many setbacks we may have, it's all part of the rocky road to recovery.

Those baby steps, which I thought so insignificant, added up over time. My mind retraces my journey: Kang's radio show; the first time I left the house; the puppies next door; that panic attack in the bathroom when Kang helped calm me over the phone; starting college; meeting Perla, Diego, Ellie; my ongoing panic attacks; my tears; my accomplishments. Everything that has brought me to this beautiful moment, here and now.

I stand up and raise my glass. "I'd like to make a toast. The world's first strawberry milkshake toast." I clear my throat. "First, I'd like to toast to Kang. I'm so proud of you. You overcame your fear of performing in front of others, of sharing the gift someone very special encouraged you to pursue, no mask needed this time."

Kang reaches out to grab my hand and plants a small kiss on it. "Thank you."

I squeeze his hand, then direct my attention to the others. "And to the rest of you, I toast to you, too, each and every one of you. You have all played such an important part in everything I've achieved. You have all been an example for me. I want you to know that I will keep fighting and that, while I will most likely fail again, I'm not as scared of failure anymore. Because I have you amazing people around me and because I know that even if I fall, I can get back up, just like I've done before. So . . . thank you."

We clink our milkshakes, smiling.

Life is complicated. It often presents us with problems and difficult situations. But then there are days like this one, good days, good moments that deserve to be acknowledged, appreciated, and celebrated. Together, let us follow the voices filled with joy, compassion, peace, love, and positivity. Let us always remember to follow our own voices.

Final Letter

From: Klara
To: Readers

By this point, I'd say you know me fairly well, don't you think? You've been with me from the beginning of my journey, before I could even leave home, when my only contact with the outside world was a radio program, when my heart and soul were so full of fear and sadness. You've seen me make progress and you've seen me have setbacks; you've seen me hit rock bottom. You've witnessed my vulnerability exposed in every word, in every paragraph. But you've also seen my small victories and celebrated alongside me. We've experienced a lifetime together in these pages.

Maybe you've seen yourself reflected in me or maybe my life reminds you of someone you know, because this story is not mine alone, but the story of many people, and someone needed to tell it, right?

I hold out hope that awareness of mental health will continue to spread so that no more precious lives like Jung's will be lost, so that people will stop downplaying depression and anxiety disorders. A person can't stop suffering just by deciding that they want to.

And my wish for you is that you may love yourself just the way you are, like Perla; that you may come out of your shell when you feel comfortable enough to do so, like Ellie; that you may keep your essence and joy in spite of hardship, like Diego; and that your painful experiences may inspire you to help others, like Kang.

But above all I want you to know that you can get through anything and that you should not give up, no matter how hard it is, because, little by little, things can and will get better. It's not easy; you saw me fall down but you also saw me get back up. You know that I suffered, but I also laughed; I had panic attacks but I learned how to get through them. And I'm just one of so many other people out there bravely giving it their all, struggling, surviving, and moving forward. You can handle anything; you are a champion.

In the case that someone close to you is going through a difficult time, I hope my story may provide a few ideas on how to help them, because it is so important to reach out to someone sinking into sadness, anxiety, fear. The simple awareness of another person's support can be crucial.

And finally, I hope that you will always know that you can be a guiding light in the midst of so much darkness and that you can help make someone else's light brighter by saying something nice or doing something for them without expecting anything in return. Help spread love, warmth, and light, because this world already has so much hate, darkness, and negativity.

My name is Klara, yes, with a K. I'm a faithful listener of the radio show *Follow My Voice*, and I'm here to remind you that you can do it, that you are amazing, and that you should fight to achieve what you want in life. I believe in you with all my heart. And I hope that you will remember the story of this girl who was confined to her room with no interests besides a radio show and Korean dramas, who suffered from catastrophic thoughts, depression, panic attacks. But who reemerged into the world. Thank you for staying with me every step of the way.

And now I ask you to write your own story in the book of your life. With a huge smile on my face, I toss back my curls and say loudly: It's my turn to follow your voice!

KLARA RODRÍGUEZ

Acknowledgments

This is the first time I've ever included an acknowledgments section in any of my books. And that's because *Follow My Voice* is more than a story; it is a part of me. It is to me what painting is to Klara: an outlet, a way to express the things I went through.

There's a lot of me in Klara and Kang. They are a mixture of fiction and reality, born from the experience of losing my father and the depression and anxiety that followed. Writing these characters was my way of venting my feelings.

I want to start by thanking you, Mom. You stayed by my side through every panic attack, every visit to the emergency room, every doctor's appointment where we were told that there was nothing wrong with me, that no one could understand why I claimed I couldn't breathe, why I felt like I was dying. You held my hand as I lay on so many hospital beds. And I know it was hard for you to see me suffering when no one knew what was wrong with me. Oftentimes you were Kamila, others Andy. You never gave up, never tired of fighting alongside me. You are the reason I'm still here. I love you, Mom.

And now you're up, Mariana, my best friend. We met in preschool and have been friends for over twenty years. But that's not the reason you're on this list. When I got sick, so few of my friends wanted to hang out with me because I was suffering from ailments that no one understood. Many people stayed away, but not you, never. You always encouraged me to venture out into the world with you and assured me that if I felt bad, we would go home, no problem. You would bring me donuts when I didn't want to go out and stay in to watch movies with me. You never judged me or asked questions; you listened when I was ready to talk. You don't know how much that meant to me. I adore you; you are my favorite person.

On to my dear Wattpad readers, what can I say? I am so grateful to everyone who welcomed this story with such respect, love, and understanding, who inspired me to keep writing even when I was so full of insecurities. It's thanks to you guys that I was able to finish this book. I LOVE YOU ALL.

To Darlis and Alex, who have picked me up when I was down and who have always been there to listen when things got ugly. You understand me, you love and support me, and for that I will be eternally grateful. As I've said before: You are the *malta* to my *empanadas*.

I also want to thank you, new reader, who may have bought this book without knowing me. I hope it may help you. Thank you for giving it a chance.

And finally, thank you, Dad. I still can't write to you without tears in my eyes, but I learned so much from you, and continue to do so even after your passing. This book is for you, to honor you and also to let you go. You can rest in peace knowing that I will be fine, that I am blessed, like Klara, to have very good people around me.

And that I am so very lucky to have readers who follow my voice.

About the Author

Ariana Godoy is an internationally bestselling author known for *Through My Window*, adapted into a Netflix film in 2022, and, most recently, *Follow My Voice*. Her books have sold more than a million copies and have been translated into multiple languages. Originally from Venezuela, Godoy now writes in North Carolina while enjoying coffee, time with her family, and the company of her dogs.